TELL ME HOW THIS ENDS

Jo Leevers

Jo Leevers grew up in London and has spent most of her career working on magazines, most recently writing features about homes and interiors. This means she gets to visit people all around the country and ask them about their homes and their lives. Some might call this a licence to be nosey . . . *Tell Me How This Ends* is her debut novel. Whether writing fiction or interviewing people for articles, she is fascinated by the life stories that we all carry with us. She has two grown-up children and lives with her husband and their wayward dog Lottie.

TELL ME HOW THIS ENDS

TELL ME HOW THIS ENDS

JO LEEVERS

LAKE UNION
PUBLISHING

Text copyright © 2023 by Jo Leevers

Published by Lake Union Publishing, Seattle

www.apub.com

Amazon, the Amazon logo, and Lake Union Publishing are trademarks of Amazon.com, Inc., or its affiliates.
ISBN-13: 9781662506383
ISBN-10: 1662506384

Cover design by Emma Rogers

Printed in the United States of America

For my mum, Maureen. With love x

PROLOGUE

DECEMBER, 1974

The neat pile of clothes sits by the side of the canal for two whole days before anyone thinks to call the police.

It's just before Christmas and everyone is busy: presents to buy, places to be.

A few people taking a shortcut along the canal pause, but something about the careful way the clothes have been folded deters them from taking a closer look. The pile looks so deliberate, as if the owner has just stepped away and might return at any moment.

But the owner doesn't return.

A brown suede jacket lies on the top, its arms folded. A striped scarf has been tucked underneath, as if to protect it from the rain. Beneath that, the edge of a yellow dress is just visible. A pair of leather boots, still shiny and new, stands to attention a little further along the towpath.

On the second day, the rain gets worse. Water collects in the folds of the jacket and its furry collar flattens to an ugly grey pelt. The boots are ruined.

The rain also churns up the usually calm waters of

the canal. The jigsaw of green duckweed floating on the surface breaks into smaller pieces, revealing mud swirling up from the silty bed.

Time passes. The mud sinks back down again.

And still, nobody comes.

CHAPTER ONE

HENRIETTA

The bench Henrietta Lockwood chooses to sit on is at the junction of three main roads. It could not be considered a peaceful spot, but it is convenient. She estimates it to be one minute's walk from this bench to the Rosendale Drop-In Centre, where she has a job interview in twenty-two minutes. She will leave the bench in twelve minutes, just to be sure.

Being late October, it is a little cold out here, but she does not wish to pay for the privilege of sitting inside a café. She can see one from her vantage point. It is called Plant Life, which she thinks is a very ill-advised name and, if she didn't have an appointment at 2 p.m., she would explain this mistake to the proprietor.

Despite the weather, Henrietta can feel a sweaty patch collecting on her back, so she leans forward to ensure it doesn't seep into her blouse. It is a result of her keeping her backpack firmly on. Granted, the only person who has even glanced at her was a sad-looking woman walking two chihuahuas, but muggings are on the rise. Henrietta knows this is true because she reads about them on a daily basis in the city's free newspaper.

The drop-in centre (why don't they just call it the I've Got Cancer Centre, she thinks) is located in the west wing of a hospital in an exclusive part of London, all Victorian squares, private gardens and tall plane trees. Henrietta can see it from her bench: a handsome double-fronted building with fluted pillars either side of glass front doors.

The building may be elegant but the people who come and go are all sorts. A rake-thin woman in a Puffa jacket and a billowing skirt is making slow progress up the ramp: she keeps a firm hold on the handrail and her body is oddly tilted. As she reaches the doors, an elderly man in a camel coat is on his way out. Wordlessly, he steps aside to let her pass, his face ashen, fingers fumbling for his buttons. The Rosendale Drop-In Centre does not, Henrietta has to admit, look like the jolliest of workplaces.

The advertisement for this job had been buried in the back pages of the *London Review of Books*. Since she inadvertently became a lady of leisure, Henrietta rather enjoys her fortnightly read of the classified section, tut-tutting at the frivolity on display. Yoga and writing retreats in Greece. People seeking a mate to share interests in poetry, hillwalking 'and possibly more'. But then she spotted this:

The Life Stories Project
Interviewer and transcriber required three days a week, including Saturdays.
Typing, copy-editing skills and

> empathetic manner essential. Six-
> month contract with possibility of
> renewal, funding pending.

A short-term job is far from ideal, but with a CV peppered with unexplained gaps and abrupt terminations, Henrietta can't be too picky. The 'empathetic manner' bit of the advertisement is also slightly concerning, so for the past week Henrietta has been practising facial expressions in front of a mirror.

In the privacy of her bathroom, she tried out a wide smile. This would be her 'hello' face. Then she tilted her head to one side, to show empathy. Even to Henrietta, the results looked alarming. There is a reason, she realised, why monkeys bare their teeth as an act of aggression.

Luckily, Henrietta's teeth are pleasingly even. Her face is round and her hair is cut to shoulder length, a style bestowed upon her at the age of eleven that she has never felt the urge to change. She does not indulge in make-up. Even at the age of thirty-two, her efforts always look like those of a child let loose with a set of crayons.

However, she knows that clothes make a good impression, so she spent an entire evening removing the lint from some navy British Home Stores trousers that served her well in her old job. A blue blouse ordered from an advertisement in the *Radio Times* some years ago is, she judges, formal and yet casual.

The hands of her Timex watch (a sixteenth-birthday present, still going strong) tell her it is time to leave her bench. Swallowing down a familiar knot of dread,

Henrietta puts on her 'hello' face and strides towards the Rosendale Centre.

* * *

'So . . .' The woman in the pink sweater is shuffling pages around her desk in a random manner that indicates she is rather ill prepared. Finally, Pink Sweater looks up at her. 'Aha. Henrietta Lockwood. Why do you think you would be suited to this job?'

Henrietta clears her throat and begins. 'I believe I am suited to this post on several counts. One: I am not prone to outbursts of emotion or sentimentality. Two: I possess excellent editorial skills, so I am well equipped to transcribe and then type up people's life stories before they die. Three, I like a deadline.'

It is almost word for word what Henrietta had written in her application letter. But Pink Sweater – 'Call me Audrey' – doesn't seem to notice. Audrey looks across the desk through thick glasses that magnify her eyes into two huge fish-like orbs.

'It's not always that simple,' she sighs, bringing her hands together. 'But, yes, here at the Life Stories Project, detachment can be an advantage.'

She swivels the computer screen around to face Henrietta. 'The final part of your interview is a proofreading test. This is Kenton's Life Story, which I wrote up myself. We lost him last week, but I got most of it down. His family would like copies in time for the funeral. That's often what happens. Unless we are caught unawares . . .' She trails off. 'Anyway, you have forty-five minutes. Are you familiar with "track changes"?'

She needn't have worried because track changes is Henrietta's very favourite thing to do. She is happiest when she can correct punctuation, spelling and facts, and highlight her superior knowledge in red. As Audrey leaves the room, Henrietta is already tapping away, scoring through words, frowning at the shockingly poor grasp of grammar.

When Audrey shows her out, she points to where Henrietta will conduct the Life Story interviews if she gets the job. Momentarily, Henrietta is confused because she had pictured herself in a private office, rather like Audrey's but with a window. And a pot plant. Perhaps one of those scent diffusers, too. But it seems that Audrey is gesturing towards a corner table in the centre's coffee bar, just by the main entrance foyer.

'People prefer the informal atmosphere. They like to talk over a cuppa,' Audrey says, as Henrietta hovers by the automatic doors. The glass panes judder, trying to open and shut, leaving Henrietta unsure whether to step outside or move back into the warmth, because Audrey is still talking.

'Officially it's called the Reith Café – after a generous donor. But all the staff call it the Grief Café!' Audrey delivers this as if it is a punchline to a joke, but Henrietta thinks it best to ignore this. Jokes, in her experience, feel like a ball thrown at great speed: hard to catch; even trickier to keep a rally going. And Henrietta has never been a games person.

'I can see how the coffee bar setting would facilitate conversation,' she replies levelly, stepping out on to the stone steps.

'I look forward to hearing from you presently,' she adds, as the glass doors snap shut.

It feels good to walk away from the fug of hand sanitiser, old, unwashed clothes and old, unwashed people. Henrietta admits she is a little disappointed by the Rosendale's down-at-heel ambiance. Having done her research thoroughly, Henrietta knows that this centre is the first to pioneer the Life Stories Project, an initiative funded by Ryan Brooks, a 1980s pop star who lost his wife to ovarian cancer. She's watched the video where Ryan does a walkabout at the Rosendale Centre, high-fiving his way round a TV lounge, then looking more serious as he talks about his wife, Skye, who had died swiftly and too young. 'If someone had helped Skye to write her life story, our little girl could read it when she's older,' says Ryan, jiggling his bald, scrunch-faced baby. 'Everybody has a story – and these life stories should be heard.'

Having so much time these days to listen to the radio and watch daytime TV, Henrietta is not surprised that Ryan's idea has hit a nerve. There are grief podcasts, cancer blogs about good days, bad days and chemo days, and vlogs on dying well and making bucket lists. Henrietta finds it all rather unseemly, but she's clearly in a minority because other people are falling over themselves to talk about grief or their own imminent death and Ryan's hashtags – #lastwords, #lifestories and #grievingwithryan – went viral for a while.

As a reward for getting through her interview, Henrietta treats herself to a scone from the Plant Life café. There is some confusion over the price, but it seems £4 is deemed perfectly reasonable for an artisan baked product in this neighbourhood. Vegan, apparently.

She carries the paper bag to what she now considers to be 'her' bench and eats her scone in small chunks, chewing and swallowing each morsel before picking off the next. It's a little dry, in her opinion. A pigeon is making its jerky, circuitous way towards her, looking at her sideways with one orange-ringed eye. Henrietta quickly drops the last of her scone back in the bag and folds over the top. She's wary of these bold, unpredictable birds, but will try not to let the incursion spoil her moment: the sun has come out and she might have a new job.

In fact, there is already a voicemail from Audrey on her phone, but she will wait until she gets home before listening to it, with Dave by her side. Dave likes to share her news, good or bad, and has seen her through some difficult times.

Henrietta is about to place her paper bag in the bin when she has a change of heart. Making sure no one is looking, she tips the remaining crumbs into a small pile on the pavement. Being a resident of Chelsea, that pigeon probably has more of an appetite for vegan scones than Henrietta.

* * *

Back in her flat, she sits on the sofa and listens to Audrey's message several times. After the third time, Henrietta allows the smallest bubble of pleasure to rise up inside her. Dave, however, has already lost interest and is busy making a burrow in the cushions next to her, leaving a scattering of coarse black and tan hairs in his wake. He's panting slightly, waiting for her toast crusts, and his breath leaves something to be desired. She loves Dave dearly, but it would be nice to have someone else to share her news with. She could ring her parents, she supposes, but she's not ready to have her bubble burst just yet.

Henrietta pads into the kitchen, drops two more slices of white bread into the toaster and, after they pop up, slathers them with dairy spread. She eats standing by the window, looking out at the street. After a while, Upstairs Woman comes out of their shared front door and sets off at a clip to the bus stop. She's wearing her blue coat, which Henrietta worries will be far too flimsy for this time of year. Henrietta steps back behind her curtain, just in case her neighbour looks back, but she never does. She's always in such a hurry.

All communication between Henrietta and Upstairs Woman is done via notes or texts. Henrietta prefers the former, which she writes in neat cursive letters and slides under her neighbour's door. Then Upstairs Woman replies by text. Their messages say things like 'Your food waste caddy is on pavement. Unsightly. Please remove ASAP' (from Henrietta). Or 'Your dog sounded lonely. Used spare key to let him into courtyard. Hope was OK' (from Upstairs Woman).

On cue, Dave saunters in, hoping for more crusts. He's starting to smell again and Henrietta isn't sure if it's his ears or his glands. She sighs. Either way, it's time to take him out for his constitutional. Pushing her feet into her Crocs, Henrietta bends down to clip on his lead. It's a special orange one that has RESCUE DOG printed along its length. This gets them a few sympathetic looks when Dave lunges, barks and snaps his way around the streets because Dave hates, in no particular order, cyclists, pedestrians, buggies, skateboards, cats, Labradors and German shepherds. Well, most dogs really. Next, Henrietta puts a fluorescent dog coat over Dave's head and fastens the Velcro. This time, its lettering reads IGNORE ME.

'Right, walkies!' she chirrups, without conviction. Already Dave's claws are scrabbling on the laminate flooring and a low growl is building at the back of his throat. As she opens the front door, Dave's furious barking begins, a sound that is surely now familiar to every one of her neighbours. His barking reaches a crescendo as they head off down the street, one woman and her dog against the world.

Henrietta's new position might not be everyone's dream job, but it will suit her just fine. There will be no team targets or bonding sessions and at least the dead can't file official complaints about 'dangerous and intimidating behaviour' from beyond the grave. The people she'll meet won't be around for long – all she will have to do is transcribe their rambling, probably quite tedious memories, sort them into chronological order and turn them into Life Story books. The drop-in centre may be in the business of death, but Henrietta is only too glad that business is booming.

CHAPTER TWO

ANNIE

At night, when the sleeping pill drags her down into its velvety hold, Annie can forget that she's dying. In many ways, it feels wrong – surely she should be trying to stay awake, watching Oscar-winning films, reading great literature, listening to opera. Well, that would be a first, she thinks.

She knows she doesn't have long to live and yet she craves sleep, from the moment she wakes until bedtime ticks around. She treasures the hazy half-state that greets her again, telling her she's about to fall headlong into oblivion.

Her doctor prescribes the pills freely now. Like there's no tomorrow, ha ha. But these days even her dreams feel tired and worn out. It's as if her brain is a record player that keeps playing the same old track, its needle skittering over the grooved surface and going back to the start.

Sometimes she's back at Chaucer Drive, where she and Terry lived once they were married, woodgrain pattern on the kitchen walls, that yellow kettle with scorches up the sides. Or in her parents' front room in Dynevor Road, with its shaggy rug that you weren't allowed to walk on. Tiptoe, tiptoe around the edges of that room she and Kath went, in their white Sunday-best socks.

But most often, her dreams are full of water. Bucketloads of the stuff, fast-moving, with weeds trailing under its surface. And beneath that is dark, brackish mud. The memory of all that rushing, dirty water clings to her when she wakes and realises she's still here.

She often wakes at this time, just before dawn. The air outside is quieter, softer, but these days nobody is here to notice what time she gets up or whether she's left a wet patch in her bed, her nightie clinging to the backs of her legs. All those watery dreams aren't helping things, she thinks.

In the kitchen she flicks the switch on the kettle and it roars into life. She puts a teabag in a mug, lines up her pills and waits. Annie likes to take her tea back to bed and has done since Terry died two years ago. Oh the freedom she felt that first night in her brand-new bed when she could spread her arms and legs out, no longer fearing she would collide with his hard, bony shins, his unyielding back.

When she moved to this little flat, the bed, the room, the whole place was hers and hers alone, unsullied by his presence. A shame, then, she won't be around to enjoy it for much longer, although the nurses were cagey about how much time she has left. All she was asking for was a rough estimate – weeks, months? – not the winning numbers for the lottery.

She holds her mug in both hands and sips carefully. She feels sure today is important, but she might be wrong. She tips her head to one side. Her left ear – her bad one – clears briefly and she hears the bin lorry chuntering up the road. Wednesday, then.

It was easier biding her time in the hospital, when she was having her tests. 'Not the best cancer,' the doctor had said, like she'd backed a losing horse. 'Go home and spend time with those you love. Make your peace.' He had a stethoscope looped round his neck that he kept touching for reassurance and he seemed close to tears. It would have felt unkind to tell him that there's no one at home, that she's the only one left.

Now she's back in her own flat, she thinks fondly of those clean, starched-white days of waking up on the ward. The rattle of the tea trolley at 7 a.m., then the chatter and the squeak of shoes on the floor as nurses came and went. Mia, the girl who runs the café, brought the teas round. She did a sideline in stationery, too: notebooks and cards, colouring books and felt tips. It was Mia who gave her the leaflet about the Life Stories thing. At first, Annie thought the whole idea was silly, but Mia had kept on at her.

'Annie, everyone's got a story to tell,' she'd said, perching on the side of her bed. 'It's social history, isn't it? Tell us what being young in the seventies in London was really like, eh? Were you a glam rocker or a hippy chick? Women's libber?'

Oh, I've got stories to tell, Annie had thought, but she wasn't sure they were the sort Mia had in mind.

She'd bought a notebook anyway, the smallest Mia had. It has daffodils on the front and it's here on her kitchen table, still waiting for her words.

The free minibus to the drop-in centre isn't due until Saturday, but she should probably make a start. She's kept things inside for so long and she hopes that getting the words out might bring her some relief. It's time to tell some truths – not everything, perhaps, but enough to lighten her load. Make her peace, like the doctor said.

It's later that Annie gets out the photo albums, because Mia says they can put pictures in the Life Story books, too. She begins with the old Doyle family album, the one she knows off by heart. It starts with black-and-white shots of her parents' wedding, everyone lined up like wax dolls, and ends with wonky shots of her and Kath sitting on a beach, the sea's horizon listing dangerously to the right.

As she turns the last page of the album, a small envelope slips down into her lap. It's the kind a florist might pin to a bouquet and that's what Annie thinks it is at first. A special message saved from an anniversary, perhaps. But as soon as she opens the envelope, she realises it's nothing of the sort.

There is her lovely sister, standing beside her bicycle on the side path to their terraced house at Dynevor Road. Kath had just got her job at the shoe shop and rode her bike there and back to save on bus fares. Tick, tick, tick went her bicycle wheels every morning, as she steered it out on to the pavement. Then she'd be off, standing up on the pedals to get going over the brow of the hill.

Glued to the back of the photograph is an official-looking form. Annie unfolds its creases. The handwriting isn't familiar, but the words are. In cramped, neat script it reads:

> Kathleen Doyle, age 18. Fresh complexion. Dark brown/black hair. Hazel eyes. Wearing brown suede jacket with fur trim, yellow dress, striped scarf and black leather boots. Height 5ft 6in. Last seen 21 December 1974, 5pm.

The police had taken away that tiny photo, she remembers that bit. They needed something for their men, they said, a description to circulate.

Kath's things had been found by the side of the Grand Union Canal, the clothes folded in a neat pile. Much later, they were returned in a brown paper bag, the jacket's fluffy collar clogged with mud, crumbling and dry.

As for the photo, Annie doesn't recall it being returned, but maybe that happened months later, once the search had been called off. Probably handed over to her dad, man to man, when Annie was back at work and her mum was having one of her bad days.

Annie peels off the form, slides the photograph back into the envelope and replaces it between crackly cellophane pages. That time feels like yesterday but also forever ago. When she looks in the mirror these days, Annie is surprised by the face that peers back at her.

Her hair is completely grey, her skin is a map of lines, all heading downwards. She supposes, to other people, she looks like an old lady. The kind who has heart-warming anecdotes and smiles at fond, misty memories.

She knows that this is what the people at the Rosendale Drop-In Centre will be expecting: a nice story from a nice old lady. If only I had a happy tale to tell, she thinks, one that's all sunshine and smiles, with all the ends nicely tied up.

Unfortunately, that's not the case for Annie Doyle, but next Saturday she will get the free minibus to the centre and she will start telling her story as best she can.

CHAPTER THREE

HENRIETTA

'If you happen to be there at the end, don't imagine it's like on TV,' Audrey says. Not much is, thinks Henrietta, but keeps it to herself. This woman is a talker and they generally don't like to be interrupted.

She is in Audrey's office for 'a little welcome chat', but Henrietta would much prefer to be downstairs in the café so she can get going on her first day of interviewing. She has been up since 6 a.m., cajoling Dave around the dark, damp streets for an early constitutional, and he was not best pleased.

'It's not often we get called to a bedside, but once or twice we're asked on to a ward to finish a story. Last words, though . . .' Audrey sighs. 'Not always what people expect.'

Audrey pauses, laces her fingers together and leans across the desk. 'One man just recited betting odds to his assembled family. Another lady sat straight up in bed and said, "I never loved him." Caused all manner of speculation and upset, that did. Which is why we are here. To make things clear, get everything down in black and white, before it's too late.

'But bedside visits are, as I say, very rare,' adds Audrey, who is wearing a different pink sweater today, in a shade closer to magenta. 'Mostly, you will be based in the Grief Café and the clients will come to you. A few are hospital inpatients but most will be our day visitors.'

Henrietta thinks this all sounds a little haphazard and wonders whether she shouldn't suggest introducing an appointments system. A form determining condition, grade of cancer, life expectancy and so forth could be filled out, to ensure people with less time are prioritised. And those who had led more pedestrian existences could be given shorter appointments . . .

But now she's missed some crucial shift in the conversation because Audrey is standing up and they are on the move. Henrietta scrabbles under her chair for her backpack and follows her boss out into the corridor. It's not easy keeping pace with Audrey, who is an expert at the whole walk-and-talk thing.

'Sometimes it's a partner, or a son or daughter who contacts us,' Audrey continues, glancing over her shoulder at Henrietta, who makes a couple of hasty skip-jumps to keep up. 'They've seen Ryan Brooks on TV or they are regulars in the café, so they've seen the interviews taking place. Often, someone just drops by to see what it's all about,' she adds brightly.

Audrey comes to a sudden halt and Henrietta realises they've reached the café. On a corner table is a laminated sign that says 'Reserved'; another shiny piece of cardboard is stuck to the wall and this one reads

'Life Stories – Because Everybody Has One'. Evidently, Audrey is a whiz with the laminator.

Henrietta starts to unpack her bag to indicate she is ready to start work. Her backpack contains her pencil case, her lunchbox (cheese and pickle sandwiches, crisps and a KitKat), her tartan Thermos flask and today's free newspaper. And, as of just now, a set of Life Story questionnaires, a notebook and a work mobile phone for recording interviews.

Audrey looks down at these objects, clears her throat and continues. 'So, to recap. Each client gets around seven sessions, each lasting about an hour. Some like to use more, others get it done in less. Some clients, well, we have to tie things up as best we can.

'Mornings are for interviews and in the afternoons you'll do transcribing, proofreading and running the stories into the book template. It has pre-set chapters to keep us nicely organised.' Here, Audrey gives a tight smile. 'Is that clear?'

Henrietta approves of everything she's heard. 'It's very clear, thank you. I'm raring to go.'

Twenty minutes later, she's still sitting in the same spot on her own, feeling rather foolish. Her appointment book is empty until 11 a.m. and nobody has 'dropped by', as Audrey promised. Is this job going to be like a series of short, unsuccessful blind dates? Not that she has ever been on one. It remains a mystery to her why anyone would willingly subject themselves to such an uncomfortable experience.

On the TV screen mounted on the wall, a video of Ryan Brooks is playing on a loop, interspersed with adverts for funeral plans and private healthcare services. 'Your memories will live on, as a comfort to others. Find a centre near you,' he encourages. But the London branch seems woefully short on custom this Saturday morning.

Henrietta has been taking surreptitious sips of coffee from her Thermos cup, but screws it back on sharpish when she sees a thin, tall man ambling towards her table. Disappointingly, it turns out that he isn't a proper client; he isn't even ill.

'I've just given my brother a lift here. He goes for counselling upstairs,' the man says, waving a hand towards the lifts. 'But I never know what he says. I saw the Life Stories thing on the TV and I thought, if Cody did a book it would be nice, you know, to look at. Afterwards.' At that, the man's voice starts to wobble and he turns away, not even thanking her for the leaflet.

An older woman seems to take this as her cue to approach the table. She's been sitting nearby for a while, wrapped in a too-big dressing gown, so Henrietta deduces she is a hospital in-patient. But this woman doesn't want to sit down either. Instead, she places her dark, veiny hand on the table to steady herself and fixes her gaze on Henrietta. 'I did my story with the last girl,' she hisses. 'But I wasn't happy with it.'

Henrietta's mind flits through its internal filing system of responses, but finds no precedent because neither she nor Audrey had anticipated getting repeat customers. 'Oh?' is all she can muster.

'Yes, all very pretty with its gold lettering on the front but she didn't put in half the stuff I told her. She just typed up the nice bits, like it was a fairy tale. And she spelt my middle name wrong. It's Lesley with a "y". Not Leslie "ie".'

At that, Henrietta smiles with relief. 'I completely understand,' she says. 'There's no excuse for such errors: one is the female version and the other is male. As in Leslie Phillips.' Henrietta reaches for a questionnaire. 'I'm sure we can rectify this. Together we can write your Life Story. Again. Because everybody has one.'

'No, no, I can't be doing with that,' the woman replies, pulling her dressing gown cord tighter. 'I just wanted to say. And she cried all the time, the girl before you. Which brought me down, you know.'

She turns to go, scratching her head as if to rub away these troublesome thoughts, then stops. 'It just didn't sound like me, the words she used.' Her tone turns angry. 'It was meant to be for my family so they could know what it was like for our generation. But I wish I'd never done it.' With that, the woman walks away, before Henrietta can give a suitable answer.

She's still trying to think of one when the automatic doors glide apart and a ragtag group of people make their way in – surely one of them must be her 11 a.m. appointment.

First through is a young man using a wheelchair, pushed by a woman in a purple fleece, a beatific expression on her face. Henrietta has met her ilk before, as volunteers in charity shops and leading lights of church bake sales. The man she is pushing looks extremely cross and is wearing a beanie hat, pulled down to cover his ears. It dawns on Henrietta that this may be because he does not have any hair underneath, and she's still processing this when she notices that a pair of checked trousers has appeared in front of her.

A tall, stern woman looms above her. She wears a large white linen shirt cinched in with a big-buckled belt and on her head is a black beret, edged in worn leather. There is a piratical air to this woman's dress sense but, thankfully, no eyepatch, just two bright eyes, hollow cheeks and a slash of lipstick in an improbably bright shade.

Henrietta can't take her eyes off the woman and the way that her lipstick breaks into fine hairline cracks as her mouth starts to move.

'Hello, I'm Annie Doyle. Your eleven a.m.,' she announces.

Thankfully, the girl who runs the café chooses this moment to appear and start fussing around with mugs and sugar and a slice of Bakewell tart. All of which seems to be for this Annie Doyle, yet involves pieces of crockery that encroach into Henrietta's paperwork. Using the edge of her clipboard, Henrietta nudges the mug and plate a few crucial inches away from her designated workspace.

'Good morning, I am Henrietta Lockwood and I am with the Life Stories Project. Together we will be writing your story, because everybody has one,' she says in a rush.

Annie sighs. 'Are you reading from a script?' she asks. 'You sound like you're out of one of those leaflets.'

'No, this is just how I talk,' says Henrietta. 'Now. We have found that our questionnaire provides a useful framework for remembering important times in your life.' She pushes one across the table.

Having spent the past hour pretending to be engrossed in this form, Henrietta knows the questions off by heart:

What is your date and place of birth?

Do/did you have brothers/sisters/pets?

Tell me about your schooldays. For example, what games did you play?

What job do you/did you do?

Have you been married?

Do you have children?

Do you have photographs you would like to include?

She has to admit they are rather uninspiring. 'A useful framework,' she says again, less confidently this time.

'Actually,' says Annie, 'I've made a few notes of my own.'

But Henrietta has a form to fill out. 'If we could just start with these questions . . .' she continues. 'And then next week you can bring in some photographs.'

Annie Doyle runs her finger down the questions and proceeds to rattle off a set of answers. 'Hmm, let's see. Born, yes, Hammersmith Hospital, 1955. Yes, one sister. Schooldays, yes. Job, worked in a nursery. Married, yes, August 1975. Now widowed – an unfortunate accident. Children, no. Photographs, I'll see what I can find.'

She slides the form back over the table, gives Henrietta a wry smile. 'Now we've done that, how about I read what I've prepared? Seeing as it's my story.'

The last thing Henrietta needs on her first day in the Grief Café is someone making a scene, so she decides to acquiesce. She will find a way to subtly reintroduce the questionnaire at a later juncture. She places the mobile phone closer to her first interviewee and presses the red circle on the screen. 'Very well. Annie Doyle, today is Saturday the sixth of November and I am recording session one of your Life Story.'

Annie gets out a spiral-bound notebook with yellow daffodils on the front, turns to the first page and begins.

'I grew up in a poor part of London that is now very rich. My father, Aidan, was Irish; my mother, Deidre, was born in Kilburn but to Irish parents. I've never been to Ireland and I think it's too late for me now. It's a shame I'll die without seeing the place.'

She holds the notebook close to her face, then at arm's length, squinting.

'I was born in September 1955 and my parents were happy to have a daughter. My parents were lucky again when they had another daughter eleven months later. My sister was called Kathleen and we had ordinary childhoods. We both went to St Mary's Primary School and they put us in the same class. I won a prize for needlework and Kath sang in the choir. Then we went up to the new comprehensive school, where we both did OK in our studies and got our O levels. We enjoyed music and fashion and going out. Some people thought we were twins because we often wore the same clothes.

'When I was nineteen I got married to Terry. My cousin Edie was my maid of honour because sadly Kath had died, presumed drowned, the Christmas before.

After Terry and I got married we moved into a council house in Chaucer Drive, out in the suburbs. Terry worked as a rep for a printing company and travelled for his work. I worked at a nursery, where I later became the manager. We were not lucky enough to have our own children.' Annie licks a finger and turns over the page.

Slowly, Henrietta leans forward and presses pause on the phone screen.

'Hang on,' she says. 'Your sister. What did you say happened?'

CHAPTER FOUR

ANNIE

The pain is back, radiating from a place deep inside, but Annie holds her head as high as she can as she walks out of the café. That new girl, Henrietta, fiddling with her forms and her phone, has no manners at all. And those questions – Mia hadn't said it would be like that. Damn Mia, with her endless cups of tea and slices of Bakewell tart. *Did you have brothers and sisters? Do you have children?* On the surface, the questions seemed so innocuous, but they cut Annie far too close to the bone.

Then, when Annie started reading out her own words, it felt even worse. Pathetic, so little to show for a lifetime – that's what the girl's face told her, with her blank, uncomprehending stare. But then, with no warning, the girl had asked about Kath – and Annie wasn't ready, not ready at all, to talk about those particular memories.

So she'd said she needed some air, and that was true too because when she stood up she realised she couldn't stay a minute longer in that place, with its stewed tea and sad people. So now she's outside, but the minibus won't be here for ages and her heart is racing and that dizzy ringing in her ears is back.

Annie takes her time walking down the ramp – the cold is making the ache in her stomach worse so she hunches forward, trying not to disturb the beast coiled inside. It would be good to sit down and there's a bench over the road, but she knows it's too far away. Instead, Annie leans against the wall of the building and does her deep breathing, like the teacher in the Stretch and Flow class tells them: 'And breathe, like the waves of the sea. In and out.'

By the time people for her minibus start to trickle out of the building, Annie's heartbeat is almost back to normal. First comes Nora, with her tightly wound headscarf. Then Stefan, still being pushed by Bonnie, that bossy lady in her purple fleece top. He's looking poorly today, his face glistening, and he raises his hand in greeting as he passes by. He can't be older than thirty, she thinks.

The ride home is all stops and starts, drawing up next to vans, Uber drivers and four-wheel drives. Most people are on their phones or talking into thin air so probably still on their phones, just not juggling them with a steering wheel. Annie always sits on her own at the back of the minibus. The fuzziness of the armrests irritates her hands, so she places them in her lap. She notices her nails are flaking, white dots under each one. I'm falling apart, she thinks.

A white Toyota Prius in the next lane nudges forward, the driver's face almost side by side with Annie's. He's young, close-cut hair and a pointy little beard: a handsome man. Annie wonders how much he makes an hour and whether it's worth it and if he has a wife and whether he loves her. The man catches her eye, looks away: nothing to see here.

Annie wants to bang her hand against the window and shout at him, 'I might look like an old woman to you, but I used to turn heads. I could have had anyone. Anyone. If I hadn't settled for Terry.'

Of course she does nothing of the sort. She closes her eyes and waits for the traffic to move on. That Henrietta had been right to look so disappointed at Annie's answers. Her expression told Annie what she already knew: this has been a waste of a life. When she was younger, she would never have believed she'd end up like this: dying alone, no children, no family. Where did it go so wrong?

A sharp vision comes to Annie, herself and her sister at the swing doors to The Bell pub. The brass fingerplate, the glossy brown paint. They are in matching dresses that sit just so on their thighs: Annie's is green; Kath's lemon yellow. They wear belted suede jackets, fake fur at the collars, and knee-high boots, bought with Kath's shop discount. She remembers the smoke, the smell of beer and the rush of noise as they pushed the pub doors apart. They always liked to wait in the doorway for just a moment, so that people could glance up and notice them, then watch as the two sisters shouldered their way towards the bar.

They had a name for themselves: Annie and Kath, the Doyle Girls, only eleven months between them and both pretty as a picture. When they were little, their mother sewed them identical dresses with puff sleeves and Peter Pan collars. The sisters would take turns to stand on a chair while she made her adjustments, a row of pins held tight between her lips. Their job was to rotate as slowly as possible, so Mum could see if the hem was straight, and if you went too fast it earned you a swift slap on the back of the leg.

Annie quite liked standing high above her mother for a change. She could look down on her black curls and see the secret white roots beginning to push their way out. But Kath had no patience and would sigh and slouch, which meant she got slapped calves and a party dress with a wonky hem.

As teenagers, the two of them had revived the tradition of wearing matching outfits, but this time around the dresses were shorter and they did their own alterations. Sometimes they shared clothes, too.

But then a bad memory swoops in, the one where Kath is pulling off the yellow dress. She throws it on the floor, swears, gives it a kick. Her face is twisted and she's messed up her hair. 'I hate this dress. Why do we always have to match? I'm not doing it any more.'

That's the problem with Annie's memories: for every nice one she wants to talk about, a worse one zips in right behind it, whispering about the bad times.

The minibus drops Stefan off first, and it's a bit of a faff with the ramp and the wheelchair brakes and all that. He chats with Annie and Nora while the clanking goes on, as if what is happening below his waist is nothing to do with him. 'Well, see you ladies next week on the fun bus?' he says. 'If we're still here,' they both say, as they always do, a joke they've shared for the few months that they have all been taking this free minibus ride.

Annie is next. Her flat is nearby but the driver has to go the long way round, via a system of one-way roads studded with speed bumps. Annie doesn't drive, never has – that was Terry's domain – so the arrival of speed bumps and parking meters made no difference to her.

Today, though, the shiny tank-like cars are bumper to bumper all along Annie's road so the driver has to double-park outside her flat. It's a low 1970s housing association block, built as an infill between far grander Victorian houses, and the four ground-floor flats are set aside for people like her. It was all down to her nice GP, who took pity on her after Terry died, when she lost her marbles for a while and was taken off for a long stay on Briar ward.

It was the shock, her doctor said, of Terry's accident that had left her in such a state. Words like 'breakdown' and 'at risk' were used. Maybe the GP already had his suspicions about Terry and felt guilty he hadn't done anything to help sooner.

Annie remembers the lady from the housing association saying she was a 'very lucky woman' to get a nice place like this. She feels less lucky these days, but it is good being back in the area where she grew up, before Terry moved her away to Chaucer Drive. The noise of traffic, even the air, it all feels familiar.

There's a silence when she closes the flat door, but it doesn't bother her – the sight of her own home, empty and just as she left it, is always a relief. It's not a big place and her furniture is from the cheap end of Portobello Road market or charity shops, because there wasn't anything she wanted to bring from her marital home. Here, everything is blissfully untainted by the past. If anything, it reminds her of a B&B room she once stayed in. She managed three nights away from Terry that time, before coming back to face the music.

With nobody here to tell her off, Annie heads straight for her bed, sliding her legs under the covers, trousers still on. She's desperate for sleep, but it won't come. She'd imagined this whole Life Stories book thing would be a lot simpler – just a matter of telling a few stories, choosing a few photos – but already it's getting more complicated.

At last, Annie can feel her eyes closing. She tucks her arms around herself, pulls up the covers and waits to be dragged down deeper. An old trick that sometimes helps is if she goes back to her parents' house in Dynevor Road and tries to picture every speck of the place. The wooden gate that you had to jiggle to make it shut, the path with its brick blocks, and the front door with its frosted glass and the dodgy Yale lock that spun round if you turned the key too hard.

Then the hallway with the telephone table, a cream phone with a dial that you put your finger in and had to wait for it to click back into place before you did the next digit. The carpet had orange, brown and gold swirls, worn thin at the front door so you could see the criss-cross of threads underneath. At tea time, the smell of boiled potatoes.

It wasn't a particularly happy house, but she can trace every corner of it without trying too hard. This time, she only gets as far as their bedroom before she starts to drop off, but then the wires in her brain get tangled and a different memory crackles into life. A flash of that yellow dress, its silky lining. A suede jacket, but this time its fur trim laced with dark mud.

Annie lurches awake, her stomach clenched. Thinking about this Life Story book is stirring everything up, bringing back all those bad memories. For so long, she's tried to ignore them, but the minute she lets her guard down they're back, nipping and tugging, crowding around her like hungry children. And now she's tired, so tired, of trying to make them behave.

But perhaps the answer is to stop trying. Instead, she could hand these memories over to that officious Henrietta, who seems so keen on knowing everything, so she can take them in hand and shut them away for good between the hard covers of a book. And then, just maybe, Annie might get some peace.

Annie hoists herself up in bed because that acrid taste is back, rising up her throat. When she first tried to describe how it felt to the doctor, Annie heard herself saying it was as if someone had been sitting next to her all night, shoving brown canal sludge into her mouth, stopping up her tongue and cramming it into her ears. No wonder the doctor had looked a little alarmed. That simply isn't possible, he said.

Still, that's how it feels, like her insides are silted up, the sour rot coming back up her throat. Acid reflux, she reminds herself as she sinks back down into sleep. That's what the doctor has said so many times. Canal sludge is simply not possible.

CHAPTER FIVE

HENRIETTA

On balance, Henrietta concedes that her first Saturday morning at the Grief Café has not been a roaring success. She thought it would be very straightforward – give the interviewee a form to fill out, press 'record' on the phone app and take a few notes. But it all proved rather more complicated.

First, she'd had to contend with a less than enthusiastic past client, then that oddly dressed woman – Annie Doyle, 66, with terminal pancreatic cancer – wasn't much easier. She hadn't been at all keen on the form and when Henrietta had asked her a perfectly reasonable question, she'd shut down completely. Frankly, when Annie had buttoned up her coat and walked out of the door without even saying thank you, it had been a relief.

Inevitably, this little contretemps did not go unnoticed – the young woman from the tea counter had been hovering nearby, making endless, damp circles with her cloth, and must have heard every word. And now, of course, she's working her way over, making a big show of putting vases of flowers on all the tables.

'New, are we?' The girl in the pinny plonks a spray of fake carnations in the centre of Henrietta's table. With her immaculate make-up and her hair in a high plait, she looks like the sort of person who would be better suited to giving make-up tutorials on YouTube and Henrietta wonders how she ended up working in a place like this.

'Good morning, I am Henrietta Lockwood and I shall be here on Tuesday, Thursday and Saturday mornings.' She slides the carnations to one side. This is, after all, her official workspace. 'I will be helping people tell their Life Stories. Because everybody has one.'

'Hiya, Hen. Yeah, I know all about that,' the girl says, nodding to the laminated sign above the table. 'I'm Mia. Everyone here knows me.' She smooths her hair, still held tight in the grip of its plait, and leans forward. 'Hen, you're not a weeper, are you? The last one was a weeper and it didn't help anybody.'

All morning Henrietta has half-watched Mia at her counter, clattering about pouring teas into mugs – white, with 'Rosendale Drop-In Centre' printed on them – and making unnecessarily noisy coffees at her machine. To one side of the counter is a glass-fronted cabinet where all manner of nostalgic cakes are laid out in neat rows: slices of Bakewell tart, wedges of Battenburg, and Tunnock's teacakes wrapped in red foil. Mia restocks it regularly and it is clearly her pride and joy.

But Henrietta won't be troubling Mia for her refreshments or her advice. She silently congratulates herself on having brought her own Thermos and resolves to bring her own mug next time, too. And she must put a stop to being called 'Hen' – in her opinion, it's best to keep things formal.

Without waiting for an invitation, Mia slips into the chair opposite. 'It's tough starting here, isn't it, Hen? I'd say you get used to it, but that would be awful, if you did. If you didn't feel for them all.' Mia looks down at her lap, where she is folding her J-Cloth into neat squares, then smoothing it out again. 'I see them come and go, the patients and their families. They're here for months and then I don't see them again and I never know if that means it's good news or bad. Sometimes they have a moan at me – the tea's too strong, the tea's too weak, the table's dirty. But I know it's not what they are really angry about.'

Henrietta ponders this. 'It is true, Mia. I too have observed that people often say one thing while meaning something completely different.'

Mia reaches out to adjust the carnations so that the blooms face the same direction as those on the neighbouring tables. 'Other people, you can tell if they are barely holding it together,' she says. 'You know that if you give them a smile they will crumble. Or start telling you things and not be able to stop. That's when they need to talk, to get it out of their system.' Mia stands up and begins collecting mugs.

'How long have you worked here, Mia?' Henrietta asks.

'Started as a volunteer, three years ago, Hen. Spent so many hours here when my fiancé, Brice, was in and out for treatment.' Mia presses the clutch of mugs to her chest. 'The nurses here are brilliant, they help you get through it. It was afterwards that it hit me, when I tried to adjust back to normal life. Going back to an ordinary job seemed so, I don't know, pointless?'

Henrietta nods, being no stranger to pointless, disappointing jobs.

'I mean, friends ask how you are for a while. But then they expect you to get over it, come out partying again. So I applied for a job here, because people here get it.'

Henrietta nods again, although 'friends' and 'partying' are less familiar territory. She notices that when Mia stops bustling about with fake flowers and slices of cake, she looks younger and a little lost. Perhaps this isn't the best moment to reprimand Mia for shortening her name to 'Hen'.

Instead, Henrietta decides to ask what's been preying on her mind. 'That woman Annie, she didn't seem very keen to talk. Do you think she'll come back?'

'I hope so,' Mia replies. 'I know she hasn't got long left, poor woman.'

'Not long?' Henrietta echoes.

'From what I've heard, I don't reckon she'll see Christmas.'

Henrietta finds herself making a swift calculation. Annie has just had her first session, leaving just six more Saturdays before Christmas. Now, Henrietta usually likes a deadline, but this one could be rather tight, especially given their unpromising start.

Mia stands up and her old toughness is back. 'But

if Annie doesn't want to tell her story, that's up to her, isn't it?'

* * *

There is a queue at the bus stop and Henrietta joins the end of the line, which places her just beyond the overhang of the shelter. This means she is exposed to the steady November rain, plus the extra run-off from the roof. She supposes she could just move underneath the structure as several other people have, creating a rather messy huddle, but a queue is a queue and should be observed.

The red blur of a bus appears in the distance and, as it gets closer, the line dissolves as everyone jostles towards the doors. As the only one who has obeyed the rules, Henrietta is last on so has to stand all the way, the sharp edge of someone's bag jabbing into her side every time the bus turns a corner. And there we have it, reflects Henrietta: the story of my life.

That evening, when she takes Dave for his walk, Henrietta lets her mind wander. This is a risk, because any outing with Dave is best conducted on high alert, but she finds herself thinking back to Annie Doyle and wondering what lay behind her few carefully chosen words.

Henrietta badly needs to make a success of this job and her previous career hiccups are never far from her mind. Fresh out of university with her first-class degree, Henrietta's first job was at an academic library, where she sat in a book-lined booth and catalogued obscure dissertations from 9 a.m. until 5 p.m. If she listened hard, sometimes she could hear the soft sibilance of turning pages from the next booth along, but she rarely saw her bookish colleagues.

As her initial high hopes for her career ebbed away, Henrietta took to slipping off to forgotten corners of the library stacks, where she would fold her cardigan into a pillow and take afternoon naps, surrounded by dusty, unread books. She liked the way the metal shelves creaked under their volumes, as if letting out a sympathetic bored sigh.

All that came to an abrupt end when a new manager was transferred in and summoned Henrietta for something he called an appraisal. She had listened in horror as he talked of a new system of Department Targets and Production Outcomes. And how, according to his estimates, Henrietta's cataloguing output over the past month amounted to less than a single day's work.

So she bought a new blouse, filled out an application form and applied for a job as a sub-editor on a petrochemical company magazine. Things had not ended well there, either. She'd never meant to wave those scissors around in a threatening manner, it was simply to make her point. Who knew that the correct usage of the Oxford comma could arouse such strong emotions?

But whatever her former colleagues might think, Henrietta Lockwood likes to get a job done. Yes, her afternoon naps at the library were an oversight, but they were born out of sheer boredom. And pressing Annie Doyle for more details of her life story is a far from boring prospect. It will be a challenge, and a challenge is something Henrietta Lockwood can rise to. Her first Life Story book needs to be carefully transcribed, covering her client's major life events. Further questions will need to be asked and any inconsistencies resolved, because Henrietta cannot countenance producing a Life Story book that falls short of these exacting standards.

Ever since her schooldays, Henrietta has been most comfortable when there are guidelines, rules and a measurable degree of success that she can tick off. If Audrey had been efficient enough to provide a job evaluation form (which, of course, she has not) Henrietta would put 'Complete first Life Story' in the Goals column. Under Performance Indicator, she would write 'Include an accurate sequence of major life events'. And, of course, in the third column would be the deadline: 25 December.

What's less easy to put into words, let alone an imaginary spreadsheet, is the way that Henrietta's mind keeps circling back to one particular thing Annie said. When she mentioned, almost as an aside, that her sister had died, 'presumed drowned', a prickling sensation had spread across Henrietta's scalp. Those same words kept coming back to her while she sat with Mia, as she walked to the bus stop and at regular intervals during her journey home. And now she can't ignore them any longer.

A set of images is flitting through her head like old-fashioned slides on a projector, each one worse than the last. It's not Annie's sister she sees drowning, though, it's a little boy, and he is being pulled out of the water by his stick-thin arms. As he's dragged, his bare back bumps over the hot pebbles and his feet flail in the air. There is shouting and she is standing very still in the shallows, watching it all unfold.

Even now, she remembers what struck her most on that hot afternoon was the way that the waves kept coming, steadily slapping against the backs of her legs, as if nothing had altered. The earth was still turning and the sun was still shining, but her whole world was about to change forever.

Audrey was right when she said life is rarely like TV. In Henrietta's experience, a dead body looks far worse in the flesh than on screen. She doesn't know why Annie Doyle refused to talk about how her sister died, but she is sure of one thing. A drowning isn't something you would easily forget.

CHAPTER SIX

ANNIE

A tapping sound wakes her. It seems to be coming from the window, like branches on the pane, but that can't be right because their dad cut the tree down last summer. It's such an effort to peel her eyes open, unglue her face from the pillow. She can see an alarm clock, a glass and a beautiful white rose. No, not a rose at all. A scrunched tissue. And now this bedroom feels empty, too full of cold air, as if something or somebody is missing.

She wakes up properly while she's sitting on the toilet and realises it's OK, she's here, in her own flat, not back at her parents' and not in Chaucer Drive, hasn't been for two lovely, solitary years. She pees, breathing out with relief. The shower is dripping again: tap, tap, tap. That must be what she heard.

She'll take her pills double-quick, before the pain wakes up too. Then she must start writing some notes for what to say tomorrow, when she climbs on board Bonnie's fun bus and heads back to the drop-in centre. Quite who will want to read her story apart from Mia in the café, she can't imagine. Yet it feels necessary to get everything down on paper, to draw a line under things. Annie imagines it will be like having a good clear-out.

After Terry died, she surprised the residents of Chaucer Drive by hiring a skip and doing just that. After forty-four years, she still didn't know any of their neighbours' names – Terry made it clear early on that he preferred it that way. But when the skip arrived, she sensed those nameless neighbours watching from behind net curtains as she went back and forth with a wheelbarrow, carrying out his stereo with its huge brown speakers, his boxes of LPs, his suits, his rowing machine and dumb-bells, the slippery piles of magazines from his tool shed.

When she'd finished, a lorry came and winched up that big yellow skip and as it swayed in the air Annie had felt a glimmer of hope, as if the weight of her past might be about to lift.

That afternoon at 53 Chaucer Drive, things didn't quite work out that way, but maybe this book is Annie's second chance. It'll definitely be her last one.

Last week, she'd been caught off guard by Henrietta's questions, and even now, it's difficult to know where to start her story. What to say, what to leave out. Annie knows she'll have to talk about Kath, but last week had felt too soon to dive straight in.

She supposes she could start by telling Henrietta about something far nicer – working at the nursery, perhaps. Or a story from when she and Kath were little – that holiday when the sun shone and shone and they spent every day on the beach. But lately, those sorts of memories elude her.

It reminds her of a lucky dip at the school fair where she paid her tuppence and reached so far down into the bin that the sawdust clung to the sleeve of her sweater. She wanted to get to the very bottom, where the best presents would be, but Mrs Sims told her to hurry up so she panicked and pulled out the first thing she touched, which was something cheap and useless. Kath got a doll, of course. It had blonde hair and blue eyes and Mrs Sims said, 'Oh, well done, Kathleen!'

Anyway, that's what delving for old memories feels like – stretching her fingers as far as she can to touch the earliest, happiest ones, but she can't find them. Each time she tries, her fingers close on something rotten and bad that's closer to the surface. These days, even her happy memories feel tainted by what came later or what was simmering under the surface all along. Even the sweetest times with Kath – walking into The Bell arm in arm, dancing by the jukebox, whispering secrets to each other in the dark – have a bitter aftertaste.

Jealousy is an ugly emotion, but it's one Annie learned to live with from an early age. As soon as her little sister could walk and talk, she was the special one. Even at school, if Annie put up her hand, the teacher's gaze would skim over her head, looking for her younger sister. And at home, there was never any effort to disguise the fact that Kath was the favourite. She got to scrape the cake mixing bowl clean, dry the dishes instead of washing up, and she could wrap their dad around her little finger.

Aidan Doyle used to sing her an old Irish song, 'I'll Take You Home Again, Kathleen', and their mum would roll her eyes and smile. He never sang about taking Annie anywhere, not even in jest.

At every children's party, school play or sports day, people doted on Kath, and Annie learned that it was best to just keep smiling. 'Isn't she a picture?' 'Adorable.' 'You must be so proud.' So she smiled until her cheeks ached, folding that hot, dark emotion back in on itself, waiting until they were home and she had Kath to herself in their bedroom.

Because sometimes, Kath needed taking down a peg or two, and no one else was going to do it, were they? And what sisters didn't fight every now and then?

But then came that dreadful night in December and Kath was gone for good. And Annie would have taken back every cross word, every spiteful snipe and secret pinch, just to have her sister back by her side.

Annie sighs and puts down her pen, feels the coil of pain twisting deeper into her stomach, bedding in for the day. She's not stupid enough to hope for absolution, it's too late for that. It's more a matter of getting the words out and leaving this world with a clean conscience. Or as clean as possible, in the circumstances.

CHAPTER SEVEN

HENRIETTA

The next Saturday, Henrietta is somewhat flustered by the time she gets to the Rosendale Drop-In Centre. Her morning got off to an inauspicious start, due to an incident between Dave and a jogger. As Henrietta made abundantly clear to the man in black Lycra, there had been 'No. Physical. Contact.' But, she admits, the barking had been intense, even by Dave's standards.

She has to rush to collect a stack of questionnaires from the office and is out of breath as she sits down at the café table. Frankly, the last thing she feels like doing is talking to anyone.

She hears Bonnie the minibus helper before she sees her, ushering her group through the double doors. First in is the man in the beanie hat, his face like thunder as Bonnie gives a running commentary – 'Here we go then! Through the door!' – like he's a child. Then comes a woman in a headscarf and, bringing up the rear, is Annie Doyle.

Henrietta takes a sip of water and notices that her hand is shaking a little. This week, she tells herself, it is important to put Annie at ease, so she puts on her empathetic face, angling her head to one side.

Then all at once Annie is right there, shrugging off her coat, dumping a large raffia basket on a chair and moving things around on Henrietta's desk to make way for her mug of tea. Then she stops, looks at Henrietta in a puzzled way. She cocks her own head. 'You alright, dear? Crick in the neck? Try a bit of Tiger Balm – works a treat,' she says. 'Or maybe Mia can rustle you up a paracetamol.'

But Mia isn't around; instead a portly man is at the counter, his lower lip protruding as he concentrates on pouring from the giant teapot.

'I'm fine, thank you,' Henrietta says slowly, taking in Annie's curious outfit.

Under her coat, Annie Doyle is dressed in a dark-blue boilersuit, the sort of thing a plumber might wear. Except she's put a thick belt around her middle and on her feet she is wearing a pair of pointy boots with big buckles, which put Henrietta in mind of a children's book about elves and shoemakers.

'So, I've had a bit of a think since last week,' Annie says, 'and I've come to a decision.'

Here it comes, thinks Henrietta. She doesn't want to do her story. Only I could manage to lose a client before she's even died.

'I'm not filling out that questionnaire,' Annie says.

'That's fine, you're well within your rights. I will simply erase your first recording. It'll be like it never happened.' Henrietta begins to tidy her papers, tapping them on the table so they line up. 'It can be difficult.

Remembering things from one's past.'

Annie, who has been busy unwrapping a mini packet of biscuits, looks up. She holds a bourbon cream over her mug of tea, about to dip it in. 'Eh?' In one quick motion she dunks the biscuit, opens her mouth wide and pops it in. 'You see, I've filled in enough forms for social workers and doctors to last me a lifetime. I want to do my story, but I need to do it my way. The things I need to say aren't about pets or what games we played in the playground.'

Annie reaches for her next biscuit. 'So how about I just talk about things that matter to me, as they come into my head? And you can put them in the book any way you like. That organising side doesn't bother me – it's not like I'll be around to read it.'

'But what about the chronology and the Life Story template? What about keeping it all in order?' Henrietta can hear the note of panic in her voice.

'The funny thing is . . .' Here, Annie pauses to drink her tea. 'When you look back, you don't see your own life in an orderly way. It's more like snapshots – like in a photo album. And sometimes it's hard to remember the bits in between, like what happened the moment before the photo was taken or just after. Do you know what I mean?'

On the one hand, it's a relief that Annie still wants to do her book, but her idea of a jumble of disconnected stories is making Henrietta extremely uncomfortable. However, they are already seven minutes into their allotted hour. Each client's story needs to be told in seven sessions and Annie also has an unspoken deadline of Christmas, just six Saturdays away. Henrietta clicks the end of her pen and taps the red circle on her phone. This unstructured approach is far from ideal but, for now, it will have to do. 'Very well, Annie Doyle, we are ready for session two of your Life Story. Today is Saturday the thirteenth of November.'

Annie smiles, puts two hands around her mug and begins. 'If you lived in our patch of west London in the seventies, you would have heard of me and my sister Kath, but in a good way. If there was a party, the first thing people asked was, "Are the Doyle Girls going?" Because if we weren't, it wasn't worth bothering with.'

She looks Henrietta in the eye. 'I know, hard to believe now. But it's true. We were good girls, mind, so we didn't start going to the pub until Kath turned eighteen. But the first time we walked in The Bell, we realised that it was a whole new ballgame. Nothing like the youth club.'

'The Bell?' asks Henrietta.

'A pub near Ladbroke Grove. Well known, back in the day. Sometimes they had live music on a Friday. All the greats hung out there – Dr Feelgood, Joe Strummer, Van the Man. Dylan played a set one Sunday lunchtime.'

Henrietta makes a note of Annie's friends' names and nods for her to continue.

'We never had much money, so we'd share a half of lager and stand next to the jukebox. It was a good one, too, had all the best stuff. 'Mama Told Me Not To Come', 'Telegram Sam', 'All The Young Dudes', 'Starman': we knew all the words . . . And because we stood there, blokes would come over to put music on, and proper blokes, they were. Not like the Catholic boys at the youth club. These were men who worked for a living, who had sideburns and flared jeans that came in tight in all the right places.

'Kath was more forward, so she'd always ask for a fag or a drink, but it never meant anything to her – she'd take her rum and Coke and leave them standing there, gawping. But she always got away with it.

'So off we'd go for a night out, arm in arm, our hair fresh out of rollers so we had the biggest flicks. It was exciting, back then, walking into a pub. The music, the smoke, the crush at the bar. We'd wear things that matched, so we looked good as a pair, you know? If Kath wore jeans, I would. If I wanted to wear a dress, she would . . .'

Annie trails off and looks around, as if surprised to find herself here, under the bright strip lighting of the café, with crumpled biscuit wrappers and dirty cups and Henrietta sitting opposite, pen poised in mid-air. Then the juddery glass doors at the entrance open and close, letting in a blast of cold air, and Annie tries to gather herself. She looks down at the phone, up at Henrietta, away again.

'Of course, that was the first place I went looking, the night Kath disappeared,' she says at last, her voice softer now. 'Being Christmas, it was packed, but the barman said she hadn't been in. I looked and looked, but the rain that night, it didn't stop. So hard to see in the dark . . .'

Henrietta does not dare speak because it'll almost certainly be the wrong thing. Her past is littered with blunders and faux pas that are immediately obvious to everyone except her. One wrong word and there's a danger that Annie will walk off again and they will never get back to talking about her sister.

On the table between them, the red numbers on the phone app tick by, recording the long silence. All around, the low murmur of other people chatting. Chairs are scraped back; the coffee machine hisses and froths.

Then Annie shakes her head. 'Perhaps this isn't such a good idea, after all.' Something has altered in the air and her face has changed. It's like when the shutters on Mia's tea counter are pulled down at the end of the day with a clatter and all the bright wrappers and cakes disappear from sight.

Henrietta's breath catches in her throat. Annie Doyle doesn't seem to understand that major points in each Life Story need to be covered, even difficult ones. Fundamental events like a drowning – the sort that can change the course of a life.

The clock says 11.30 a.m. and she is aware that Annie's time is running out – not just today's one-hour session but the number of weeks she has left to live, whether she knows it or not. And Henrietta can't make a book out of a few recollections about jukeboxes and hair rollers. It just won't do. This is what comes of people ignoring the rules and diving into random anecdotes.

She decides to chance it. 'Annie, we have a limited number of sessions in which to cover your story, so time is of the essence. A chronological framework is favoured, but your book can be, how shall I put it, "episodic", if you insist. But I do need material. I am going to fetch us some refreshments and when I return, I would very much like to resume with a key event. The loss of your sister.'

CHAPTER EIGHT

ANNIE

Truth be told, Annie isn't even that keen on Bakewell tart, but as soon as she sees the glistening white icing, she feels hungry all over again. And it's nice, this feeling that someone is looking out for her for once.

'Thanks. All I seem to be able to eat right now is sugar,' she says, scooping up the jammy crumbs with shaking fingers. She can't work this Henrietta out, but her no-nonsense manner makes a pleasant change. She's done with therapists and their careful sympathy, their half-smiles and the way they repeat your own words back to you like an echo. If anyone can help her get her story out, maybe it's this girl with her long silences and her blank, round face.

'Alright, Henrietta Lockwood, I'll tell you about my sister and the night in 1974 when she didn't come home.'

Henrietta springs into action and presses her red button. And Annie begins.

'Kath was eighteen and I was nineteen and it was the last Saturday before Christmas. Kath had been working in the shoe shop all day and we'd planned to go out. But six o'clock teatime came and went and there was no sign of her. At first I was put out, because I thought she'd gone somewhere with the girls from the shop and forgotten about me. Most of the time we got on, but sometimes Kath could be sneaky like that.' She looks up at Henrietta. 'You know how it is. With sisters.'

But maybe Henrietta doesn't know, because she just stares back, unblinking, so Annie carries on.

'I didn't have any other plans. I wasn't seeing Terry so much then and he was out with his boys from the printing works, which was fine by me.

'While I waited, I watched TV with my mum and dad. I remember there was a man with huge sideburns who was absolutely rubbish at *The Generation Game* – he couldn't tell Bruce Forsyth anything that was on the conveyor belt. Not even the cuddly toy. We had a good laugh at him; even my dad cracked a smile.'

Annie can almost hear the audience's shrieks of laughter – her dad always turned the volume up high. 'If I've paid for my TV licence, I want to get my money's worth,' he used to say. But even with all that noise, they were all keeping an ear out for the sound of Kath's key in the lock.

By the time *Kojak* came on TV at 9.30 p.m., her dad wasn't smiling any more. He started pacing up and down, going on about Kath stopping out, how he'd give her a piece of his mind when she got home. Her mum moved over to the front window, holding an inch of net curtain to one side, getting ready to say, 'Ah, Aidan, here she is.' But she never did. When it got to 10 p.m.

and her dad pressed the clunky 'off' button on the TV, Annie knew things were getting serious.

'I pretended to go up to bed, but then I slipped out of the house,' she tells Henrietta. 'At that point, I just thought Kath was out having a good time without me, so I was cross. I imagined her already in the pub, flirting with some new bloke, not bothering to ring me from the payphone to say, "Get yourself down here." I went to The Bell first, but it was just faces and music and shrieking laughter and the barman said he hadn't seen Kath, not all evening. Then I tried another pub around the corner, but she wasn't there, either.'

Annie had even gone past the shoe shop and peered through the windows. She doesn't know what she was looking for – a clue of some sort – but of course it was all shut up and dark inside.

'Then I just walked and walked in the rain, in case I saw her. I pushed open the doors of a few more pubs, I walked past a big house party that was just getting going in Powis Square. A couple of girls we knew from school were going in, but they hadn't seen Kath. They invited me along, but I said no, I had to keep looking.'

Annie couldn't say for sure which roads she'd been up and down that night, she'd just kept going in the rain and the dark. It was like she was on some drunken mission, except she was stone-cold sober. What she does remember very clearly is creeping back into the house and seeing the slice of yellow light under the living-room door.

'I could tell my dad was still sitting up in the front room and I guessed my mum had gone up to bed. As I got to our bedroom door, just for a second I thought, wouldn't it be wonderful if I opened it and saw Kath right there, tucked up in bed? I imagined how I'd rip that cover off and call her a cow for going out without me. But when I flicked on the light, Kath's bed was as smooth and empty as before.'

Annie stops to catch her breath and when she looks up, Henrietta is staring at her, an unreadable expression on her face. There's no judgement, no pity, as Annie says these terrible things, and that's what gives Annie the courage to carry on.

'It wasn't until Sunday morning that I thought of ringing Debbi, one of the girls from the shoe shop. My dad watched me dial the number, then put his head close so he could hear the ringing tone, then Debbi's mum answering.'

It had felt all wrong, her dad letting Annie take charge. His cheek was rough with stubble, his clothes rumpled and his breath sour, but in that brief moment, standing with their heads together to the telephone receiver, she'd felt an unexpected tenderness towards him.

'Debbi said that Kath had asked to leave work early – closer to five p.m. – and Debbi kept moaning about how it wasn't fair because she'd had to manage on her own: people were buying slippers and wanted them gift-wrapped and some woman trying on heels couldn't decide which she wanted. When I put down the phone I wished I was Debbi, because all she had to worry about was that she'd worked extra hard the Saturday before Christmas. Then I told our dad he'd better get down Notting Dale Police Station and me and my mum watched as he laced up his best shoes and set off to do that. There was no talk of going to church that Sunday.'

It was hours before Aidan Doyle came home. He said they'd kept him waiting at the police station, but the beer on his breath made it clear he'd stopped off for a few pints on the way back.

'When my dad got in, he was furious – he had a temper, our dad. The police had sent him away, practically laughed at him. He kicked the kitchen door, said they were lazy gobshites and should be ashamed of themselves. Even before that, Aidan Doyle was not a fan of the local constabulary, and vice versa.

'The shoe shop manager found Kath's bike on Monday morning, propped up against boxes of old stock in the store room – he said he often let her leave it there if she forgot her bike lock. That made me think she wasn't coming straight home. That she'd been planning to go somewhere she couldn't take the bike.'

Until now, Henrietta has been as silent as her recording app, just scribbling away in her notebook, but now she leans forward. 'And the police, when did they realise it was more serious and mount a search?'

Oh, this girl with her neat notes and her recordings, she's such an innocent. She still doesn't get what it was like back then. 'I'm not sure they ever did,' Annie says slowly. 'Debbi told us she'd seen Kath zip up her jacket and step out into the high street. Then nothing – no trace. CCTV wasn't really a thing back then and I'm not convinced the police interviewed anyone over the next few days.

'They could have asked all the bus conductors on shift or the man in the ticket booth in the Tube station or the newsagent on the corner, where Kath bought cigarettes. Then there must have been hundreds of Christmas shoppers, all out buying bubble bath and handkerchiefs and boxes of chocolates, with only four days to go. They could have asked them, put out an appeal . . .'

Annie trails off and the tiny spark of hope inside her goes out as she remembers she's here, in the café, and all this was a long time ago. She picks at a loose blue thread on her boiler suit, tugs it until it comes free.

'Anyway. Then it was Christmas and, with time off and the usual drunks and thieving, the police didn't do much. All they had to go on were her clothes, which were found under a bridge by the Grand Union Canal. They said she was probably off with a boyfriend and would breeze back in once she'd had her fun. But that never happened. Kath was never seen again.

'In the new year, they put up some posters, but no witnesses ever came forward. They questioned a few people, but that was just for show – they all had alibis. Then the policeman in charge started talking about "death by misadventure", how she'd probably gone to a party, taken a shortcut home and fallen in and drowned.'

Annie remembers the rumours that had gone round the neighbourhood, words muttered over pints, in the supermarket queue or after church. That Kath liked a drink and had always been a bit wild. Then there was the version that she'd got herself in trouble and drowned herself to save the family from shame.

'When they started talking about suicide, that was what pushed my mum over the edge. She never really recovered.' For a moment Annie's back there, in that house where the air was thick with grief, sitting by her mum's bed while, downstairs, her dad raged. That was the darkest time.

'In the months and years afterwards I used to go and walk along the canal on my afternoons off. I needed to see it, to imagine the worst, and in an awful way it made me feel closer to her. But I wish I hadn't because I've never been able to get the thought of it out of my head. All that silty black water . . .'

Her words are tumbling out now, fast and breathy. 'I dream of it, Hen. All the time. And I can't bear it any more. That she ended up down there, alone with all the mud and the weeds.'

Now Henrietta is peering at her oddly and Annie knows she's said too much. She puts her head in her hands, tries to breathe deeply. But perhaps Henrietta isn't bothered about Annie losing it among the Bakewell tart crumbs and the cold dregs of tea. She seems more worried about the lapses in police procedure.

'But that is deplorable,' Henrietta says. 'Surely, the longer they left it, the less likely they were to find any evidence.'

Annie sighs and lifts her head. 'As I say, we weren't a priority. When my dad walked into the police station that Sunday morning, do you know what they said?'

Henrietta shakes her head.

'They said, "Mr Doyle, if you can't control your teenage daughter, that's not our problem."'

In the silence that follows, Annie takes a good look at Henrietta, because she's hard to work out, this one. 'How old are you, Hen, twenty-something?'

'I'm thirty-two.'

Not what Annie had been expecting. Somehow, Henrietta seems so much younger.

'Well, this was way before your time, but in 1974 London was on high alert for IRA bombings. It was on people's minds, you know, and if you had an Irish accent, well . . .'

'And your father was involved in that?'

'Nooo!' Annie scoffs. This girl is so literal-minded. Not big on nuances.

'Aidan Doyle was small fry, didn't have the nous to be political, either. What I mean is that the police were in no hurry to go looking for an Irishman's daughter who had stayed out too late. So, no, Henrietta, nobody worked out what happened on that night back in 1974. And they haven't bothered to wonder since.'

It's nearly twelve o'clock and Annie's time is almost up. She feels the weight of her words settling into the air, the two of them thinking them over. Henrietta seems on the verge of saying something. Her hand hovers, as if reaching towards Annie's, but then there is a commotion at the glass doors – it's Bonnie, waving her purple-fleeced arms like she's flagging down an aircraft – and the moment is gone.

Annie stands up and, as she passes behind Henrietta, she pats the girl on the shoulder as if it's her, not Annie, who has just been through something difficult. It's only once she's on board the minibus that Annie lets go. She rests her forehead on the fogged-up window and her tears feel thin and mealy, as if they've dried up after such a long time. She cries for Kath, for herself, for the whole damn mess. And as she cries, she feels a knot in her chest beginning to loosen.

Saying those words hadn't been so bad in the end. Henrietta's quiet acceptance helped, the way she seemed to let her mind drift off, leaving behind a polite expression and a pair of hands that wrote things down and tapped at the phone screen. But then a coldness runs through Annie as she remembers the reasons why someone might feel the need to switch off and retreat from the world.

Maybe talking to Henrietta was easy because she reminds Annie of herself. Not Annie as she is now and not even Annie as a naive nineteen-year-old who just wanted to have fun on a Saturday night, but Annie of the long, empty years after she was married. The woman who had lost a sister, married a bully and moved out to suburbia, where she discovered that making herself very small and quiet was the best way to survive.

And then one day, many years later, she looked in the mirror and realised that life had silently passed her by. Her grey hair, that ache in her knees, the muffle in her left ear – they weren't going away. While she'd been busy washing up and cooking Terry's tea and wiping kids' noses, she'd grown old.

Henrietta doesn't wear a wedding ring, so maybe there isn't a man like Terry waiting for her at home, but

Annie is pretty sure that someone in that girl's life has made her feel like she's no good, told her to shut up, put up and behave. For the rest of the journey, Annie keeps her forehead on the cool window and her eyes tightly closed, right up until she feels the minibus rock up and over the first of the speed bumps, the sign that she's nearly home.

CHAPTER NINE

HENRIETTA

After Annie and her companions have filed out of the doors, Henrietta methodically gathers her things together and heads for the women's toilets. She needs to be on her own, out of the bustle and noise and false cheeriness of the Grief Café.

She stands at the sink for a long time, holding both her hands under the tap. It is the sort of tap that works on a sensor, so every now and then she has to waggle her fingers to keep the flow coming. Stop, go, stop, go – it works so efficiently, washing everything away, and it carries on working whatever people feel when they stand here: grief, sadness, loneliness, fear. For some, relief and joy. The tap just keeps on going, and this is how Henrietta likes to think of herself, too: efficient, unflappable.

Eventually, she looks up at the mirror and is surprised to see that she looks exactly the same as when she left for work this morning. Untrammelled, a little pale, but certainly nothing like the swirling maelstrom inside her. Yes, from the outside, she probably seems entirely composed, but inside Henrietta feels weakened, as if she's been chopped up into pieces and put back together in a haphazard way and none of the bits join up properly.

For as long as she can remember, Henrietta has been very good at keeping things under control. She prefers to think of it as part of her overall efficiency – like that splendid modern tap. She keeps going. She keeps up appearances.

The facial expression she assumes at times of stress – what she thinks of as her mask of indifference – is part of this. Sometimes she can even feel it forming inch by inch, and that's what happened just now with Annie. As this elderly woman talked about her sister's drowning, Henrietta felt her own face hardening like quick-drying plaster.

She had wanted to say the right thing – something empathetic, for example. She could have simply said 'Sorry for your loss', but no words came out. The truth is, what came into her head were some wholly inappropriate words that her father imparted to her many years ago. 'Drowning is thought to be rather a peaceful way to die,' he'd said, rocking back and forth on his heels as if delivering a lecture. 'When water incrementally seeps into a person's mouth and then their lungs, their brain shuts down and they feel virtually no pain.'

At least she hadn't been foolish enough to blurt out these words to Annie, because she's never believed that explanation. She didn't fall for it when she was nine years old, when she'd seen a little boy's lips turn the colour of a bruise, his eyes wide, with a dreadful emptiness to them. And she certainly doesn't believe it now. Instead, she can far more easily imagine the mute panic of opening your mouth, desperate to breathe, and feeling not air but water rush in. And she's pretty sure that Annie has imagined that moment too.

Eventually she has to leave the safety of the women's toilets and she heads towards the lift that will take her up to Audrey's office. As she crosses the café, the morose man is clearing her table so Henrietta raises a hand to say goodbye, but he carries on wiping, as if he hasn't even noticed her. This happens a lot to Henrietta.

But not to worry, she has plenty to keep her busy. This afternoon she has Life Story proofs to read and emails to answer and then she will go home and she will walk Dave and watch Saturday-night TV and make sure that her mind does not wander. She will try very hard not to picture how the final minutes of Kath Doyle's life might have played out. The panic as she struggled to breathe, then a numb dizziness as the strength drained from her body. As Henrietta steps into the lift she sees black water, a slick jumble of limbs. A bundle of clothes left on the water's edge. She gives her head a sharp shake and presses the lift button.

* * *

That evening, she and Dave trudge around the deserted roads of the industrial estate, their favoured walk since they became *persona et canis non grata* at the local park. When she picked Dave out from a line-up at Last Chance Dog Rescue, Henrietta had imagined quite a different future for the two of them. 'He has some socialisation issues,' the woman with the lanyard had told her. 'Not to worry, I have experience in this area,' Henrietta told her firmly.

Dave was an unspecified terrier-mix, squat with wiry fur that resisted brushing and ears too big for his face. His greying muzzle indicated he was a 'senior', the kind of dog that usually got overlooked, but Henrietta knew he was just right for her. Here, she decided, was her passport to joining the merry band of dog walkers that she'd seen congregate at the park.

All last summer, she'd observed these women and their hounds from a safe distance. She'd eavesdropped on titbits of doggie news, learning how Monty the labradoodle 'desperately needs a haircut' or Luna the dachshund 'is literally obsessed with her tennis ball'. She saw how their dogs would sniff each other politely, then bound off to play in a loveable rough-and-tumble way. And afterwards, the women would call out bright and easy things like 'See you at the gym' and 'Don't forget – book club tonight!'

On their first outing to the park, Henrietta had a spring in her step. She couldn't wait to introduce Dave to his new friends – and perhaps open up a whole new world of opportunities for herself. Unfortunately, Dave didn't wait for introductions: he made straight for Trinny the Lhasa apso and tried to sink his teeth into her fluffy nape. Thankfully, all he came away with was a mouthful of fur, but it was made quite clear that Dave was not a welcome addition to the merry band. And neither was Henrietta.

Tonight, as they pass by the shuttered garages and empty car parks, Henrietta feels her thoughts returning to Annie Doyle and the troubling aspects of her story. First and foremost is the police's inaction. 'Nobody worked out what happened on that night back in 1974,' Annie had said. 'And they haven't bothered to wonder since.' In Henrietta's view, a more thorough investigation is well overdue. In fact, she can't contemplate writing a Life Story in which an event such as this is glossed over, dismissed as a footnote.

Apparently 'a few people' had been questioned, but no action was taken, while the search for Kath's body sounds half-hearted at best. What made Annie and her family accept the police blithely saying it was 'death by misadventure'? It wasn't even an official coroner's verdict. Henrietta badly wants to untangle these strands of Annie's story and lay them out so they make more sense.

Then there's the question of how much she can rely on Annie Doyle's recollections. It could be that Annie doesn't want to dredge up her past (something Henrietta can understand), or it may be that, aged nineteen, she wasn't told the full details of the case. Either way, Henrietta has the feeling that she's not getting the whole story from Annie. What Henrietta needs to set her own mind at rest are hard facts.

Of course, the best source of information would be the police, but she knows she can't just dial 999 and ask to see an ancient missing person file. Henrietta has watched her fair share of cold-case TV dramas and she can picture what Kathleen Doyle's file would look like by now: a dusty manilla folder with her name written across the top; inside, sheafs of paper held together with rusty paperclips; typewritten statements, the ink smudged and faded. Her best chance of locating this file, Henrietta believes, is to get in touch with the original police station and hope for a sympathetic officer.

She and Dave are approaching the halfway mark of their walk, the point where they usually turn and head for home. It's the car wash that she frequents once a month, treating her Nissan Micra to their 'Executive Super Wash', and tonight three men are sharing a cigarette under its awning, sheltering from the first spatterings of rain. Are they working late, she wonders, or maybe they just never leave the place? Silently, the men pass the cigarette back and forth and one of them looks up. He's the youngest, the one who attaches the pine-scented car freshener to her rear-view mirror – a personal touch she always appreciates.

She hesitates, on the verge of waving hello, but then stops. Don't be so silly, she tells herself. He won't even recognise you. All he sees is a lone woman in a duffle coat, walking her antisocial dog in the rain.

Henrietta gives Dave's lead a gentle tug. They turn for home and she lets her mind return to that image of Kathleen Doyle's long-forgotten police file. This is what she needs to find and she has an idea forming for how to track it down.

* * *

An hour later, her laptop on her knees, Henrietta discovers her brilliant plan has one fundamental flaw.

Notting Dale Police Station, where Aidan Doyle first raised the alarm one Sunday morning in 1974, has long since been sold off to a developer, and its nearest neighbouring station at Notting Hill is about to go the same way. Already it has no desk service because, its website tells her, 'Ninety-two per cent of queries from the public are submitted by phone or online'.

Actually, this could be preferable, Henrietta reasons. In her view, a politely worded email is always far better than a rambling, unpredictable phone conversation. She is gratified to find a central Metropolitan Police website with the option to 'Request information about someone'. She clicks on the correct box and waits.

But this takes her to a page with far less comfortable choices. No, she is not requesting information for a Family Court case. Neither does she need to know if her partner has a conviction for domestic violence or a sexual offence against a child. Not surprisingly, there is no box to click for those who are curious about a cold case from the 1970s that is, strictly speaking, none of their business.

Dave snuffles into her side, so she scratches under his grey muzzle, then moves on to the matted fur on his belly. Henrietta needs to try a different tack. She keeps clicking and searching until she discovers something called the Missing Persons Unit. Henrietta feels a flutter of excitement as she enters Kath's name, age and the year 1974 into their search engine. This is excellent: it will confirm or refute the information Annie has given her.

But her enthusiasm evaporates when she sees a

short, morbid set of results appear on her screen. It brings up just three unsolved cases, each woman's body so decomposed or damaged that the only hope of identifying them is their clothes. She glimpses a snapshot of a grey hoodie, rumpled and stained. A muddy trainer. A cheap bracelet with silver charms.

None of these is Kath. In fact, these three cases are far more recent, all within the last fifteen years, and now Henrietta doubts whether the database even goes back to the 1970s. She thinks of the youngest of these women, who put on her hoodie one day to leave home but never came back. And how, fifteen years later, still no one has come forward to claim her. Henrietta gently closes the lid of her laptop: she's not sure she has the stomach for this line of enquiry.

This has been a sobering experience and Henrietta can well imagine what would happen if she were to turn up at a police station tomorrow morning. 'So, Ms Lockwood, you want access to a file that's nearly fifty years old. What, precisely, is your interest in the case? Do you have new evidence? Are you a relative? A legal representative?'

No, none of the above. She's just a failed librarian, prone to overreacting, who should keep a tighter lid on things. Her best option is to keep talking to Annie and hope that she is more forthcoming about the case.

Come to think of it, it might also be worth asking Annie about the demise of her husband, the one who met with an 'unfortunate accident'. What are the chances, she wonders, of losing not one but two people close to you in fatal accidents?

Her father would know: Edmund Lockwood can be counted on to have a little-known statistic or a probability rating for most things in life. And death, for that matter. She will be seeing her parents – emphatically not dead, just buried deep in Tunbridge Wells – tomorrow. For Sunday is when Henrietta makes her weekly journey home for lunch and listens to her mother and father conduct their post-mortem on The Disappointing Life of Henrietta Lockwood.

She turns on the TV just as the theme tune to *Strictly Come Dancing* is starting up. She's about to switch channels when who should pop up on the screen but Ryan Brooks, Mr Life Stories Project himself, shimmying around the dance floor in a sequinned pale blue one-piece. It's alright for him, she thinks, telling everyone to share their memories and then waltzing off, quite literally, without thinking about the consequences. Meanwhile, Henrietta is beginning to suspect that digging around in the past is a dangerous business.

She clicks off the TV, and all the glitter, wide smiles and whooping disappear in an instant, leaving Henrietta alone in the gnawing silence. There's a bad feeling in the pit of her stomach. Something about Annie Doyle's story is deeply wrong. It's just that she can't quite work out which aspect troubles her the most – or what she should do about it.

CHAPTER TEN

Annie

Well, this isn't quite how I imagined spending my Saturday night as a newly single woman, Annie thinks to herself. She's been sitting in this armchair for hours now, the one she sank into after Bonnie's minibus dropped her home, and she still hasn't got the energy to move. No, Annie Doyle is not exactly living it up tonight.

In fact, she keeps nodding off, but then jolting awake as she remembers the things she told Henrietta. Already, she's said more about Kath than she has in years, and there's so much more to come out. It's as if Henrietta has unlocked something and now the words are bubbling up at her throat, waiting for their chance to escape.

Everything feels churned up inside her – and that slice of Bakewell tart she had this morning isn't helping. Some days her guts seem to grind to a halt, like they've forgotten how to work, and she can picture her tubes silted up, black and solid as the mud that haunts her dreams. Other days, everything abruptly turns to liquid and she has to run to the loo, waiting it out until the cramps finally ease. She suspects today is one of those days – and that bad things are destined to come spilling out of Annie Doyle in all sorts of ways.

There's plenty more to say about Kath, but when she thinks about those nights at The Bell it gets all jumbled up with images of Terry, because he's hovering at the edges of those good times, tainting her memories. She's not sure she can burden Henrietta with him just yet but, yes, she needs to get Terry Vickerson out of her system too.

Maybe she can tell Henrietta about the first time she met Terry, dress it up a little so it sounds a bit more romantic. Because it wasn't exactly love at first sight – Terry was just another bloke in The Bell who bought them drinks and tried his luck. The only difference was, on that first night he made a beeline for Annie instead of Kath. She knows why now – she was an easier target – but at the time, she'd been flattered.

'Wasn't you two in the class below me?' he'd asked. 'I remember a pretty face.' Then he looked from Annie to Kath. 'Or two.'

He swayed a little, Annie remembers that much, and his breath was beery as he steadied himself and leaned in. Wiry ginger hairs sprouted from the top of his T-shirt, struggling to escape. She and Kath had exchanged knowing smiles.

'Buy us a drink? Go on.' Kath stepped forward, always the pushier one and used to getting her way.

That was how it started, then Terry's mate Brian tagged along to make up a foursome. It wasn't like they were dating, they were just hanging out together, a regular Friday thing. Terry usually had wads of fivers (he said he won it on the dogs at White City, but nobody believed him) and Brian was his shadow, always there with his lighter at the ready but mostly tolerated because he had a car.

Sometimes, if there was no lock-in at The Bell, the four of them would get two bags of chips to share and sit in Brian's Vauxhall Viva. Then Annie snogged Terry and Kath went with Brian, but neither of them went too far. At first, it was good fun. But then came a night when it stopped being fun and Annie realised that Terry was bad news.

It was last orders in The Bell and none of them were ready to go home. 'I've got a mate called Leon,' Terry said. 'His dad's a school caretaker. His mum's done a bunk and his dad's never there. Leon lets us into the classrooms – it's a laugh.'

They were already drunk by the time they arrived at the school, Kath hanging on to Annie's arm, so it took a moment to realise where he'd brought them. They saw the looming red-brick Victorian building with tall windows, the goal marked out on the asphalt: it was Annie and Kath's old primary school.

Terry pulled a handful of coins out of his pocket and started aiming them at a window in a flat high above the classrooms. To them, the sound of the pennies hitting the glass was deafening. 'Terry, you'll break it,' hissed Annie, knowing he wasn't going to listen.

Terry cupped his hands around his mouth: 'Leon! Leon, mate!'

A window opened and a dazed-looking boy appeared, rubbing his eyes and squinting until he made out the figures below. 'I was sleeping,' he said.

'Mate, it's me, Terry, remember? Let us in, eh?'

The window slid shut and a few minutes later the boy appeared at a side door. His hair was mussed up from sleep and he was a skinny thing, long legs in too-short tracksuit bottoms. He looked nervous, but a bunch of keys dangled from his hand.

'Yeah, alright, Terry, Brian, long time no see.' Leon had put some glasses on, NHS specs with black frames. Annie felt sorry for him and wondered what could have been so bad to make his mum take off and leave her kids behind.

'Your dad out, I hope?' Terry asked, lighting up a cigarette, passing one to Leon.

'Yeah, at his girlfriend's, as per usual. Just me and my little brother up there. We were sleeping,' Leon said again. The scent of bed was still on him as he drew hard on the cigarette, cupping it in his palm like old men did. Annie could see from the way the smoke trickled back out of his mouth that he wasn't inhaling.

Leon led them through the side door into the school and, like they already knew the place, Terry and Brian started switching on the lights, click, click, making it all too dazzlingly bright.

Annie and Kath looked around one of the classrooms. Everything was so small they felt like clumsy giants. Teeny-tiny plywood chairs, low tables covered in Formica. Even the blackboard looked smaller than they remembered. There was a reading corner with cushions on the floor and books they recognised on the shelves. It felt weird being here, dangerous too.

'Right, music time!' said Brian, opening the cupboard behind the teacher's desk to reveal a stereo turntable. 'Leon, bring down your dad's records, eh?'

Leon stood for a moment, wondering if there was any way he could say no. His fag had burnt right down and Annie watched a length of ash fall on to the reading mat.

'And some of that rum.' Terry clapped his arm around Leon's shoulders, guiding him to the door.

Leon's dad had good taste in music, with records he'd collected since the sixties. The volume was turned right up so there was a loud crackle before each track started. There was old stuff like Millie Small's 'My Boy Lollipop', then James Brown, Curtis Mayfield, Marvin Gaye and the Rolling Stones. Things that weren't on the jukebox in The Bell, but were great to dance to.

A bottle of dark rum appeared and soon they were all dancing, even Leon, with his lanky legs and wonky glasses. 'Woah, look at Leon dance!' Brian shouted out. Leon grinned back, like he couldn't believe his luck at this instant party with friends. Then Kath got up to dance and she moved the way she always did, swaying and sexy. The boys stood back to watch her, slack-jawed. 'She's a nice little mover, your sister,' Terry said slowly. 'Why don't you dance like that?' Annie had just smiled, given the smallest shrug.

But then it was alright again, because Annie and Kath went off to find the girls' toilets. Neither of them could stop laughing as they sat on the miniature loos, knees nearly touching their chins. There was even the same shiny loo paper from when they were little.

'Remember how Mrs Sims used to ration this paper?' Kath said, pulling a long streamer of it off the roll.

'Yeah, you only got two sheets of toilet paper each time. "If you need more than three sheets, you're not well enough to be in school" – that was the rule. What a cow!'

With a whoop Kath sent a ream of paper over the wall of the stall. Then they both started pulling and pulling at the rolls, running back to the classroom with armfuls of the crispy, shiny paper.

That was like a green light to the boys, who'd been left too long on their own and were getting bored of playing records. 'Enough of this old crap,' said Terry, zipping the needle off Otis Redding.

Leon's smile fell and he waited for Terry to show that he was only joking. But Terry turned his back to Leon, picked up the LP and held it in two hands before skimming it through the air towards Brian. The rest was a blur, but Annie remembers the crash when the library shelves went over. Chairs that had been neatly stacked were scattered. Finger paintings were ripped off the walls.

At some point Terry pissed on the reading mat, but the worst thing was the goldfish. It took the two of them, Terry and Brian, to lift the big tank. It hadn't been cleaned in ages and the sides were a cloudy green. When they tipped it over it seemed to happen in slow motion, letting loose a deluge of water that seemed to go on and on, spreading towards them – more than you would imagine was contained in that one tank.

Bright orange fish wiggled and gasped on the parquet flooring, the water still cascading out to mingle with broken glass, sticks of chalk, books and sodden toilet paper. Some fish landed on the reading mat, their gills helplessly opening and shutting against its rough surface. Kath tried to save one, running back to the little girls' sinks with it cupped in her hands, but then the squirming made her scream and she dropped it on the dusty hallway floor anyway.

For weeks, Annie could picture those fish thrashing and looking around wide-eyed for water that would save them. And Leon, raw panic in his face, his arms limp by his sides, fists clenching and unclenching at all this wrongness. 'My dad's gonna kill me, like really kill me,' he kept saying to himself.

When they left, Terry gave Leon a playful slap on the back of the head and grabbed the bottle of rum, holding it up high as the four of them stumbled out into the night. Breathing in the cold, clean air was a relief after all that mess.

Later, Annie liked to imagine she'd done things differently. That she'd stopped at the classroom door, called Kath back. How she and Kath could have calmly saved the fish, then swept up the glass and helped Leon make up a story about a break-in. She ran this version through her head so many times that she almost convinced herself that she'd done the right thing. But she hadn't.

Annie and Kath tried not to hang out with the lads

so much after that. 'I think we should give it a rest with those two,' Kath said as they did the dishes after Sunday lunch. As usual Annie was washing, Kath drying.

'Yeah. More trouble than they're worth,' Annie replied, handing her sister a plate dripping with suds.

'It wasn't Brian's fault,' Kath said. 'It was all Terry, really. You want to watch him – he's trouble.'

Yes, Kath had tried to warn her, but a few months after that night at Leon's Kath was dead and Annie was left all alone. And on your own, you didn't stand a chance against Terry.

Somehow this story feels too shameful to tell Henrietta, worse than all the things that happened once she was married, because that night she still had the chance to walk away from Terry. If she'd recognised him for what he was right at the start, her life could have been so different.

But Annie's hope is that if she keeps talking, all the stories she's held inside her so tightly and for so long will rise to the surface and escape. She can feel the words getting ready to float to the top, like bubbles from deep water, shiny and clear against the murk below. It's hard to know how much will come to the surface and what will have to stay buried, but she'll keep talking and hope for the best.

Outside, Annie can hear the swish of tyres on the wet road: people going to the cinema or fancy restaurants for their Saturday nights out. It's been a while since she had one of those. After losing Kath, she'd gone out with the girls from work a few times, but it felt wrong, disloyal somehow, having fun without Kath. And then

Terry explained how he would really prefer it if she didn't, so then it was just easier not to go out at all.

This evening, all she wants is her bed, but it seems a very long way away, so she might just stay in this chair a bit longer. Sleep is nipping at the edges of Annie's consciousness now, starting to drag her down, so she tries to think of good things, of sunshine and beaches and sandcastles. Her hope is that these sunny thoughts will set her on the right course and stave off that dream, the worst one, where Kath is sinking under the black water and the canal mud billows up around her like a cloud, then slowly settles again, falling into the creases of her skin and the whorls of her ears until her sister is hidden for good.

CHAPTER ELEVEN

HENRIETTA

Henrietta's drive to Tunbridge Wells takes her in the opposite direction to her local police station, so she won't need to be reminded of last night's foolish idea to go asking about police files and missing people. In fact, she is determined to put that whole troublesome Annie Doyle business out of her head for today.

When she's at the wheel of her Nissan Micra, Henrietta feels like she is queen of the road, and she always drives with her hands at ten to two, elbows out. 'It's not a tank, Ms Lockwood,' her instructor used to say.

She has to keep the car window open a crack, due to Dave's malodorous nature, but that has its drawbacks. As Henrietta pulls up at a set of traffic lights, a man with a jaunty spaniel crosses the road in front of her. From his back-seat lair, Dave catches a whiff of the dog and leaps into action, teeth bared, his crate bashing against the seat with each lunge. 'Sorry,' she mouths, too late: Dave's latest victims have already hightailed it down the road.

By the time Henrietta and Dave arrive in Tunbridge Wells, a steady drizzle has settled in. But that barely matters, because The Pines is the kind of house that never gets sunshine and lends itself to hush and shadows rather than a lightness of mood. Built in a faux Arts and Crafts style with fussy awnings and leaded windows, it hides behind a thick bank of glossy rhododendron bushes that rarely dare to bloom.

It's the house her family came to live in after her father's stint of missionary work in Papua New Guinea. From the age of five until nine, Henrietta led what she supposes some might consider an unusual life. Her father had been appointed the headteacher of Masura Missionary School in Papua New Guinea, bringing his family along as an afterthought. Edmund Lockwood had expected to stay on in Masura indefinitely – 'It is a calling, not a job,' he used to say. But when an unfortunate incident abruptly cut short their tenure, the Lockwoods returned to England and moved into The Pines, conveniently bequeathed by Great-Uncle Malcolm. 'The Lord has provided,' her father had said. Many times.

So at the age of nine, Henrietta was transported from the high plains of Masura Mission Station to the shaded byways of Tunbridge Wells, where the air felt too cold to breathe and her teeth wouldn't stop chattering. The house's dark warren of rooms came with its own furniture – 'Such beneficence! What bounty!' – in dark polished wood. There were table lamps trimmed with twisted gold fringing that draped cool and heavy on your arm if you dared to reach in and click on the bulb.

On the floor, rugs were in complicated patterns of red and brown, huge eyes and dragons' teeth hidden within their swirls.

For Henrietta, the move heralded a switch from a sun-blasted outdoor childhood to a gloomy Edwardian half-life that still dampens her spirit. For her, the Garden of England will always be a place of stifled yawns, ticking clocks and overwhelming guilt. Nothing is ever said, but every moment she spends in The Pines is a reminder of why they had to return so suddenly from Masura.

Henrietta parks outside the house and yanks up the handbrake a little too early, giving the car its customary jolt. On the back seat, Dave has opened one wary eye. Henrietta tries to humour him: 'Time to go and see Mummy and Daddy.'

Virginia Lockwood is already standing in the front porch. 'Henrietta, you've arrived!' she exclaims breathlessly, as if the journey from south London is fraught with danger. She peers at Henrietta's face, looking for clues of wrongdoing, small failures to unpick. 'Oh, you *do* look tired.'

Dave is straining on his lead, keen to investigate the house's smells. 'And you've brought the dog,' adds her mother, who can be relied upon to state the obvious. Together, they follow Dave into the ever-chilly hallway and continue to the kitchen, where her mother has been peeling carrots.

'There you are!' her father booms, making Henrietta jump. Ever the teacher, he's wearing cream trousers and a checked shirt, but no tie: his concession to relaxed weekend dressing.

'Yes, here I am. Hello, Daddy.' Henrietta turns, tucking her hair behind her ears to present herself.

'Hmm. Still got the job, I hope?'

'Yes, Daddy. It's going rather well, actually.'

'Good – we're not made of money,' her mother adds.

The carrots are coming to the boil. 'Shall I lay the table?' asks Henrietta, as she does every time she visits, and her mother waves her away, as she always does.

'All done. You just have time to freshen up.'

Henrietta hadn't realised the journey has left her so visibly soiled, but she dutifully heads upstairs, her feet heavier with every step. She feels nine years old all over again. Pausing at the top, she registers how the smell up here never changes: a musty mixture of old clothes, mothballs and furniture polish from another era. After splashing cold water on her face, she reaches for the threadbare orange towel, one of a set that came with the house. Praise be, once again, for Great-Uncle Malcolm.

She sighs as she steps back out on to the landing – never her favourite part of the house. Its red walls used to terrify her in a predictable sort of way (she'd read her *Jane Eyre*), but mostly because while walking its length one often dipped in and out of cooler pockets of air.

When Henrietta first encountered these patches, it had reminded her of learning to swim in the ocean, when her toes brushed a colder, deeper current and she knew it was time to kick hard and swim back to shore. But in The Pines there was no escaping those chilly spots.

No wonder sleep had not come easily to the schoolgirl Henrietta. At night she would lie stiffly awake until her parents had come upstairs. First, her mother, a soft padding and dithering. Then her father, heavier, humming a hymn as he brushed his teeth and then urinating thunderously, which made her blush in the dark. Those were the nights when she lay awake, haunted by thoughts of what had happened in Masura. How a little boy had drowned and it had all been Henrietta's fault.

But now, downstairs, Virginia Lockwood is ringing the little silver bell in the shape of a milkmaid, to signify that Sunday lunch is ready.

* * *

'Do you believe in ghosts, Daddy?' she asks, as her father carves slices of dead bird and lays them in careful fans. She has a feeling she asked this question many years ago when they first moved here, but didn't get a satisfactory reply. 'I was just wondering, because in my new job I'm meeting people who are not long for this world. So it's on my mind,' she adds, helping herself to carrots, then peas.

Edmund Lockwood unfolds his napkin and sits a little taller in his chair, ready to give an impromptu lecture. But Virginia cuts in. 'Are you sure this job is quite right for you?'

'Yes,' replies Henrietta, 'it has the potential for high levels of job satisfaction, as grief is a major life trauma and the Life Story books can help relatives process their loss.'

Against her better judgement, she can't resist ploughing on. 'Also, it throws up some interesting questions. For instance, some clients have lived a straightforward life, while others have experienced greater misfortunes. Already, I have met someone who lost both her sister and her husband to accidents. Which made me wonder about the chances of such bad luck.'

There is an unexpected clatter as her mother drops her knife, but her father ignores the interruption. 'An interesting question,' he says, for Edmund Lockwood fancies himself something of an expert on statistics. 'Evidence shows men are over sixty per cent more likely to meet with a fatal accident than women – car crashes and the like. Men also lead in self-inflicted deaths.'

Henrietta looks up.

'Suicide,' her father says brusquely, putting his cutlery down. 'Although women do lead in the high jump.' Here, he uses his finger to trace an arc in the air, going up, up over their dining table, then plummeting down fast towards the cruet set. 'Off cliffs and so on.'

Virginia Lockwood, who has had enough of this talk spoiling her Sunday lunch, turns to Henrietta with her iciest smile. 'Any nice people at your new job?'

Henrietta knows exactly what her mother means: she wants to know if there are any young men, one of whom might eventually be invited for Sunday lunch at The Pines. Romance came into Henrietta's life only once, at the end of her second year at university. He was a medical student and Henrietta had what she believes is called a one-night stand. But there was no standing involved, just her lying on her back as he investigated her body in a detached manner, turning her limbs this way and that. She has not felt inclined to repeat the experience. 'No, I have not met anyone you would approve of,' she replies.

But for once, she is grateful that her mother has steered the conversation back to more familiar territory. She does not wish to let any more details slip about Annie Doyle, to betray her confidences in this house where nothing of true consequence is ever spoken.

Her parents would never understand Annie, with her eccentric dress sense and her sad stories. And they certainly wouldn't understand why, even now, over the chicken bones and cold gravy, Henrietta's thoughts keep returning to Annie's drowned sister – and the wrongness of not knowing exactly what happened all these years later when Annie's own time is running out.

Before she leaves, Henrietta slips upstairs once more, but this time she goes into the guest bedroom with its tightly made single bed and a mahogany cabinet that contains a set of Encyclopaedia Britannicas and the Lockwood family photo albums.

From a young age, it had been made quite clear to Henrietta that she was not a photogenic child, so she is not in the habit of seeking out pictures of herself. But the Life Stories Project has made her curious about what photos she would put in her own book, should the need arise.

She sits on the hard bed and opens the album that begins with her family arriving in Papua New Guinea. There they are, gleaming white and squinting into the sun as they step down from a flimsy light aircraft and into the shimmering heat. A few pages on, there's a picture from a church outing, Henrietta eating fire-scorched sweetcorn in the wide shade of a rain tree, a hat jammed on her head. Then come a few gaps in the album, just photo corners marking out empty squares where someone has removed the pictures.

All at once she remembers running through hip-high sharp grasses, blue flip-flops slip-slapping against her heels, smaller footsteps just behind her. In the dry season, the air was almost too hot to breathe and everyone longed for the storm to break. Then, when it finally did, the rain drummed so loudly on the corrugated-iron roof that you couldn't hear yourself speak. Sometimes the rain knocked out the power in the middle of the night and her mother would go from room to room, lighting candles to show they were awake. It was nice to look over to the nearest house, where Esther lived, and see the same glow in their windows.

Esther was the same age as Henrietta and they always walked back from school together. Sometimes, they would look up at the fruit bats flying home too, darkening the sky with their devilish black rubbery wings, filling the air with shrieks until they found their perches and swung upside down, smiling their ratty smiles in the branches of the rain tree.

Esther had been Henrietta's best friend. She tries not to think about Esther and Masura too much, but occasionally something takes her back there: the smell of rain hitting dry earth; the oily growl of a motorbike's exhaust that reminds her of the plane taxiing on the day they left.

The three of them had to hurry towards the little plane, her mother pulling her in a too-firm grip, so her feet barely touched the ground. An urgency to get on board, knowing their tiny cargo was already stowed in the back. Then looking down through the aircraft's window at the red earth, the palm trees, the corrugated-iron roofs, leaving it all forever.

Once they were back in England, their time in Masura was rarely mentioned. And definitely not that day when they had to rush for the plane because Henrietta had done a terrible thing and a little boy's life had been cut short. She never did get a chance to say goodbye to Esther.

As Henrietta heads back downstairs, she absent-mindedly trails her fingertips through the largest cold patch on the landing. These days, it almost feels like an old friend.

CHAPTER TWELVE

ANNIE

Annie had Henrietta down as a stickler for punctuality, but she's been waiting at an empty table in the café for a good ten minutes with nothing but a laminated sign and a tartan Thermos flask for company. Then the lift doors open and she spots Henrietta. She walks with a laboured gait, like she's wading through water, and her blue synthetic trousers make an unpleasant rasping sound. They are an unusual choice for a woman of Henrietta's age and Annie can't help thinking how a style with a wider leg and a higher waist would work better with those brown lace-ups. Team them with a white shirt and she could go for more of a Katharine Hepburn look. Then Henrietta would stand out for all the right reasons.

Finally, Henrietta plumps herself down. 'Sorry I'm late, Annie. I got waylaid by Audrey, my boss.' Then she starts muttering about an appraisal, which is of no interest to Annie, but she notices that every time Henrietta says the word, it sets off a slight quiver at the corner of her left eye.

'Still, that's a few weeks away. Not fired yet!' Henrietta says with a nervous laugh, and there it comes again, the twitch. Annie waits patiently until Henrietta has laid out her pens and notepad and phone in a neat row, as she likes to do.

Finally, Henrietta seems calmer. 'My apologies. Now, Annie, I would like us to resume where we left off. There are a number of unresolved queries, which I have been unable to verify.'

Annie sighs. She hopes Henrietta isn't going to start banging on about that questionnaire again. 'Actually, I made a few notes myself since we last met,' she says, rummaging in her bag for her notebook. She has to flick her wrists a couple of times because she's wearing her favourite seventies stripey shirt-dress, which she dearly loves, but the huge cuffs do get in the way a little.

But it's as if Henrietta barely hears her and she has her own agenda. 'I am finding it hard to establish whether the police launched a proper investigation into your sister's death. From what you've said, it sounds as if they failed to do this. But why didn't you and your family press for one? And who was brought in for questioning?'

From nowhere, a heat rises up in Annie, and it's not just because she was kept waiting. 'I don't think you realise what my life was like back then,' she says. 'Like I said, the police didn't give my dad the time of day. My mum was in pieces and I was only nineteen – do you think they would have listened to me? Then, once I was married to Terry . . . well, my life was very different. And I was even less able to go marching into the police station, demanding answers.'

Annie opens her notebook and looks down at the pages. Her words are scrawled in several different pen colours because over the past week she kept coming back to this book in the small hours, when she couldn't sleep and her memories kept rising up, jumbled but so vivid. She needs to get them out in the open, hand them over to Henrietta to organise.

'Henrietta, things weren't that simple. If I tell you how losing Kath destroyed my family, then maybe you'll start to understand.'

Chastened, Henrietta presses the red 'record' button. 'Very well. Annie Doyle, this is session three of your Life Story. Today is Saturday the twentieth of November.'

At the top of her page, Annie has written *January 1975, Dynevor Road.* She glances down at her notes and she begins to talk.

'The days after Kath didn't come home, our house was full of people,' she begins. 'The priest visited a few times and neighbours came and went. Some left us meals on the doorstep, but it always seemed to be fish pie, I've no idea why. Even now, the thought of fish pie turns my stomach.

'Then, of course, it was Christmas, and people had their own families to look after. Auntie Rita did our shopping and ran the Hoover around, but by New Year, most people stopped coming.'

It pains her to say the next bit, but it's true. 'Apart from Rita, the only other person who kept visiting was Terry. I hadn't seen him for ages, but of course he'd heard what had happened. Then in January, he started dropping by on his lunchbreaks. "Just popping in," he'd say. He'd pick the post up off the mat or bring in the milk.'

Annie remembers the muffled clunk as Terry set the bottles on the kitchen table, still four pints, because nobody had thought to change the order yet. The flare of his match as he lit the gas under the kettle.

'You could set your watch by him. He gave us a reason to get up, to keep going.' Terry would make a pot of tea, passing Annie the first cup to carry upstairs to her mum.

'My mum took it badly when Kath went missing,' she says for the recording. She doesn't add that Deidre Doyle had gone to bed on Christmas Eve and refused to get up again. Or how Annie would take up glasses of Lucozade and cups of weak tea and, at the end of each day, she would collect them all again and tip their contents down the sink. How she'd change her mother's sheets, bundling them up so neighbours in the launderette couldn't see the stains, and then run a bath for her mum. The way she'd gently sponge her mother's shoulders, then look away as her mother pulled herself up unsteadily, all jutting bones and fear in her face. Those are not things that need to be recorded and put in a book. But that had been Annie's life, for months and months.

'Terry could see what life was like for me in Dynevor Road. That house, it was suffocating me. But, to give him his due, he kept visiting and I suppose that made me think more kindly of him again. Before Kath went missing we were on and off, if you know what I mean. I'd been hoping it would fizzle out: he certainly wasn't what me and Kath called "forever man" material.'

She can't help smiling, remembering the nights she and Kath would lie in the dark, whispering and wondering about how it would feel when you finally met 'the one'. But when she glances at Henrietta, she's busy writing things down with her arm curved around her paper like she's in an exam, and Annie wonders how much, if anything, Henrietta knows about men and their ways.

'As I say, on and off, but mostly off. But then after we lost Kath, Terry was there for me. Like at Kath's funeral. I mean, it wasn't a proper funeral, because there was no body for a coffin and the church wouldn't let us hold a service. So Auntie Rita took charge. She said, "Sod them, we'll have one ourselves", and invited everyone to what she called a Celebration of Life in her front room. Very forward-thinking, was Auntie Rita.

'It took me and Dad a long time to get my mum dressed and out of the house. Then, at Rita's, she just sat in the corner while the neighbours filed past and lit candles and said, "Sorry for your loss."'

Annie remembers how apt that phrase had felt at the time, because no one knew exactly where Kath's body was lost in the depths of the Grand Union Canal. But back to today and telling Henrietta about Terry.

'Oh, I knew he wasn't perfect, but Terry did get me through that day. He had this way of holding me by the elbow, steering me through this room full of people in black suits. At the time, I liked the way he took control.

It made me feel safe.'

'And when was this ceremony?' Henrietta asks, turning the pages of her own notebook.

Oh, Henrietta, what is this obsession with dates and facts? This is meant to be my Life Story, not a police report, thinks Annie. This girl is wasted at the Rosendale Centre – the Metropolitan Police should give her a call. 'It was June,' Annie says patiently. 'June 1975. Six months after we'd lost her.'

'So, Annie, you had a funeral and then your own wedding within a couple of months of each other.'

Annie runs a finger around her mug, wipes away a crescent of her pink lipstick. 'I suppose so,' she says quietly. 'In fact, it wasn't long after Kath's funeral that Terry asked me to marry him. At the time, I thought he felt sorry for me.'

She can't quite bring herself to tell Henrietta how unromantic the marriage proposal had been. He'd dropped by as usual on his lunch break, but this time he'd persuaded her out of the house. 'Let's get some fresh air,' he'd said. So they'd been sitting on the grass in the local park, Annie idly tugging at the prickly, dry tufts, when Terry had turned to her and said, 'The council's got a couple of houses going up Dollis Hill way. Let's get married, get one of them.' The word 'married' had been buried, almost a throwaway comment – but it was a lifeline and she grabbed it.

The red numbers on Henrietta's phone are still scrolling and Annie finds it oddly reassuring, the way her words will be captured inside that machine. And she's glad she's said something about Kath's poor excuse for a funeral, because she should never have been forgotten so easily and now, at least, she'll be in this book, her name preserved in black and white.

'As I said, my cousin Edie was my maid of honour. Big bruiser of a girl, she was, and that peach dress didn't do anything for her. Not that I looked much better in mine.'

Annie lets out a rasp of a laugh, remembering that cheap, itchy lace, the too-tight neck and the way the skirt crackled when she walked down the short aisle of the register office. She hadn't dared to look to the left, because it had been touch and go whether her parents would come. They had, in the end, but Aidan Doyle had not been by her side to walk her towards Terry and married life.

'I'm afraid my father did not support the marriage,' Annie says. 'In fact, when I told him I was engaged, he was furious. He said he'd already lost one daughter and my place was at home, taking care of my mother. "If you leave, you're dead to me too." That's what he said.'

Annie stops for a moment. It's important that Henrietta understands why she had to take her chances with Terry, even though she knew from the start it wasn't love. She had to get away from that house. She looks over and Henrietta's eyes are wide with concern, and knowing she's finally being listened to gives Annie the strength to continue.

'My parents came to the wedding, but they left the minute it was over. They didn't even stay for the photographs. Later Auntie Rita told me that as soon as I'd finished my vows, my dad hustled my mum and her out and hailed a black cab for the short journey home. And I reckon Aidan Doyle could count on one hand the number of times he'd sat in the back of a cab.'

Here, Annie tries to smile, but Henrietta's expression reminds her that it wasn't really that funny, so she stops trying to make a joke of it and keeps going, to the bitter end.

'Auntie Rita said that once they got home, my dad didn't say a word. He went straight up to our old bedroom and gathered together everything I'd left behind and some of Kath's things too. He took it all – my old schoolbooks, all our old dolls and teddies, a few clothes and bits of make-up – and he threw it all out into the backyard. Then he took a can of lighter fuel and set fire to the lot. I suppose you could say that forgiveness did not come easily to Aidan Doyle.'

CHAPTER THIRTEEN

Henrietta

As the silence stretches out, Henrietta gives the red circle on her phone a tap. 'It's just calibrating, but I think we have all that,' she says softly. Looking over, she can see Annie's notebook still has pages and pages of words and she is flicking through them with a wild look in her eyes.

'There's more,' Annie says, 'so much more. I need to get it all down before I forget. It's like I'm only just starting to remember all these things that I put to the back of my mind for so long.' She raises a hand to her hair, as if she can feel those uncomfortable thoughts pushing their way out, and Henrietta can't help noticing that Annie's dress needs a good wash. Those floppy long cuffs are very grubby and there's a tea stain near the hem, the sight of which makes Henrietta feel inexplicably sad. Someone should be taking care of this woman, she thinks. Helping her.

First thing this morning, Henrietta had been determined to get answers from Annie: about the investigation, whether a proper search and dredge operation had been mounted and how many suspects had been questioned. She'd intended to be as methodical in her approach as her teacher father, Edmund Lockwood. But now, she feels an unfamiliar urge to reach out for Annie's hand.

Then, as if from afar, she watches herself do just that and notices how the older woman's skin under her own is surprisingly supple and warm. She pats Annie's hand again, to show it wasn't a mistake. But then it all begins to feel a bit much, so Henrietta does what any sensible person would do in these circumstances: she goes to fetch them both a nice cup of tea.

Standing at the counter, she looks back at Annie sitting at the table, all on her own. It might be her too-loose dress or it might be the effort of saying all those words, but today Annie looks smaller than before, as if she has lost some of her essential stuffing. Henrietta feels an odd stirring in her chest. It's akin to homesickness, both sorrow and warmth mixed together.

'Here we go,' Henrietta says as she puts down the tray, immediately wishing she hadn't because now she sounds like one of those sing-song people who makes light of things, pretends nothing is wrong.

'Thank you. Just what I need.'

By Henrietta's watch, they still have fifteen minutes left, and this puts her in a quandary. She would very much like to steer the conversation back to her outstanding queries. Who was brought in for questioning? What about the men who bought Kath drinks in The Bell on a Friday night? And what about the manager of the shoe shop who found her bike and seemed to know a lot about Kath's routines? Then she would like to follow up on witnesses – surely someone must have seen or heard something that Saturday night down by the canal?

She's still wondering how to broach these questions when the lift doors open and the guy in the beanie hat emerges and heads towards the café counter. To Henrietta's consternation, Annie calls him over, waving her hands so her cuffs flap up and down like ragged wings. 'Stefan! Come! This is Henrietta, who does the Life Stories thing,' she says, brushing away some stray biscuit crumbs from around her mouth. Stefan does a 180-degree spin and glides over. 'Hello, Annie, Henrietta.' He nods to each of them in turn. 'Mind if I join you ladies while we wait for the minibus?'

Now Henrietta finds herself in a difficult position. She wants to continue with her questions, but Annie has issued an invitation, which it would be impolite not to honour. 'Of course,' she replies, hoping she won't be expected to fetch him a tea, too. But it's OK because the sad-looking man at the counter has already come over and is removing a chair so Stefan can take a place at the table.

'Alright, Stefan, mate. Cuppa for you?'

Stefan looks up and smiles – 'Love one, Mike, thanks' – and Henrietta catches the glint of metal from inside his mouth. One of his front teeth is gold and she wonders if this is a fashion choice or the result of long-term poor dental hygiene.

'No Mia today, then?' asks Stefan, scanning the café as if she might be hiding behind a pot plant or under a table. Unlike her mother, Henrietta has never believed that stating the obvious passes for conversation, so decides not to respond. Thankfully, Mike the tea man is back and he and Stefan talk about football for a bit. Even Annie joins in, saying something about 'Lucky Arsenal' and Stefan laughs and says, 'As ever, Annie, as ever'.

Here it comes again, thinks Henrietta, that old feeling of being on the fringes of a club, discovering that everyone else has been a fully paid-up member for ages while she's still trying to figure out the rules.

She pulls her own chair a little closer to the table. 'Have you been coming here long?' she asks Stefan, trying to reassert her pivotal role in this gathering. They are sitting around her table, after all.

He stops laughing and takes a good look at her. 'On and off, three years. One year of remission in the middle,' he says. 'And what I've learned' – he leans in, and Henrietta does too, ready to receive his words of wisdom – 'is to go for the Tunnock's teacakes. Every time.'

This causes more hilarity between Stefan and Annie. Even Mike has a smirk on his face and they are still laughing when the lilac-fleece-wearing Bonnie appears at the front doors.

'Look out,' says Annie, 'here's the purple peril. Best get going.'

Henrietta feels a lurch of panic. 'But Annie,' she starts. 'Your story. Your sister's case. There's so much to discuss.'

Already, another session has gone, their third

out of seven, and she still has so many unanswered questions. And today she wasted time getting distracted by pointless emotions and chat about football, of all things. No, no, this will not do at all. She grips the sides of the chair, trying to keep calm, but Annie and Stefan are standing up and beyond the glass doors Bonnie is hopping from one foot to the other, keen to get away on time.

Annie turns back and her face softens. 'Don't worry, Hen. I'll be back next Saturday on Bonnie's fun bus. Lots more stories where that came from.' And with that they are gone, leaving only a gust of cold air in their wake.

Mike goes back to his counter, shaking his head at some last joke about a referee needing spectacles, and it's oddly quiet in the Grief Café – far emptier, somehow, without Annie.

Transcribing is only meant to be done in the afternoons, but Henrietta has an urge to listen to a bit of today's recording, just to make sure she didn't imagine the whole thing. She steals a look left, then right, to make sure there's no sign of Audrey, then unwinds her headphones and plugs them into the phone. And there it is again, Annie's voice, saying every word, loud and clear.

Until now, Henrietta has been unable to stop imagining how Kath drowned, the panic in her eyes as the black waters closed over her head and rushed into her mouth. But after today's session, what stays lodged the longest in Henrietta's mind is the image of a man so full of rage that he left his daughter's wedding to go home and burn every reminder of her.

* * *

That afternoon, as Henrietta starts to type up Annie's words, she cannot ignore a growing sense of unease. It's not just the subject matter, it's the fact that Audrey will expect her to reproduce all of this verbatim in a book when, in her view, the case of Kathleen Doyle is far from closed.

Annie has told her the bare bones of the case, but Henrietta senses that there's more, that Annie is holding things back. She should have pressed Annie for more information, but then Stefan had barged in and, before they knew it, their time was up. And now it's another whole week until Annie is due back in.

Henrietta looks down at her right hand, the one she laid over Annie's, remembering the surprise of the warmth she felt. Then comes a hot wave of embarrassment as she sees the state of her nails, ragged and bitten as a schoolgirl's, and she wonders if Annie noticed them. A nasty habit, she knows, and one her mother has always detested. She scrunches her hand into a fist, determined not to think of home, steering herself back to the unsolved case of Kathleen Doyle.

Realistically, going to the police is a non-starter, so it's time to look elsewhere for solid, verifiable information. She is well aware that background research is not in her job description but, she reasons, it falls well within the *spirit* of her job – to record people's life stories as accurately as possible.

For the rest of the afternoon, Henrietta makes

good use of Audrey's super-fast broadband and extra-large computer screen. She starts by typing the name Kathleen Doyle into Google – every amateur detective's first port of call. She's not hopeful: it seems the case barely caused a ripple in 1974, so it's unlikely to have made it on to the internet – but she needs to tick this first line of enquiry off her list.

She is unsurprised to find that Kathleen Doyle is a very common name – her initial search brings up over 16,000 results. There are professors, writers, dentists and plenty of students, including ones in Ireland and America. Then there are a fair few obituaries for Kathleen Doyles, but none of them sounds like Annie's Kath.

As Henrietta begins to sift through these listings, she hears voices out in the corridor, a group of nurses laughing and calling out to each other about where to go tonight and whether they will make Happy Hour. It is Saturday night, she realises. She can imagine them jostling each other as they go and how they will probably get very drunk and by the end of the night someone will be sick and her friend will hold back her hair and, for a moment, she feels plunged back into Freshers' Week.

She had endured hers alone in her room, ears stuffed with cotton wool as her cohort rampaged up and down the stairs, spraying each other with cans of squirty cream, drinking tequila and then vomiting in the communal kitchen sink. She remained in halls for the duration of her degree, which meant she had to endure Freshers' Week twice more – except by then nobody expected her to join in.

Then she remembers that, much like those students, the nurses don't even know she's here, and she goes back to her solitary work with renewed zeal. Working in the library may have done little to improve her social skills, but it did teach her how to access historical records, and she registers for a free trial with the British Newspaper Archive. Then she types 'December 1974', 'Grand Union Canal', 'drowned' and 'Doyle' into the search field.

Miraculously, a list of news reports from the now defunct *Kensington News & Post* appears on her screen. All are brief and only the first one has a photograph, a black-and-white image of a young woman standing beside a bicycle, holding the handlebars with pride.

The dots are grainy, but Henrietta can tell her hair is dark and thick and the tilt of her jaw is a bit like Annie's, but narrower. Her smile, too, is similar, but more mischievous. Or maybe it's just that Annie doesn't have much to smile about these days. This young woman looks in a hurry to be off, like she's got things to do, places to go, without any inkling of what will happen to her. 'Full of life' is what people would say, looking at that photo.

She screenshots the short report that appeared in the bottom-right-hand corner of the newspaper's front page:

Shopgirl missing for Christmas

Kathleen Doyle, 18, is missing from her home in Dynevor Road, W10. She was last seen leaving work on the evening of Saturday 21 December, wearing a suede jacket with furry trim. Miss Doyle works in Ravel Shoes on Kensington High Street. 'We are desperate for information about our daughter,' said Mr Aidan Doyle, the girl's father. He added that it was very out of character for Miss Doyle to go off on her own without notifying her parents of her whereabouts.

The police's search is ongoing. 'It's a very busy time of the year but we are making efforts to trace this missing person,' said Detective Chief Inspector Williams of Notting Dale Police Station. 'We have every hope that Miss Doyle may be staying with friends and has simply forgotten to tell her family.' If members of the public have any information, they are asked to telephone the station.

That issue of the *Kensington News & Post* was published on 27 December and the rest of the front page is taken up with a huge photo of someone's grandad dressed up as Father Christmas, his fake beard skew-whiff and a small boy in an anorak sitting uneasily on his lap. 'It's Christmaaas!' was the unoriginal headline.

The next issue, dated 2 January, is a particularly short edition. The lead story is a photograph of a woman holding a new baby, both of whom look like they could do with a good night's sleep. The caption reads: *Welcome to 1975! Bouncing baby girl Michelle Louise was born in the early hours of 1st January to proud parents Mandy and Mark Dowler, weighing in at 8lb. Mother and baby are doing well. 'She's the best New Year's present ever,' said Mandy.*

This irks Henrietta. Who ever heard of a New Year's present? The sub-editors must have been half asleep or drunk when they sent down that issue. Rather heartlessly, the story on Mr and Mrs Doyle's missing daughter (once their bouncing baby girl, after all) has been relegated to page five.

'Find in missing shopgirl case' is the headline. Henrietta shakes her head in disgust. Calling Annie's sister a 'shopgirl', as if she didn't have a name. She scans the short update, but all it tells her is that items of clothing were found by the canal towpath, believed to belong to Kathleen.

A final report appeared three weeks later:

Search called off for missing shopgirl

Officers searching for Miss Kathleen Doyle of Dynevor Road, W10, have drawn a blank. Miss Doyle went missing on Saturday 21 December. Items belonging to her were found beside the Grand Union Canal, under the Ladbroke Grove bridge.

'Despite our efforts, we have not found any trace of Miss Doyle,' said Detective Chief Inspector Williams. 'Due to

the busy Christmas period and inclem-
ent weather we were unable to carry
out an extensive search of the canal at
the time. Unfortunately, no leads have
proved fruitful.'

DCI Williams added that Miss Doyle
was not previously known to the police and seemed of good character. 'We
would urge anyone visiting the canal to
stay away from the water, as there are
risks that can't always be seen from the
surface. Unfortunately, we also see an
increase in suicides during the festive
season and this cannot be ruled out,'
said DCI Williams.

Several members of the public have
been helping the police with their inquiries, but were released without
charge. The Doyle family was unavail-
able for comment.

'Helping police with their inquiries.' When Henrietta first heard this phrase as a child, she had imagined a
jolly scenario where public-spirited individuals popped
into their local police station to offer advice and ideas. Now she knows it means almost the opposite: that
someone gets a knock on their door and is brought in
for questioning with little choice in the matter.

Annie said very little about the suspects – only that
'a few people' had been questioned and then released
– but she was right about one thing: the police did the

bare minimum. They stumbled upon a pile of clothes but failed to carry out a wider search or track down any witnesses. Surely somebody must have seen or heard something: a splash as she went in, a cry for help?

If Henrietta is going to do this book, she's going to do it properly, with facts, dates and information that will establish whether Kath's death was murder or an accident. She looks back at the inky photograph of eighteen-year-old Kathleen Doyle with her open smile, a face so like Annie's and yet so different. Flicking through the scans of these old pages, she can almost imagine what it must have been like that Christmas in 1974 when Annie and her family sat waiting for news. How hope must have ebbed away a little more each day, when still no news came.

She reads over the newspaper pages again, searching for something she might have missed. Then she notices the small byline for each report in the *Kensington News & Post*. What's remarkable is that it's the same name as appears regularly in her mother's favourite magazine, *Country Days*. Each month their columnist Sharon Sharpe writes about the ups and downs of life in an English village, and each month Virginia Lockwood recounts these adventures to Henrietta, almost word for word. Henrietta knows all about Sharon's bantams (they escape on a regular basis, causing much havoc) and her blossoming romance with the local vet.

Henrietta had always assumed that Sharon Sharpe and her countryside capers were the figment of a ghostwriter's imagination, but perhaps there is a real Sharon Sharpe who, many years ago, cut her teeth as a rookie reporter on the *Kensington News & Post*.

* * *

On her bus journey home, Henrietta discovers that not only is Sharon very real, but she and her bantams have a loyal following on social media. Her last Instagram post, detailing a visit to a donkey sanctuary, has 6,000 likes and 89 comments. Despite Sharon's ash-blonde highlights and suspiciously smooth forehead, Henrietta judges that she is probably well into her sixties, which means she could well have started her career at the harder end of journalism back in 1974.

To date, Henrietta has never felt the need to interact on social media (neither socialising nor 'liking' are her forte), but by the end of her bus journey she has created an account for herself, using the moniker @ failedlibrarian. By the time she reaches her front door she has left a comment on Sharon's post: 'My mother finds your column most amusing.'

Sharon must have nothing better to do on a Saturday evening because when Henrietta sits down on her sofa, there is already a reply. 'Hi @failedlibrarian Super news! Next month, Roland the rooster is back to his old tricks!'

Henrietta pauses to say hello to Dave and give him his customary belly rub. Now it's time to get to the heart of the matter. With one hand, she types her next message: 'Sharon, would you be the same reporter who covered a botched police investigation into the death of Kathleen Doyle in west London in 1974?'

The next time she checks her phone something odd

has happened. There's no reply and when she checks Sharon's profile again the feed is blank and it says 'User not found'.

Henrietta has reason to believe she has just been blocked by Sharon Sharpe.

Henrietta purses her lips. This is entirely unacceptable. Not just being blocked (Henrietta is no stranger to rejection) but the sheer breadth of incompetence she's uncovering. In 1974, the police were almost certainly negligent in their investigation, and now it seems a trainee crime reporter failed to hold them to account.

Annie Doyle deserves to know why no proper search and dredge operation was carried out. Henrietta would also like to know exactly who the suspects were and the justification for releasing them without charge.

She looks at the calendar. There are only four more Saturdays before Christmas – the immovable deadline for completing Annie Doyle's Life Story. Henrietta is not done with Sharon Sharpe just yet.

CHAPTER FOURTEEN

ANNIE

That hollow ache inside her is back, the one that feels akin to hunger but might flip into nausea at any minute. An image of the perfect slice of toast comes to Annie – gently browned with butter pooling on top – and she hopes this might be the answer. By some miracle there is the crust of a loaf in the breadbin and, as it warms under the grill, the smell is delicious. Once Annie sits down with it, she knows she's eating it too fast, shoving the last bit in with the back of her hand, but it's too late to stop. Please, she thinks, let it stay down. Let me get away with it this time.

So she's told Henrietta about her wedding, but what's harder to explain is why Terry was still in her life after that night at Leon's. Because she'd tried to get rid of him, she really had. She didn't return his phone calls and she and Kath stopped going to The Bell on Fridays, switching to Thursdays, when he was at the dog racing at White City.

There were a few short weeks when it seemed like he'd got the message and she almost forgot all about

Terry and his sidekick, Brian. It felt like a reprieve, a golden time when it was back to just her and Kath. She'd meet Kath after work and sometimes Debbi from the shoe shop came too. They went to a tiny narrow café that played Radio Caroline, a pirate radio station, and they drank frothy coffees as guitar solos by Led Zeppelin ebbed and swelled with the radio static.

In the evenings, she and Kath would sit facing each other on one of their beds and do each other's make-up, copying looks from magazines with sweeps of glittery blue eye shadow and thick layers of mascara. She liked to study every inch of Kath's face as she dabbed and daubed with her brushes – that tiny butterfly-shaped scar on her forehead, her cupid's bow, just that bit fuller than Annie's. She treasured those times because she had Kath all to herself. She wasn't chatting to blokes or laughing with Debbi or disappearing off on her bicycle to work.

Annie didn't like it when Kath did things without her. She felt it as an absence, like when you go out in the cold without a scarf and you can't think about anything except how much better it would be if you had that nice warm scarf wrapped around you. But during those weeks, life was exactly how Annie liked it. Warm and cosy, with Kath by her side. Just the two of them; sisters. Practically twins.

All that changed one Sunday, when Terry barged his way back into her life. The day was off-key from the start because Kath had refused to get up for church, lying in bed with the covers drawn up to her neck. 'No, Mum, I can't. My time of the month is really, really bad, honest to God. I think I'll bleed out in front of Father when I go up for Communion.'

Disgusted at such talk, their mum clicked her handbag shut and hustled Annie out of the door. Annie knew Kath's excuse was a barefaced lie so she slouched her way through the service, resenting how Kath always got her own way.

On the way home, Annie's dad strode ahead so he could nip out for a swift pint before lunch. 'That dog's not going to walk itself,' he called over his shoulder to Annie and her mum, but they all knew the dog's walk would be a short route to the local pub.

The front door was still wide open when Annie and her mum reached it, and she could tell something was different. For a start, her dad was talking in a booming voice and he was standing in the front room, which was kept for special.

They must have a visitor. They never had visitors. Annie and her mum peered in, trespassers in their own home. The lounge was taken up with male bulk; not just their dad, but there was Terry, hair slicked back, grinning like he'd pulled off some hilarious trick. It felt all wrong seeing him there, among the antimacassars and her mum's needlepoint pictures.

Kath was there too, trying to edge her way out of the room. 'Dad, this is Annie's friend Terry,' she said quietly, trying to make herself smaller and sneak upstairs.

Annie knew something bad was about to happen. Without knowing why, she had an urge to reach out, grab Kath by the hand and make a run for it. The two of them could fly down the street and keep going, not come back until they were sure their dad had got rid of Terry.

But already it was too late and their dad was doing quite the opposite, puffing himself up and playing the avuncular host. 'We've got a visitor, Deidre,' he announced. 'Better lay another place. You a beer man, Terry?'

Finally, Annie stood facing Terry, this not-really-boyfriend, and something inside her turned hot and liquid. He was still grinning, like this was the best joke ever. 'Alright, Annie.' He ran his eyes over her. 'Long time no see.'

She had to hand it to him, Terry put on a good performance for the Doyle family. 'I'm working my way up at the printworks,' he said over lunch, adding another dollop of mint sauce to his plate. 'Learning the ropes. But one day I'll run my own operation. How about yourself, Mr Doyle? You a man of business?'

Terry knew full well that their dad was nothing of the sort. He'd worked as a postman since coming over from Ireland in 1952 and did all the local rounds.

'Public service. Royal Mail,' said Aidan Doyle, chewing vigorously. 'People will always need the post.'

'And now two clever daughters, too,' replied Terry.

Thin ice, thought Annie, he's pushing the joke too far. But, no, their dad was lapping it up. 'Take after their mum, there, I'm afraid, Terry. The women are the brains in this family.' And together they laughed long and loud at the very idea.

Annie had left school at fifteen and worked at the

local nursery ever since. Wiping bottoms, getting toys out, putting toys away. Scraping soggy rusks off plastic plates, rinsing cups, putting plasters on grazed knees. The kids were OK, but up close they smelled of wee and she hated the way they climbed all over her with clumsy heels and elbows. It was as if they couldn't imagine she might not want a damp bottom plonked in her lap; they assumed devotion and love. In her own home, Annie had never been so presumptuous.

Kath was doing fine at the shoe shop: the customers liked her and the manager was teaching her bookkeeping.

'She's got a head for figures, our Kathleen,' her dad said, topping up Terry's glass. Oh, how they laughed at that one.

Afterwards, Kath disappeared upstairs and Annie was left to walk Terry to the bus stop.

'Did you like my surprise visit, then?' he asked, looping a meaty arm over her shoulder.

'Not really. I mean, I didn't realise you knew where we lived,' she said. They walked on. They were a few yards from the bus stop when in one swift move he pulled Annie towards him and pushed her up against a pebble-dashed wall. He was breathing hard, cigarettes, her dad's beer and roast lamb, all mixed together.

'I was missing my Annie,' he said, through gritted teeth. 'Me and Brian haven't seen you girls in ages.'

He wedged a practised knee between her legs, suctioned his mouth on to hers and started kneading her breasts. The motion reminded Annie of her mum making soda bread on the floured kitchen table, rolling the dough over before patting it into shape and cutting a cross on top with two quick gashes. But that daydreaming made her lose her concentration and Terry had progressed to fiddling under her dress. Top, bottom, top, bottom: it was impossible to fend off both at the same time. She plumped for bottom.

'Terry, babe. Not now,' she said, moving her head to the side.

It wasn't like in the Vauxhall Viva with Brian and Kath in the front, which kept things decent.

'It's my time of the month,' she blurted out, taking a leaf out of her sister's book.

That stopped him. 'Alright, no need to tell the world.' Up close, she could see Terry's Adam's apple bobbing, the way his two front teeth overlapped. He was nicer from a distance.

Then his bus came careering around the corner and Terry let go of Annie so he could stick out his hand – the one he'd just had up her dress – to hail it. 'See you in The Bell, then. Been missing my girlfriend.'

Annie walked home, shaken. A bloke had said she was his girlfriend. She should be pleased, but all she felt was deep-down dread.

When Annie walked into the lounge, her dad was making a show of reading the paper, but she knew what was coming.

'A word, young lady.' Aidan Doyle might have knocked the edges off his Irish accent since coming to London, but he was still old-fashioned when it came to how he expected his girls to behave.

Annie could hear her mum washing up in the

kitchen and the tinny sound of her sister's radio upstairs. But there was no point in trying to back out now; it would just put off the inevitable.

Her father folded his newspaper with great care, set it aside. 'How long you been seeing that Terry, then?'

'Not long. I don't really know him, to be honest.'

'He looked pretty bloody familiar with you, my girl,' her dad said. 'Gave him your address, did you? What else you been giving him?'

'Sometimes we share a bag of chips,' said Annie, knowing as soon as it was out of her mouth that it sounded like she was giving him cheek.

The punch, when it came, hit her square on her left ear, and she couldn't work out which was worse, the hot, black pain or the way everything had gone ringy and muffled. 'Dirty slut. If either you or your sister gets yourselves in trouble, you'll be out on the street. Now get out of my sight.'

Annie's ear was never quite right after that and is still prone to muffling. Not that it matters much now, when this sticky pain is spreading through her guts, stopping her from eating much more than soggy biscuits and sweet, milky tea. And slices of Mia's bloody Bakewell tart.

What would Henrietta make of that story? she wonders. She's an odd mix of contradictions, that girl. On the one hand she seems a complete innocent, out of step with modern life – not to mention fashion. But at the same time there's a world-weariness about her, as if she's already seen too much. What, she wonders, happened in the Life Story of Henrietta Lockwood to make her quite so unreachable?

This weekly unburdening is leaving Annie a little lighter each time. But perhaps it can help Henrietta, too. Of course Annie never had her own daughter, but if she had, she wouldn't have sewn her party dresses and told her to look pretty as a picture. She'd have warned her about men like Terry. So next week Annie will tell a cautionary tale so that if Henrietta ever meets a man like Terry, she'll know to run a mile.

CHAPTER FIFTEEN

HENRIETTA

The fact that Sharon Sharpe blocked Henrietta on Instagram has only made her more determined to track her down: this woman definitely has something to hide. After spending a considerable part of her Monday morning loitering among the magazine racks of WH Smith, she discovered Sharon's email address in the front of *Country Days* magazine and set about sending her a series of emails.

You seem to have blocked me in error, she ventured in her first email. By her fifth email, she was feeling more bold. *It's clear, Ms Sharpe, that hard-nosed investigative crime reporting was not your forte, given your more sedate journalism these days.*

Her sixth was more conciliatory, with a dash of melodrama: *I am writing a memoir with Annie Doyle, the sister of Kathleen Doyle, presumed drowned in 1974. I cannot access police records. You covered the case and are my only hope of more information. I implore you to help.*

Twenty-four hours later, she hasn't received a single reply. It's a good job that Henrietta is due back at work today, because she will benefit from the distraction.

Tuesdays in the Grief Café bring a different type of client, people who don't need a minibus to the drop-in centre and come and go as they please. First up is Neil Marshall, who is in remission but is still a regular in the café. He says he keeps coming because 'Mia makes a damn fine cup of tea.'

He was her 9 a.m. appointment, but he is still talking at 11 a.m., which, strictly speaking, is against the rules. But things are quiet today, so she keeps listening and recording. This is just as well because Mr Marshall is in no hurry to get through his Life Story. He's already clocked up six sessions with Henrietta's mysterious predecessor and after today's two hours they still haven't even reached his secondary-school years.

She suspects Audrey would not be impressed by this failure to adhere to the correct timetable, but Henrietta can't help being drawn in by Mr Marshall's words. He has a brilliant memory for details, talking of how his mum would send him down the hill to collect fresh milk from the milkman's horse-drawn cart and how he and his brother would spend summer days out in the local woods, making camps and eating blackberries, then go home for tea with purple-stained teeth.

She sees from his file that he's well into his eighties, but somehow Neil Marshall reminds her of a child, with just the faintest wisps of white hair on his head, rosy cheeks and an expression of permanent wonderment. But he's not had an easy time of it. The whole of last year was a write-off because of the chemo, he tells her. 'But there's no point in feeling hard done by. I'm simply happy to be here. So every day, I try to find something that brings me joy,' he says. 'The counsellor upstairs suggested it – keeping a gratitude diary. I know, it sounds very American. But, you know, it's not a bad idea.'

Henrietta tries hard to think of anything joyful that has happened to her today. She has walked Dave around the streets before dawn, been stuck on a bus in traffic and is now sitting in the corner of the Grief Café, trying to focus on what Mr Marshall is saying and resist an increasingly strong urge to check her phone to see if Sharon Sharpe has replied.

She can picture Annie sitting here last Saturday, and the memory of her dangling, tea-stained sleeves touches Henrietta in some inexplicable way. She wants so badly to piece together what happened to Annie's sister that night. How wonderful it would be, she thinks, if she can tie up all the loose, lost threads of her story and knit them together into one satisfyingly complete Life Story book, neatly bound in time for Christmas.

Unaware of these machinations inside Henrietta's troubled mind, Mr Marshall is still extolling the virtues of keeping a gratitude diary. 'For yesterday's entry,' he tells her, 'I wrote about my walk to the post office. I was passing by a Greek café when I heard a snatch of music coming from the doorway. It took me right back to holidays in Corfu, when our children were little,' he says with excitement.

'Then, today, I got into my car and I realised how much I absolutely love it. It's a 1973 Citroën DS.' When Henrietta looks blank, he reaches into his wallet and pulls out a photograph. 'It never starts and it costs me a fortune in repairs. But the smell of the leather seats, the feeling I get when I'm on the road – such pleasure!'

'I too have a car,' Henrietta replies. 'It is called a Nissan Micra and it is yellow.' She wishes she had a photograph to show him in return.

Something about his enthusiasm is infectious, and when Mia brings Mr Marshall a mug of tea, she pulls up a chair to join them. Henrietta is about to remind her that this is actually her workspace from 9 a.m. until midday, but then she sees how Mr Marshall is smiling and she thinks maybe she will leave it a little longer. But if Mia is still sitting here in ten minutes, she will have to say something. Because rules are rules.

Mr Marshall beams at the two of them. 'Well, look at you, Mia,' he says, as if he's greeting an old friend. 'Radiant – simply radiant!' Mia blushes and does something peculiar with her hair, twisting an escaped curl round and round her finger, which Henrietta thinks is probably very unhygienic for someone who works in the food and beverage service industry.

Then Mr Marshall turns his attention to Henrietta. 'And you, my dear, are looking very fetching today. Isn't she, Mia?' And suddenly Henrietta finds herself equally lost for words, ducking her head down in a coy manner.

'She is indeed,' says Mia, looking her up and down. 'That is a very striking top, Hen.'

Henrietta beams with pride. This is her very favourite top: a pale blue sweatshirt with a huge polar bear's head printed on the front, so lifelike that the artist has even included a dusting of snow on the bear's black nose. 'Why, thank you both very much. If you wish to purchase a similar sweatshirt, I can direct you to the relevant market stall in south London.'

She pulls her shoulders back and stretches out the bottom of her sweatshirt so Neil and Mia can appreciate the full effect. Their admiration leaves them quite lost for words, so Henrietta explains that the stall does a range of wild animals. 'I am thinking of buying the elk next time, although I am also tempted by the koala,' she explains. 'But perhaps that Australian marsupial would be more appropriate on a summer T-shirt.'

Mia says that reminds her that she needs to buy her nieces something for Christmas, but they are what she calls 'ungrateful madams' so she'll probably just give them vouchers or money. 'Since I lost my fiancé, Brice, Christmas feels like a bit of an effort,' she says. 'I put up the decorations at home and help my mum with the cooking to make it nice for everyone else, but inside . . . I could scream, sometimes. But you have to get on, don't you? Look to the future.'

Mr Marshall nods. 'You've been through a lot, Mia. Don't forget to be good to yourself too. Not long until Saturday and your favourite customer,' he says with a wink.

Mia taps him on the leg. 'Oh, be quiet. He's just a friend.'

Henrietta has somehow lost the thread of their conversation, but it all seems very jolly and light-hearted, so she puts on her smiley 'hello' face.

But then she realises Mr Marshall and Mia have

stopped laughing and are looking at her in an odd way.

'You alright, my dear? Not a migraine, I hope?'

Thankfully, Mr Marshall doesn't wait for her answer. Instead, he tells them that this Christmas he'll just enjoy being with his wife and their children and grandchildren, because it might be his last, which should be sad but makes him happy. And before Henrietta knows it, it is twelve o'clock and time to pack up her equipment and head to Audrey's office for an afternoon of admin. It's only as she gets in the lift that Henrietta realises she has just had a perfectly pleasant chat with two people who seemed equally happy with the arrangement, a novel and rather pleasant experience.

* * *

Henrietta is settling nicely into the routine of transcribing, typing and proofreading that she does in the afternoons, although it took a while to set things up correctly in the office. In fact, Audrey has yet to thank Henrietta for adjusting her chair, reorganising her desktop icons, deleting the extensive browsing history and separating the email inbox into fourteen separate folders.

Today, when Henrietta reaches the office, Audrey already has her coat on and is halfway out of the door. 'I'm off to a branding meeting,' she says. 'We're going to be doing Life Stories mugs, badges, stickers, pens, that sort of thing. I've got exciting ideas for the logo . . .' Audrey begins to button up her coat. 'Trust your morning went well? Everything ticking along?'

Henrietta gives a quick nod.

'I've left the new project handbook out for you. It should have been in your welcome pack but, well, it wasn't ready in time.'

Henrietta takes a step closer to the desk, sees a thick spiral-bound booklet with a laminated cover. The words 'Life Stories Handbook' are jauntily arranged above a clip art image of a pile of books. Audrey has been busy.

'Please do have a read, with particular reference to Chapter Three: Maintaining Professional Detachment,' Audrey is saying. 'In our line of work we hear some difficult stories, some of which may engage our emotions or pique our curiosity. But please remember that the Rosendale Drop-In Centre has trained counsellors at the ready, should a client need to discuss upsetting events in their past.'

Henrietta can feel the tickle of a twitch in her left eye. Has Audrey been spying on her? Or perhaps Henrietta slipped up last week and left an incriminating internet trail from her searches for Kathleen Doyle. But now Audrey is moving on to her next topic, which is only marginally less alarming.

'. . . So I'll send you that agenda next week,' she's saying.

Henrietta tries to look as if a sensible answer is on the tip of her tongue. 'Agenda?' she tries.

'For your appraisal, remember? We discussed it and put it in the work diary. It's right there, next to the handbook.' With that, Audrey disappears in a flash of magenta.

Her appraisal. No, Henrietta hasn't forgotten that particularly unappealing prospect. She waits until she can hear the clip-clop of Audrey's heels fading away, then the ping of the lift doors. She lifts the handbook up in both hands, feeling its heft, then risks a glimpse inside. Just as she feared, it's been printed double-sided in a small font size, with only a few illustrations. She catches a glimpse of a line in bold type: 'Each Life Story book should take no more than seven sessions to complete. Eight, if the client is a slow speaker.'

This is another uncomfortable reminder that Annie's Life Story book is woefully behind schedule. But, she reasons, if she starts wading through Audrey's handbook now, it will only slow her down further. No, she can't let herself get bogged down with Audrey's directives today – she has far more important work to do.

Someone has interfered with the seat height of the office swivel chair again so she has to waste more time putting it back to the correct level. Then she skims through the Life Stories Project emails, flagging the more important ones and filing them into her new system of sub-folders. She sends PDF leaflets to several people who want to know more, tells two families when their books will be delivered and then she deletes some rather unsavoury spam purporting to be from a gentleman called XXXL Larry.

Next on her list of jobs is transcribing Mr Marshall's session from this morning, but she is dismayed to discover that while her two-hour recording has plenty of chit-chat and pleasantries, there is surprisingly little she can add to his book. Clearly, her interviewing technique needs finessing.

It's not on her list for today, but she can't resist bringing up Annie Doyle's file again. *Just to remind myself where we're at,* she tells herself. But when she sees it on her screen in black and white, it's impossible to ignore the fact that this Life Story is in deep trouble.

The finished books are similar to the photo albums people order online to celebrate weddings, birthdays and so on, but with more space set aside for words. These are organised under Audrey's pre-set headings, starting with Early Years, progressing to Family Times, Achievements, Love & Marriage and then Golden Years.

So far, Henrietta has tried to paste Annie's random recollections into this format, but as she scrolls through, the effect is somewhat unsettling. Under Family Times, random lines jump out at her: *Kath was never seen again* and . . . *threw it all into the backyard.* Under Love & Marriage, she glimpses *If you leave, you're dead to me too.* And when she reaches Golden Times, all she has is one long, blank page.

She's pretty sure that this is not the sort of material Audrey will be expecting.

This is all getting a bit much to cope with. Henrietta thinks longingly of the KitKat nestled at the bottom of her backpack and wonders if it's too early to take a tea break. Instead, she allows herself to check her emails again and is surprised to find not one but two new emails. One is from Jane at Stationery Supplies, who kindly keeps her informed on all the latest offers on inkjet cartridges. The other is from Sharon Sharpe.

She glances down at the shiny handbook, no doubt

full of advice on Maintaining Professional Detachment and setting clear boundaries. Henrietta is a firm believer in rules, but sometimes it is the spirit of the rule that one must follow. She opens the email.

Dear Henrietta,

You are clearly not going to take no for an answer. Perhaps you should retrain as a crime reporter – you certainly have the tenacity. Yes, I did report on this case in 1974 and, if I'm honest, it is a case that has played on my mind over the years. Because you're right, Henrietta, this was not my finest hour as a journalist. I was three days into my traineeship on the Kensington News & Post. *It was Christmas and my boss disappeared off to the pub, leaving me to cover the crime beat.*

The officer in charge of that case, a DCI Williams, was not a pleasant man. He was old-school: not used to having a jumped-up reporter, a woman at that, asking nosey questions. He told me the bare facts of the case, supplied me with a photo of the missing girl and then he told me to bugger off and stop bothering him.

I did try to get more information, Henrietta. I asked when they would mount a full search. I asked about suspects, if there had been any similar cases and if any witnesses had come forward. But they stonewalled me every time.

After that placement, I continued my training on Fleet Street, where I soon toughened up and learned how to deal with intimidating police officers and chauvinistic bosses. These days I am enjoying semi-retirement in the Cotswolds. I hope you and Annie Doyle find what you are looking for.

Henrietta feels she's done Ms Sharpe a disservice. If she spent the rest of her career as a woman on Fleet Street, she's earned her right to spend her later years tending her bantams and judging entries for the oddest-shaped vegetable at the village fete.

She chances one last email.

Dear Sharon, I am grateful for your reply. One last thing – who were the suspects brought in for questioning? I did wonder about a boyfriend, or even the manager at her shoe shop?

The reply is almost immediate and, as Henrietta reads it, she lets out a gasp.

No. There was only one serious suspect. The girl's father.

Henrietta returns to her computer screen, skimming through Annie Doyle's words. She stops when she finds the bit where Annie had talked about sneaking out on the night of 21 December to look for her sister. And how, when she got home, her mum was already in bed, but a slice of light under the living-room door told her that her father was still up. Anxiously waiting for his daughter to come home.

But a light left on all night is hardly a solid alibi. What's more, if Annie had been out walking the streets in the rain, how could she be so sure that her father had been home during those hours? Henrietta keeps scrolling until she finds the words she's looking for: *Forgiveness did not come easily to Aidan Doyle.*

CHAPTER SIXTEEN

HENRIETTA

It's Wednesday, Henrietta's day off, and she is determined to focus on the task in hand, which is her weekly grocery shopping trip to Poundland. When she goes shopping, Henrietta always likes to leave the house on the dot of midday, but it's still only 11.43 a.m. so she sits on her sofa, her shopping bags folded neatly on her lap, until the minutes tick by. She's waiting for the pleasing symmetry of seeing both hands of the clock overlap on the number 12, marking the middle of the day on Wednesday, the middle day of the week.

Sitting here, she hears the scrape of a chair from the flat above. Upstairs Woman works from home, mostly in silence except for the odd one-sided phone conversation. She seems fond of the afternoon drama on the radio and, in the evenings, there is sometimes an energetic pummelling on the floorboards – initially alarming until Henrietta realised it was only a Davina workout DVD.

As Henrietta's mother would say, 'Good fences make good neighbours.' Although her mother's favourite phrase is 'Least said, soonest mended.' It's something of an (unspoken) family motto, but Henrietta is beginning to doubt its wisdom. Since hearing Annie's complicated life story, she's finding it harder to lock away her own difficult, watery memories quite so efficiently. Her job may involve tying up other people's loose ends, getting their lives in neatly bound order before they die, but Henrietta is increasingly aware that she, too, may have unfinished business.

It is now 11.59, almost time for Henrietta to leave. She hides some of Dave's pungent liver-flavoured dog treats among the sofa cushions to keep him occupied while she's out and puts her shopping list in her duffle coat pocket. She always takes a list – the same one every week – so that she can shop efficiently and swiftly, buying the same set of tinned products each time. She notices her list is getting a little ragged around the edges and wonders idly if Audrey might allow her access to the Life Stories Project laminator.

She closes her flat door softly and steps into the corridor when an alarming sound makes her freeze. It's the clunk of Upstairs Woman's door, followed by light, rapid footsteps. Even if she makes a dash for it, Henrietta won't make it out of the front door in time. Some form of interaction now seems inevitable. She grips her shopping bags tighter, presses her back to the wall.

'Hi,' says Upstairs Woman, with a wide smile. 'Off out?'

Oh dear, yet another person who can't help stating the obvious. Upstairs Woman is wearing her running gear and fiddling with a shiny wristwatch that lets out a series of sharp beeps. Next, she rolls her shoulders this way and that. 'Just off for a run,' she adds, unnecessarily. 'Get the old endorphins going.'

The two women stand facing each other. The hallway is not wide and yet everything about this woman is so dazzlingly clean and healthy that Henrietta can barely look at her. She's close enough to smell her neighbour's zesty deodorant and feels her own armpits prickle with discomfort. Henrietta is suddenly shamefully aware of her unwashed hair, her shabby duffle coat and sensible footwear.

She begins to scissor-step her way towards the front door and unlatches it with one hand, all the while trying to think of something to say. Despite her many years of observing people, Henrietta is at a loss when it comes to small talk. 'I'll be off, then. Time for my weekly shop,' she tries. Really, is that the best she can do? She'd been aiming for jolly and it came out as brusque.

But Upstairs Woman doesn't seem to mind. 'Great, great,' she says, joining Henrietta on the front step, adding some twists to her warm-up. 'Wish I was more organised. I always end up getting takeaways by the end of the week. Terrible, I know.'

'Yes, I've noticed,' says Henrietta, who hears the put-put of the delivery driver's moped every Friday night.

'Ha, ha, yes, guilty as charged.' Upstairs Woman is fiddling with her watch, getting ready for the off. 'Anyway, nice to chat.'

Henrietta steels herself. She always thinks of her

neighbour as Upstairs Woman, but she does have a name. 'It's Melissa, isn't it?'

'Melissa or Mel, either's fine.' She smiles. 'I'll see you around.' With that, her neighbour gives a wave and sets off at a bouncy jog.

Henrietta watches her go, observing the way her shiny ponytail swings from side to side. Melissa, she reminds herself. Or Mel. Who will see me around.

Sitting on the bus, she observes the familiar sights of the high street: the newsagent's with its faded postcards in the window, advertising cleaners or old furniture that no one wants; the shouty red hoarding of Pizza Pizzazz, which never seems to close. She idly wonders if that's where Melissa orders her Friday-night takeaways and, unbidden, an image pops into her head. It's of her and Melissa laughing as they open up a giant pizza box: Henrietta imagines it's a Hawaiian, but then she wonders if Melissa might prefer the Vegetarian and how she'd happily agree with that choice, because it has sweetcorn and pineapple on it too. But now she's getting quite carried away, so she shakes her head at such silliness.

As they approach her usual stop for Poundland, she stands up and rings the bell in good time. But then, as the bus slows and begins to pull in, a strange thing happens. Henrietta slowly sits back down and watches as other people barge their way out of the doors. Then the bus pulls out into the traffic and she finds herself still here, on board the top deck of a number 2 bus heading towards central London. She's not thinking about shopping any more, not even about Melissa.

She's thinking about Annie Doyle and their Saturday sessions, when there is never enough time to answer all Henrietta's questions. And a new plan is forming in her head.

Stepping outside her usual routine feels dangerous yet exciting. Aside from going to work – a straightforward journey that she planned out in advance of applying for the job – she does not like to venture beyond her south London postcode. But as the bus continues northwards, Henrietta looks down from the fogged-up window and sees eddies and streams of people going in and out of less familiar shops. Most of them have looks of grim determination indicating that, with December only a week away, serious Christmas shopping is in progress.

In Brixton, they pass a brightly lit shop selling rolls of sparkly wrapping paper, blow-up Santas and giant Christmas cards. There's a blast of music – 'Walking In A Winter Wonderland', a tune that Henrietta finds unexpectedly uplifting. She taps her foot along, although because she is wearing her favourite Millets' walking boots it requires more effort than she expects.

Yes, this impulsiveness is most irregular but, Henrietta reminds herself, these are exceptional times. She might not have read Audrey's Life Stories Handbook cover to cover, but she feels sure that she can prove she is the best transcriber the project has ever hired, willing to go above and beyond the call of duty. And, right now, an incident in her first book requires more background research. A field trip, if you like.

The traffic is torturously slow, so she will have plenty of time to change her mind en route. But, if not, the bus will take her all the way to Victoria Station, where she can pick up a number 52 bus. Even then, she will be free to ring the bell and step off anywhere she desires. But if she does choose to get that next bus, her travel app tells her that it will wend its way around Hyde Park Corner, past Knightsbridge, then on towards Notting Hill Gate and finally Ladbroke Grove, which, at its very top end, crosses over the Grand Union Canal. It was underneath this bridge in late December 1974 that a bundle of clothes was found, the last recorded trace of Kathleen Doyle.

Some ninety minutes later, Henrietta stands by the canal's edge, peering at the trails of weeds under its surface. Ever since reading those reports in the *Kensington News & Post* she's tried to imagine this spot, but in her mind's eye it's always been a far darker and lonelier place. Admittedly, this area has probably changed a fair bit since Kath Doyle stood here – and since Annie took her afternoon walks up and down the towpath, looking in vain for signs of life, or death. But today, on a Wednesday afternoon in late November, this stretch of waterway does not feel especially significant or ominous.

A steady flow of people passes her by: cyclists and joggers, a group of schoolgirls and an elderly man with a stiff-legged dog, all going about their daily business. Henrietta walks up to where some narrowboats are moored. There are a few older ones, raddled and tatty, then a couple that have been smartened up with glossy red paint and gingham curtains. One is getting into the festive spirit with a mini Christmas tree on its deck, looped with flashing lights. She wonders if any boats were moored here back in 1974. If so, had anyone caught a glimpse of Kath? They might have seen whether she was here alone or with someone, or even if someone followed her to this spot.

There's also an apartment block on the opposite bank, which she judges to have been built within the past couple of decades. She would like to know whether a house stood there before – although the chances of tracing anyone who might have been looking out of a window on a rainy night in 1974 are, she concedes, rather slim.

Moving underneath the iron girders and heavy bolts of the bridge, it feels dark and damp and her footsteps echo in a far spookier way. The walls here are spray-painted with indecipherable words and the bare skeleton of an abandoned bike lies on the ground, no wheels, no saddle, no good to anyone. Was this the spot where Kath's clothes were found?

Today the air is crisp and the sun is out, but on a rainy night in late December it would have felt quite different. She can easily imagine how cold the black waters of a London canal would be on such a night, if you fell, slipped – or were pushed in.

She walks a little further and a breeze picks up, sending a takeaway carton spinning out on to the water. Beyond the carton, Henrietta notices a set of numbers painted on to the far wall of the canal, the greenish waterline sitting just below the number 4. Being rather ill prepared for this field trip, she has a pen but no paper in her pocket except for her shopping list. It's a shame to spoil it, but with no other option, she writes 'depth 4m' in very small letters at the bottom of her list. Pocketing the slip of paper, Henrietta heads back up the path to wait for the first of the two buses to take her home, her empty shopping bags still looped over one arm.

* * *

Dave, never effusive in his greetings, opens one eye as Henrietta comes through the flat door, then closes it again. A warmer welcome would have been nice, after what feels like an epic journey across London. She has stepped outside her comfort zone and while it was not easy (comfort zones are called that for a reason) she has returned safe and sound. And, as she had reminded herself at various points during the lengthy journey, thorough research is essential. Editorial accuracy is non-negotiable.

Because she never made it to Poundland, she and Dave share a simple repast of tinned tuna for their evening meal and then Henrietta gets out her ancient laptop. She has new leads to follow. As the fake coals of the gas fire warm up, sending the not unpleasant smell of singed dust and old dog into her living room, Henrietta soon finds what she's looking for.

A local history website tells her that the waterside apartment block she saw was built in the 1980s, replacing a run-down pub called The Red Lion. Interestingly, in 1974, a pub, not a house, overlooked the spot where Kath Doyle left a pile of clothes and entered the water, willingly or unwillingly.

Next, Henrietta turns her attention to more official sources of information: a Health and Safety Executive report that estimates survival times in open water and the Canal & River Trust's website, which helpfully lists the various depths of the UK's inland waterways. Essential information, she supposes, to ensure the nation's narrowboats aren't left high and dry. She discovers that while some canals are as deep as 11 feet, urban passages tend to be less easy to navigate and are far shallower. In fact, along the stretch of the Grand Union Canal that she walked today, the depth is rarely more than 4 feet 10 inches.

Henrietta snaps her laptop shut. How could she have been so stupid? The number she saw on the canal wall measured the water's depth in feet, not metres. Which means an adult of average height would be exceptionally unlucky to drown in that particular spot.

To Henrietta, there are four possible reasons why Kathleen Doyle could have left her clothes on the towpath, entered the relatively shallow water and never emerged. One: she was drunk, fell in and drowned by accident. Two: she was drunk and jumped in for fun – Henrietta is aware that such horseplay is common around Christmas time – and accidentally drowned. Three: as DCI Williams thoughtlessly implied in 1974, Kathleen had found a way to weigh herself down and take her own life. But possibility number four, that Kath was held down or weighed down by a person or persons unknown, is looking increasingly likely, given the depth of the water.

Of course, there is also possibility number five, that

Kath Doyle never even got her toes wet. She had simply left those clothes there as a cover and escaped into the night. Perhaps she needed to get away from their father or had a secret boyfriend that Annie didn't know about.

Then something that Annie told her in their very first session comes back to her: 'Some people thought we were twins because we often wore the same clothes.' Who was to say that it was Kath who had left that neat pile of clothes on the towpath? Annie could easily have helped lay a false trail when she sneaked out that night, ostensibly to look for her sister. Could this be the information Annie is holding back – that she knows far more about the events of 21 December 1974 than she's letting on? Perhaps the sisters were in cahoots all along and Kath is alive and well and living in an executive home in Milton Keynes, and sends Annie a Christmas card every year.

Except then Henrietta remembers how utterly alone Annie had looked on Saturday and everything she's said so far. The fact is, losing her sister changed the entire course of Annie's life, prompting her to rush into an ill-advised marriage and lose touch with her family. No, she can't picture this scenario at all: if Annie had helped spirit her sister away, Henrietta feels sure she would be listening to a far happier Life Story.

But when Henrietta starts to imagine the numerous ways in which Kath might have ended up in the water, her mind is far more alive with possibilities. It's as if she's right there, watching Kath gasp at the sudden coldness of the water. She can picture how she might have struggled to find a handhold on the slippery banks and that, even in that shallow water, the silty mud would be surprisingly deep and heavy. She might have tried to get a handhold on the weeds, but they would come away, slick and slimy. And then, at that point, how panic would really set in.

All this comes too easily to Henrietta, from years of thinking about what happened to a little boy called Christopher, all those years ago on a beach far away in Masura, Papua New Guinea. The way the water ran off his body in runnels, his baggy shorts hanging from his skinny legs. How the pebbles on the beach were so hot that the dark trail of seawater evaporated almost immediately. The rubber swimming ring left to drift out to sea, a bright dot of orange in the blue that became smaller and smaller until it disappeared entirely.

Saturday is still three days away, but at Annie's next appointment Henrietta will be far more organised and ready to make the best use of their time. She will have a set of questions ready and this time she won't allow herself to be distracted by stories about clothes and jukeboxes and burnt schoolbooks. She needs to know everything that Annie remembers about that night and about her father. Because she has the horrible feeling that Aidan Doyle, strict with his daughters and prone to anger, has taken the truth of Kath's death to his grave.

CHAPTER SEVENTEEN

ANNIE

Today is Friday and Annie is getting ready for her weekly trip to the vintage clothes stalls down Portobello Road. She didn't sleep well and her eyelids feel gritty on the inside, but she's determined to make an effort. She's decided to wear one of her favourite dresses – a beautiful deep-blue Jean Muir number with tiny fabric-covered buttons and floaty sleeves that gather at her wrists. It's ever so comfy, once she's done up all the fiddly buttons.

Annie loved it from the moment she saw it and she guesses that its previous owner was a terribly chic lady who swanned around cocktail parties in Kensington in the late seventies, around the same time that Annie was five miles up the road cooking pork chops for a man she was scared of and wiping noses and bottoms for children who weren't even her own.

But this morning, even her favourite dress doesn't feel right and, before she knows it, she finds herself imagining how Kath would have looked in it. Her sister has been gone so long, but every time Annie buys something new, she still does this. The habit of a lifetime, she supposes – compare and contrast these two girls. Because the truth was, while the Doyle Girls looked similar from a distance, up close, the differences were easy to spot. It was as if Annie had been the trial run and then, when Kath came along eleven months later, everything had been refined and made perfect. Her nose a touch smaller, her chin slightly less square and her eyes a prettier brown.

Just stop it, she tells herself, and concentrate on those last tiny buttons. If only her hands would stop shaking. She'll need to get a move on if she's going to make it to the market in time for the best bargains.

The Portobello Road Friday market was a revelation to Annie when she moved back to this corner of London two years ago, once she was finally free of Terry. She loves to sift through the rails of the second-hand clothes stalls, stroking the vintage dresses or skimpy tops and imagining what she would have worn if she'd had the chance the first time around. Today, though, it's slim pickings at her favourite stalls. Even Chantal, the nice stallholder near the flyover who puts things by for her, doesn't have anything interesting. 'It's coming into the party season, Annie,' she says. 'As soon as I hang something up it goes. And they don't even blink when I name my price.'

Annie likes the way Chantal wears her hair in a 1940s-style chignon, with red lipstick and a wraparound wool coat with big buttons. In summer, she switches to tea dresses with tight nips and tucks that fit her like a glove. It's a crying shame, Annie thinks, that she won't be around next summer to admire Chantal in those outfits again.

After a lifetime of wearing the dull-as-dishwater dresses Terry approved of, Annie has bought lots of things from Chantal – and the less appropriate, the better. Shiny, sequinned tops, shirts with fringes and frills, a silver-green faux fur coat that felt like wearing a big hug. Or she got the 23 bus up to Oxford Street and bought cheeky vests, a pair of something called Mom jeans and a whole new set of undies from New Look, which seemed appropriate.

Not all of her outfits were a success. A sparkly gold polo neck was unbearably itchy and she stopped wearing her stripey Breton top when she saw that it was something of a uniform for the mums that cruise the streets in SUVs at school-run time. The Mom jeans dug into her waist, so she replaced them with some thick canvas trousers that Chantal called 'French workwear'.

Such wanton extravagance was unknown when she and Kath were growing up. Clothes had to be saved up for, or their mother ran up identical frocks on her sewing machine. But even back then, the differences between the two girls were impossible to disguise. 'Annie, she tries hard, but she's not a patch on our Kath,' she'd once heard her mum tell Auntie Rita. That's what you get, she supposes, for lurking outside closed doors.

Of course, it wasn't just their parents who noticed the way that Kath outshone Annie. Boys, teachers, friends' mothers, even Sister McGhee at the youth club – they all fell for Kath, with her sunnier smile and her easy laughter. By the age of fifteen Kath had mastered a tinkling sort of laugh that everyone loved but set

Annie's teeth on edge because she'd heard it a thousand times.

So Annie found her own way of levelling things out, once she and Kath were alone in their bedroom. She can't remember exactly when the fights started, but it must have been when they were at primary school, because of the scar. That time Annie went a bit too far.

She hadn't meant it to happen: she'd felt her nails pincer into the skin in a tight pinch and couldn't resist digging in that bit further, just to see what would happen next. She was curious, too, to see if Kath would break their code of silence and cry out. But she didn't. Blood bloomed under Annie's nails and Kath still kept her lips pressed together. There was no sound except for the two of them breathing, fast and hot, their heads pressed together in combat. Afterwards, they'd sat on the bed, working out a way to brush Kath's hair over her forehead so it wouldn't show.

These secret squabbles always began with a sly poke. Then came the niggling, a tit-for-tat until one or the other lashed out, and then it would begin properly: a tight, silent tussle that ended up on the floor. Annie liked to pinch; Kath preferred to grab a fistful of hair. Annie would twist her sister's arm until it burned; Kath would bite where it didn't show. Then, a pinch or a twist to the ear until one of them whispered, 'You win.'

These fights were always conducted in silence. No one must hear, least of all their dad, who would hit the roof if he found out what they were up to. He saw it as his right to raise a hand to the women in his household, but they knew that in some illogical way their skirmishes would have offended his sense of propriety. But he never did find out. After each bout, almost refreshed, they would brush their hair, smooth out each other's clothes and trip downstairs in their white socks, in time for tea.

Yes, having a sister like Kath wasn't always easy. But then Kath was gone forever and, without her sister by her side, Annie's life got so much worse and soon she realised that it was herself, not Kath, who had been the problem all along.

Her retribution for all her years of jealousy was her marriage to Terry. And after a few years with him, she found herself looking back on those sisterly bedroom scuffles with a sort of fondness. They were nothing but child's play. Compared to Terry, she and Kath, even their dad, they were all rank amateurs in the business of cruelty.

Annie is almost home, but the walk seems to be taking longer than usual and her heartburn is back. That was how her illness started, a feeling like the worst indigestion, a burning that never let up, whether she lay down, sat up or walked back and forth all night. She fumbles in her pocket and finds a foil sheet of Rennie tablets – she has several packets on the go these days, scattered all around the flat, in her bag and in all her coat pockets, so she never has to look too far for them. They used to help, but not so much now.

Tomorrow, when she sees Henrietta, she needs to talk about how life changed after she lost Kath. The way that Terry had swooped down like a crow that spots fresh roadkill, scraped up what was left of Annie and carried her off to suburbia. And after a few years of living in Chaucer Drive, Annie didn't feel like herself any more, more a quiet shadow that floated from one tidy room to the next, with no strong feelings about anything in particular. Those were her blank years, the numbness partly down to the pills the doctor gave her, but mostly down to Terry.

When everyone whispered about Kath's death they said, 'What a waste of a life.' But what about Annie? Annie carried on living and breathing and putting on her shoes each morning, going to work and cooking and washing up. But that wasn't a life, that was just existing, marking off the days and then the years. Doesn't that count as a waste of a life, too? But how typical, she thinks, that even in death, Kath still managed to get all the sympathy.

At unexpected times this week, staring out of the kitchen window, listening to the radio as she waits for the creep of the grey dawn, she's found herself thinking of telling this to Henrietta. Someone in Annie's position really shouldn't be wishing the days away, but she's been looking forward to Saturday. In fact, she must have been thinking about Henrietta too much because she could have sworn she saw her moon-like face staring out from the top deck of a number 52 bus on Wednesday, but her mind must be playing tricks on her again.

Back at home, as Annie takes off her coat and starts to unbutton her dress, she realises that, in a funny way, this dress will outlive her. She should tell someone, so it doesn't get tossed out as rubbish. And that Ossie Clark number that she treated herself to for her birthday must be worth a few bob, too. That's another thing to tell Henrietta about: her second-chance clothes and why she loves them and wants to squeeze every moment of pleasure out of what little time she has left. She wants to tell Henrietta that it's high time she started doing that too, because you don't get a second chance at life.

CHAPTER EIGHTEEN

HENRIETTA

Today there will be no fussing around with cups of tea or slices of Bakewell tart. They have sixty minutes, which is inevitably closer to fifty-five by the time Annie has sat down, and Henrietta is determined to make the very best use of this time.

She has a set of questions, which she typed out neatly last night, adding a bullet point next to each one. She has placed the sheet of paper on her table and she glances at it again, to give her the courage she needs.

Questions for Annie Doyle:
- Witnesses?
- Eg, in The Red Lion pub?
- Suspect – Aidan Doyle?
- Kath's boyfriend/s?
- How long in water? (cf chart)
- Why clothes left there?

And now Annie has arrived, although, annoyingly, she is walking even more slowly than usual. It doesn't help that she's wearing a pair of the most impractical boots, with lots of buckles and straps that jangle, and a silvery faux fur coat that makes her look like a bedraggled snowman. Henrietta watches as Annie tries to tug one arm out of the sleeve and then gets stuck, coat half on, half off, beside Henrietta's table.

'Sorry, love. Can you give me a hand? Truth be told, it's a size too small, but I couldn't resist buying it. So beautiful, this coat . . .'

Henrietta sighs, stands up and holds the coat by its shoulders so Annie can shrug it off. Beneath the silvery fluff of the coat she can feel Annie's bones, bird-thin and sharp in unexpected places.

'That's better.' Annie is still busy arranging her coat over the back of her chair and waving at Mia, forming the letter 'T' with her fingers, as if they have all the time in the world. But Henrietta needs to get on: she clicks her pen impatiently, looks over her list and presses the red button on her recording app.

'So, to business. Annie Doyle, today is Saturday the twenty-seventh of November and we are recording session four of your Life Story.'

Annie still seems oblivious to the urgency of the job in hand. 'I thought I might talk about my married years today,' she says. Henrietta sees that she's wearing a new lipstick, a sugary eighties pink that goes surprisingly well with her grey hair, but she mustn't lose her focus.

'I'm afraid I have a number of outstanding queries before we proceed with further material,' Henrietta says sharply. 'Several facts about the death of your sister simply do not add up. I have been doing some background research and it's clear to me that some foul play was involved.'

Annie's face falls, colour leaching from her cheeks. 'Foul play?'

'Indeed.' Henrietta glances down at her list. 'First and foremost, I find it hard to believe there were no witnesses. I believe there was a local pub by the canal, The Red Lion, which would have been busy that night. Was that establishment familiar to you?'

'No, The Red Lion wasn't the sort of pub we went to. Like I said, we were good girls,' Annie says. 'And no, no witnesses ever came forward.'

'No witnesses at all?' Henrietta wants to be sure about this.

'Think about it, Hen. It was the last Saturday before Christmas and it was raining: no one was interested in anything except shopping and then going out boozing.'

Annie's tea arrives and she starts to spoon in the sugar.

It's important that Henrietta asks her next question carefully because she already knows the answer, but she can't let that slip.

'And what about the suspects? Was there anyone of special interest?'

Annie carries on stirring her tea. 'Oh, there was never any mystery about that.' She taps the spoon on the edge of the mug and looks up. 'It was our dad. But don't get too excited – it was nothing but harassment. Like I said, the police weren't fans of Aidan Doyle, so they brought him in. Wasted everyone's time when they should have been out looking for Kath.'

Henrietta's pen hovers over her paper; she is far from ready to cross Aidan Doyle's name off her list. 'And they questioned him thoroughly?' she presses.

'That's one way of putting it. They gave him a good going over. But our dad was home all night and his only crime was being Irish.'

Henrietta writes this down. Something tells her that it's best to keep quiet for now about the obvious flaw in this statement – that Annie herself was not at home for the entire night. And that her mother, Deidre Doyle, a woman probably well versed in doing as she was told, might not be a reliable witness either. Henrietta busies herself with her list. 'And was anybody else questioned?'

'Well, yes. But it was the same anti-Irish prejudice. They pulled in a couple of my dad's mates too, but soon released them. Solid alibis.'

'So, your father's friends . . .' This new information could be relevant – crucial, in fact – but Annie gives a wave of her hand, as if all this is as bothersome to her as a fly.

'All nonsense, down to rumours,' she says. 'In the weeks after Kath went missing there were plenty of stories going around. That Kath was a drinker, that she killed herself. Complete rubbish. That my dad had a temper. True, but he wouldn't have done anything like that. He adored her. Kath was his favourite.

'Then people started to talk about my dad's mates. They said he had run into a spot of bother with them, because he'd been forgetting his obligations.'

Henrietta keeps quiet, willing Annie to continue.

'My dad was a postman, see, and now and then he might notice a nice house was looking a bit empty, that the family might be away on holiday. So he might mention it to a couple of mates. And if those mates happened to be passing that house one night they might just take a closer look. Do you get my meaning?'

Henrietta does get her meaning, and she likes the sound of Aidan Doyle less and less. However, she has a new appreciation for Dave and his habit of sitting at her front window and barking indiscriminately at anyone who approaches her front steps.

Annie continues. 'So apparently my dad stopped feeding these blokes tip-offs. Not out of the kindness of his heart, mind – only because his supervisor got wind of it. So the rumour was, those mates wanted to remind my dad of his commitments. They knew where Kath worked and might have followed her after she left work, brought her down to the canal to give her a scare – as a way of passing our dad a message. And then something went wrong.'

'And did the police follow this up?'

'The police did nothing. Like I said, they didn't bother searching the area properly until it was too late. All they did was bring in my dad and then his two mates, but they had alibis. His friends were playing in a darts match in Kilburn all night and my dad was at home, with me and my mum.'

Again, something tells Henrietta that now is not the time to challenge this because Annie is eyeing the sheet of paper that's lying on the table. In a flash, she reaches out and grabs it.

'What's this – *How long in water? Why clothes left there?*' Annie reads out the words in a flat monotone, then slams her hand down, making Henrietta jump.

'Don't you think I've wondered that myself, all these years?' Her voice rises to a shout. People stop talking and Mia is looking up, deciding if she needs to step out from behind her counter. 'Over and over, I've imagined exactly how my sister drowned. And now you swan in like this is some sort of detective game. Like you can solve it and get, what, a gold star? This isn't a game. This is the nightmare I've lived with since I was nineteen.'

Henrietta has done it again; she's said the wrong thing in the wrong way and now she's hurt Annie, this frail woman who doesn't have long to live and has shared so many sad secrets with her already. She's got carried away and hurt a person who trusted her.

Annie jabs her finger at the list again. 'What's this chart, then? Something that tells me how long my sister suffered for?'

'I found it online,' Henrietta says. 'It estimates how long a person can survive in cold water.' The rattle of plates and cups and the hiss of the coffee machine have picked up again, but she wishes they were louder still, so no one will hear her words.

'And?' Annie barks.

'It depends on the wind chill factor and the water temperature. If the water is five degrees and there is no wind, a person of average build could last forty-five minutes. With a gentle breeze, it would be less. Perhaps under thirty minutes.' She should stop talking now. 'In normal clothes. I mean, not a wetsuit.' Enough, Henrietta, she tells herself. It hadn't sounded this bad in her head.

They sit in silence, Henrietta not daring to say another word, watching the numbers tick round on her app. She can see how, in retrospect, her questions might be in poor taste. She can't possibly tell Annie about the rest of her background research or how, just three days ago, she stood on the edge of the Grand Union Canal, peering into the dark water. Perhaps, Henrietta thinks, she should stop cross-examining poor Annie and take a closer look at her own motives and whose mind she really wants to put at rest. 'I'm very sorry, that was insensitive,' she says.

Annie sighs. 'It's nothing I haven't thought about already, to be honest. As for your other questions, her boyfriend was a nobody. One of Terry's printworks boys, a dull bloke, Brian Neville. Married someone in the accounts department a few years later. Two kids. It wasn't anything serious, anyway. Kath didn't do serious.'

'You never wondered if she had someone else? Someone you didn't know about?'

Then Annie does something that takes Henrietta by surprise. She gives a serene smile. 'That's simply not possible,' she says. 'Kath and I shared everything. If she had a boyfriend, even an admirer, I would have known. Kath and I didn't have secrets.'

Annie peers at Henrietta's list of questions again. 'As for why she left her clothes there, I've wondered about that myself, whether she was getting ready to jump. But, like I say, Kath wouldn't have done that to me. She would never have left me alone on purpose.'

Annie leans forward, as if something has just occurred to her. 'I had to go with my dad to identify her clothes. And do you know what they said to us?'

Henrietta shakes her head.

'They said finding her clothes was "Not necessarily evidence of foul play". Then, to my dad's face, they said, "Maybe Kathleen Doyle just liked taking her clothes off." Sniggered like schoolboys.'

Henrietta thinks of Sharon's comments about DCI Williams and police attitudes in 1974 and she can well believe this.

'You see,' Annie went on, 'I've gone over these possibilities. For a while, I dared to hope that she might have survived and that one day she'd breeze back in and surprise me, then rescue me from my marriage. Every birthday and Christmas I waited, just in case. But there was never anything.'

She looks straight at Henrietta. 'We had our moments, me and Kath. But if Kath was still alive, she'd have let me know. She wouldn't have left me alone all these years.'

Annie crosses her arms. 'So, if you're done playing detective, I did have something I wanted to talk about – my marriage,' she says. 'If you listen to this, I think you'll understand why, once I married Terry, I wasn't in any position to go chasing the police for answers.'

Perhaps this is a way to make amends, thinks Henrietta. She feels thoroughly ashamed of herself. Annie's right – this isn't some sort of game. First and foremost, it's Annie's Life Story, and she's running out of time to tell it.

'Of course. We still have twenty minutes left.' She scrunches her list of questions into a tight ball. 'As you rightly said when we first met, this is your story.'

CHAPTER NINETEEN

ANNIE

She wants Henrietta to listen, listen and learn. This girl with her gauche words, racing into things without thinking them through – she's annoying but, oh, she's such an innocent. She talks like someone from another age, like she's been plonked down in the twenty-first century without even glancing at a phrase book, let alone a fashion magazine. Yes, she's all businesslike with her bullet points and lists, but underneath there's something soft and almost indecently vulnerable about her. She's the sort that gets taken advantage of, just like Annie was.

'Maybe you'll have guessed by now, Henrietta, but my father was a classic bully, a small-minded man who ruled his household with slaps, kicks and punches. With Kath gone, things got even worse. I thought marriage was my chance to escape, but with Terry I learned a whole new kind of bullying.

'At least my dad was predictable – if he was angry, he'd lash out. So if you spotted trouble brewing, you just kept quiet and remembered to hold your arms over your head. "Not the face, Aidan," my mum used to say. But Terry was cleverer than that. At first, I thought it was a strange kind of love, that he couldn't control his emotions. But now I realise it was all about control.'

Annie sees that Henrietta's face has changed, as if she's listening properly and this is good. Because these things can creep up on you until you barely mind any more.

'If I describe some of the things Terry did, they don't sound so bad at first. Every mealtime, he would reach over and shake salt on my food for me. That sounds OK, doesn't it? Caring, even. But what if I told you that if he came home in a bad mood, he kept shaking and shaking until my food was inedible, but I had to eat it because it was his wages that put food on the table.'

It was a good job their dining room had been wallpapered in a murky pattern of flowers and ferns, because a fair few dishes got thrown at it over the years. A bowl of too-cold custard left a yellow stain beneath a tangle of rose briars. A splatter of brown gravy (judged too weak) blended in surprisingly easily. It was the waiting that was the worst, wondering when it would come.

'Then there were the clothes he bought for me. That sounds quite nice, too, doesn't it? But it meant I only had three dowdy dresses that he picked out for me in a catalogue and one dress for special. So, Mia, if you ever get to read this, no, I'm afraid I can't tell you any stories about shopping in Biba and I didn't wear Mary Quant or hot pants or sequins. Once I was married, I dressed like a middle-aged woman and tied my hair back in a sensible bun.'

She slides her hands into her trouser pockets, the stiff workwear ones that Chantal found her, points her toes and gives her boot buckles a jangle. 'I see the way you look at my clothes.' She smiles to save Henrietta the bother of trying to find a polite reply. 'It's OK, you're not alone. But I'm just making up for lost time, having some fun while I can. Because, let me tell you, Henrietta, the years fly by quicker than you think.'

Then Annie stops her jingle-jangling. She needs to get this bit right, so this girl understands. 'Terry was always watching me, Hen. Even if I ran a bath, he'd come in and sit beside me. After a day at the nursery, I longed for a deep, relaxing foam bath like they showed in the Badedas adverts. Instead, I'd sit in a few inches of water and he would watch me wash myself with a flannel. "Go on, get in there, wash that stinking fanny, Annie. You reek." Things like that, he'd say. Fanny Annie, that's what he called me when no one else was around.'

At this, Henrietta's grey eyes grow wide and Annie feels a wave of shame. She falters, almost stops. But she's kept quiet for long enough.

'Not that we saw many people. As for family, well, my dad cut me off after I left. Like I said, it was the undoing of our family, losing Kath.'

Now Henrietta is looking straight at her. 'It's hard,' she says quietly. 'When you don't have anyone to talk to.'

'I don't think the neighbours had any idea. From the outside everything looked perfect: the window boxes, the car on the drive. Terry insisted on all the latest stuff. He'd tick things in his Argos catalogue and I'd smile and say, "Lovely, what a treat." The three-piece suite, the plate warmer, the electric carving knife – none of it made any difference. Those echoey rooms were never going to feel like a home. And, of course, it was also empty because we never had any children.'

Three times she'd felt the glimmer of hope and three times she'd felt that dreadful loosening as the babies let go and bled away.

'The longest I carried was ten weeks. I still had to go to work that day and I hoped the bleeding might stop if I didn't think about it. But there I was, reading *The Very Hungry Caterpillar* to the children, and one of them tugged at my hem. "Miss, you've got a cut. It's gone all over your dress," he told me.'

At this, Henrietta's face turns a touch paler and she blinks hard, several times.

'When I told Terry, he looked at me with such disappointment. Actually, I'd call it disdain. But I think a baby would have made things worse. They take up so much of your time, you see, and he liked my full attention. No, he was disappointed because I'd failed as a wife.

'That third time, he lost his temper. He stormed out of the house, saying what the fuck was he going to tell the boys at work. Nev, Smithy, Wills, Mikey, all the printing boys, they were looking forward to wetting the baby's head. Maybe that baby knew best, though. It could see what was in store and decided, no thank you very much, I won't be growing up in that family.'

There's a terrible irony, Annie thinks, in the way that those clusters of barely knitted cells slipped out of her so easily but now these cancerous cells have succeeded in taking a far firmer hold, multiplying until their job is done.

She can tell Henrietta is itching to ask: why didn't you leave? 'Hen, I did try to leave him a couple of times. I had to be a bit crafty because all my wages went into his bank account and he gave me my housekeeping. I had to write down everything I bought and if it was a few pence out, he'd hold out his palm, not say a word, just wait for the change. But down the market, the fruit and veg was cheaper and they didn't give you receipts. So I added a few pence on to the apples, rounded up the amount for potatoes, a little bit here and there. It took a year to save up a decent amount the first time, and I went to Auntie Rita's.

'It didn't take him long to work out where I was. Rita gave him a piece of her mind, but he won her over, like he did with everyone. He was in bits, crying, begging to be let in, telling her how much he loved me. So I went back.

'The second time I left, I didn't tell a soul. I booked into a cheap B&B in Paddington. I used money from the nursery's petty cash, and I still feel ashamed of that. But after three nights, I realised I didn't know where to go next. I was tired of lying awake in my single room waiting for him to come and thump his big hands on the door. Because he would have eventually – he just knew things, he knew people everywhere.'

She glances up at the clock; it's nearly midday and

soon Bonnie will be here, waving her arms, and she and the others will all climb back in the minibus and she won't see Henrietta for another long week.

'So, yes, I stayed, Henrietta. It was easier to give in, to go back to what I knew. At least I had a nice house. And the kids at the nursery, they did make me happy, although sad in a way too.'

It seems her cheeks are wet. Silently, Henrietta passes her a tissue. 'Oh, Annie,' she says. 'I'm so sorry.'

CHAPTER TWENTY

HENRIETTA

It's a Tuesday, which means Henrietta has had plenty of time to think about last Saturday's session: the things Annie said but also her own mortifying attempt at interviewing Annie. Interrogating, she concedes, might be closer to the mark. Still, Henrietta Lockwood has never claimed to be a people person: more a researcher, a watcher of other people from the sidelines. And now, in this job, an impartial and thorough recorder of other people's life stories.

The problem is, the more she gets to know Annie, the less impartial she feels. She admires the way that each week, Annie finds the strength to talk about difficult things. Henrietta has never felt able to 'share' or 'open up' about anything, and it's certainly not a trait that's been encouraged. Secrets have been the mainstay of Lockwood family life for as long as she can remember.

Today, back at her table in the Grief Café, she unpacks her pens, her Rosendale-issue phone and her Thermos flask, and places them on her table, ready to greet her first client of the day. But she still feels out of sorts. For the umpteenth time this morning she runs her hands over her head, trying to smooth down the frizzy mass that has developed overnight. Inspired by seeing her neighbour Melissa's flaxen hair at close quarters, Henrietta invested in a new brand of shampoo. But she must have bought the wrong kind, or missed out some extra stage, because her usual lank hair has become supercharged and doubled in size. She keeps catching glimpses of it waving at her out of the corner of her eye and can't decide whether this is a good thing or a bad thing. It's just not very Henrietta-ey.

It's a relief when her first client of the day sits down and starts to tell a Life Story that is delightfully straightforward and devoid of drama. Samuel Gregory is an octogenarian teacher who has reached his Family Times section and he speaks eloquently about travels across Europe by train in the 1980s. He shows her photographs of a rounder, plumper Samuel and his wife, Beverley, smiling from railway carriage windows in Paris and Milan; the two of them standing on snowy station platforms in Lausanne and Innsbruck. 'Then we went on to Vienna and Budapest, what an adventure!'

Next she has an appointment with Eric, who spent his career on the assembly line of Ford's at Dagenham, but confesses he always harboured a secret ambition – to become an artist. 'I went to work straight from school and my parents wouldn't hear of me doing Art O level,' he tells Henrietta. 'I did what was expected, but I regretted it every day. I know that must sound pathetic to you.'

'Actually, I am no stranger to familial obligations,'

she replies. 'So I sympathise entirely.'

The mood turns jollier when Eric tells Henrietta how he's recently bought himself a set of oil paints. 'Now I can't stop painting – I even dream in colours and shapes.'

'If you take some photographs of your work, we can include them in your book. Take as many photos as you like,' she says, and Eric promises to do just that.

'What a wonderful idea – a book of my art. With just a few words about my life, if that's alright? Thank you, love,' he says.

Her afternoon is spent in the calm seclusion of Audrey's office, proofreading several Life Stories before they are sent to the printers – the perfect task to keep her absorbed and stop her brain from drifting back to murkier matters. Annie Doyle isn't her only client, she reminds herself, and she needs to focus on all aspects of her new job if she's to make a success of it.

The last book on her proofreading pile turns out to be a reprint and Henrietta instantly recognises the story because it's Kenton Hancock's, the one she was given as a test during her job interview. It turns out Kenton was more popular than his wife had anticipated when she asked for a modest ten copies. Unbeknown to her, Kenton was a regular at a local gym, where his fellow pumpers of iron – all twenty of them – have asked for his book.

Henrietta opens up Kenton's layout, trying to put aside the painful memory of all those split infinitives and dangling participles she eliminated during her interview. But when she sees Audrey's final version, she spots several more. She also sees there is a wasted blank page at the end, where another photograph could easily be inserted. 'If a job's worth doing . . .' she mutters to herself as she goes over to the squat grey filing cabinet in the corner.

This is where Audrey keeps all the materials that are scanned into the Life Story books, before they are sent back to relatives. The drawers are heavy, each hung with rows of swinging pocket files, and they make a satisfying rumble and clunk as she opens them. Henrietta peers in and glimpses letters, certificates and photographs, the detritus of lives lived.

She finds Kenton Hancock's file and soon locates an unused photograph: Kenton and a fellow birdwatcher, by the looks of it. Kenton looks rather happy and she can't imagine why Audrey didn't include it before, so she scans in the new photo and inserts it on the last page. Then she gives Kenton Hancock's story a final read.

Before she's even made it past the Early Years chapter, it's quite clear to Henrietta that this is a work of pure fiction by a most deluded narrator. Self-important bluff bounces off every page:

> *My intelligence was recognised from an early age and I was awarded a scholarship to Helmsford House School. It took me some months to settle into the routine, but the masters took a firm approach. Very soon I was a popular and valued member of the class.*

There followed Sandhurst, two stints serving

abroad, then a long, unexplained gap before some voluntary work. There was a wife, Irene, and two sons, Euan and Roland. Finally, a move to Ipswich, where Kenton's story ends, with a paragraph on his retirement hobbies:

> *I was fond of sailing and birdwatching. Colin, my friend from Sandhurst days, often accompanied me on trips to the Norfolk Broads. Irene did not share my interests but always provided a hot dinner when I returned after a weekend away.*

As Kenton's recollections had come to a premature halt, his eldest son, Euan, had stepped in to write the final paragraph of the book:

> *Our father found the transition back to civilian and family life a challenge, particularly when my brother and I were young and boisterous, so he was not a very 'hands on' father. In his later years he discovered an appreciation of nature and I think he found this calming. I am glad he found the companionship he needed towards the end of his life and I hope he achieved something close to peace.*

Not exactly an effusive tribute to one's father, but Henrietta can sympathise with this. She has corrected the punctuation, added some paragraph breaks and inserted an extra photograph, but what, she wonders, lies between the lines of Kenton's story?

Had she been given the job of interviewing him,

she would have pressed Kenton on his experience of boarding school at the tender age of eight and whether it had made him feel lonely. She would have asked him how many people he had killed during his army career and how he felt about those deaths now he was nearing the end of his own life. He might have liked to reconsider whether he could have spent more time with his sons when they were young.

And what about his birdwatching trips with Colin – was it a case of what happened on the Broads stayed on the Broads? Her questions would not be out of prurience, simply in the interests of accuracy. Because in her view, Kenton's story lacked veracity – and what is the point of a Life Story book that doesn't tell the truth?

As she sends the revised file to the printers, Henrietta congratulates herself on how she has used her initiative to improve this version of Kenton's book. She will be sure to tell Audrey about this at her upcoming appraisal.

Henrietta leaves the drop-in centre at 5 p.m. sharp, flipping up her duffle coat hood. Waiting at the bus stop, she tries hard to ignore the cold wind and the messy muddle of a queue and to remember the more uplifting stories she's been documenting: Neil, who finds joy in the smallest things; Samuel, the erstwhile railway traveller; and Eric, who has finally found his artistic streak. But the one she keeps coming back to is the still-unfolding story of Annie Doyle.

Then an unsettling thought comes to her: what would fill the pages of the Life Story of Henrietta Lockwood? It would be a slim volume, because there are certain memories she'd prefer to omit. Chiefly, what happened twenty-three years ago on a stiflingly hot day in Masura, the event that is never spoken of but hovers around the edges of every Sunday lunch with her parents like an invisible guest. It's the reason why her father's glittering career came to an abrupt end and why the family's photo album is punctuated with empty squares. It's why she and her parents had to run for a plane that would take them away from Papua New Guinea and back to England, to the silent, unsunny rooms of The Pines.

It's also the reason why Henrietta has not been near the sea since she was nine years old. A pity, because she used to love the water. In Masura, one of the mission teachers offered to give some of the older children swimming lessons. He took them down to the small harbour, lined them all up in the shallows and showed them how to move their arms and legs. Henrietta remembers Father Jacob's curly white hairs on his chest, thick as a rug, as he called out '*Kikim lek blo yupla osem ol frog*' – kick your legs like frogs – and she and Esther splashed towards him, shrieking when the salty water went up their noses.

The picnic, the day when everything went wrong, came later, on one of those hot, still days when the ceiling fan barely cut through the air and sitting indoors felt like hard work. It was her mother who suggested they take a drive out to a beach further along the coast.

As they were packing their picnic basket and towels and Henrietta's orange swimming ring in the back of the car, Esther from next door came out to watch.

'Oh, look, Henrietta,' her mother had said. 'Would you like to invite your friend?'

Esther's mum, Flora, came down her steps, smiling shyly. She taught typing and shorthand to the older girls and was liked by everyone. 'Thank you,' she said. 'Very kind.'

When Esther ran back with her towel, Henrietta and Esther jumped up and down with excitement and Christopher, just four years old, joined in the jumping too. Then they all climbed on to the back seat with little Christopher sandwiched between the two girls. The air streamed in, hot as a hairdryer on their faces, and she and Esther talked over his head and giggled and sang silly songs. Even then, she hadn't spared a thought for poor Christopher.

Back in England, she tried to write to Esther, to say sorry for the things Esther had seen that day. She'd written in her best handwriting, but the woman in the post office said she needed a special stamp that was more expensive, because Papua New Guinea was a long way away. And when she'd asked her father for the money, he'd grabbed the envelope, torn it in two and thrown it in the bin. And told her that she was never to speak of Esther or Masura or what Henrietta had done ever again.

After Esther, Henrietta found it easier not to seek out any further friendships and Annie is the first person she's even considered talking to about what happened to Christopher on that unbearably hot day. She senses that, having weathered sadness and loss in her own life, Annie would understand.

Henrietta makes a decision. The next time they meet, she will return the favour and share her own story with Annie. Then perhaps Annie will forgive her for her bluntness and blunders and she'll understand why, ever since that day in Masura, Henrietta has felt the need to keep a very firm grip on things. She's stayed on the fringes of life, observing rather than participating. She lives by her own strict set of rules and she has her routines, which keep her safe and stop unexpected things happening.

She supposes that was one reason why she had applied for this job, where she would only meet old, ill people who wouldn't be around for long, who would fill out their forms and recall their golden memories in a quaint yet organised fashion. There would be little danger of her becoming too involved in them or their stories. But that was before she met Annie.

CHAPTER TWENTY-ONE

ANNIE

It's a Wednesday and Annie is standing in front of a painting in a new art gallery on Portobello Road. At least, she thinks it's a painting. It could be a piece of floor that someone has just stuck straight on to the wall, as it's made of floorboards covered in paint splodges and coffee stains and what is almost certainly a dried wodge of chewing gum. Of course, the label is no help at all. It reads: 'Pretty Messed Up. Mixed media. £6,000'.

She can just imagine Kath's face if she saw this. 'What? A bit of dirty floor for six grand? They're having us on!' Then she and Kath would have creased up laughing. When the two of them got the giggles there was no stopping them; they'd be doubled over, laughing until it hurt. One sister might manage to stop, but all she had to do was catch the other's eye and it set them both off again. It drove their mum mad.

The art gallery is warm and smells of something musky and fruity. Annie moves on to the next exhibit: a sculpture in the shape of a railway girder, but bright orange. A snip, at £3,000. She holds her bag close to her body, fearful she might knock into something. The rise and fall of voices float out from the back of the gallery, where a woman in a tight black jumpsuit perches on the side of a desk, talking earnestly to a man, also in black. Both of them simultaneously scroll through their phones, but there's no break in their conversation.

She knows she's on borrowed time and soon one of them will come over to shoo her away. Her left ear has gone all muffled again, her bad one, and out of habit she tilts her head to one side. It clears and the rush of clean, loud air makes Annie gasp. The gallery woman glares at her, as if she's only just noticed she's there.

'Sorry. Forgot myself,' she says, putting her hands in her coat pockets to keep them from mischief. Now the gallery owner is looking right at Annie, trying to work out whether her odd clothes mean she is someone of importance or just another Ladbroke Grove eccentric, so Annie decides it's time to go. She pushes the door and is gratified to see that her fingers leave several smudges on the glass. That whippet-thin woman will need to use a bit of elbow grease to make them disappear.

The walk home takes an age because she has to keep stopping to let the tight belt of pain around her middle loosen, just a little. Once she's back, Annie takes her pills and climbs into her bed and when sleep comes, it's the heavy kind with no silty, muddy dreams and she's grateful.

She wakes to the clanking, creaking sound of the central heating coming on. It's 5 p.m., then. Her legs feel weighed down and at first she fears it's yet another symptom of her decline, but when she looks, she sees someone has spread the old photo albums over her bedcovers again. Ah, she remembers now: it was her. She got them out just before she nodded off because she'd promised to take some pictures in for Henrietta next Saturday.

Carefully, she edges herself up to a sitting position. She knows the pages off by heart, but she can't resist flicking through the old family album again. It's like going back to a bad tooth, poking it with your tongue to see if the pain is still there.

Her favourite is of a rare beach holiday when Kath was thirteen, she was fourteen. They are both shy in their new swimsuits, but already, Kath looks more beautiful, her body leaner, a cheeky tilt to her hips. She's looking straight into the camera, while Annie, dumpy with puppy fat, looks down at the sand.

The next one must have been taken by a passing holidaymaker, because all four of them are in it: her mum wears a wide-brimmed hat that covers her eyes and her dad wears his usual grim-faced frown. Oh, Aidan Doyle, cheer up – if only you knew what was to come, she thinks to herself. And poor Mum, thinking that as long as she got her daughters to Sunday Mass each week, that would keep them safe.

She peers at the grainy dots of the photo, remembering how it was, being Kath Doyle's sister. First born, but always second best. Yes, love and resentment were twin threads of the rope that bound them together as sisters. But in the months before Kath died, the rope either twisted too tight or fell slack; there was nothing in between. One minute, there was that wonderful warmth of having her close by. The next, Kath would pull away, almost as if she was repulsed by Annie, like she couldn't bear to be near her.

She stopped wanting to wear the same things, too, saying that Annie cramped her style. It all came to a head one Thursday night when they were getting ready to go out. Kath had been standing in front of the mirror, but suddenly she'd ripped off that lovely yellow dress and thrown it across the room. She said she was sick of it, that she didn't want to match any more.

But Annie knew the real reason why. The truth was, for once, Kath didn't look as good as Annie and she didn't like it. That yellow dress didn't suit her any more; it stretched tight across her chest and hips, like she'd put on weight. But the problem was, Annie was already wearing her green dress and the Doyle Girls always had to match. So Annie had picked the yellow dress up off the floor and put it back in the wardrobe. 'OK, I'll get changed too then,' she'd said, flicking through the hangers. 'I know. We can both wear jeans. And cheesecloth tops.' Then she'd turned back to Kath. 'Can't we?'

Off they went to The Bell like nothing had happened, but she knew Kath was still in a mood. Right away she'd gone off to dance on her own, leaving Annie by the bar, guarding their bags. As soon as Kath started to dance, people stopped talking and turned to watch, and Annie did too. Because when Kath danced it was like she could slide inside the skin of a song. She closed her eyes and every sway and twist took her further into the music, away from this pub with its sticky carpet and its leery men and away from Annie, too.

It was only when the lights came on that Kath seemed to remember that Annie was still there. Blinking as she looked round for her bag – oh, and her sister – who she'd discarded like a tatty old coat in the corner. Something that didn't suit Kath any more but was useful for the walk home.

Back outside in the cold night air, she had to put Kath straight on a few things and, by the time they were nearly home, Kath had fallen in step with her and they linked arms for the walk up the hill. Her sister needed her again and that tantrum with the dress, the way Kath had danced all night without her, were forgotten. 'Sorry,' Kath had whispered. 'I'll wear the yellow dress on Saturday. And you can wear the green one.'

Annie closes the album again. She's not sure about taking these pictures in after all. There's already been enough talk about Kath and no good will come of speaking about the bad blood between them. Anyway, this story isn't all about Kath. It's Annie's story and, unfortunately, that means it also has to include Terry. And how he came to his unpleasant end. Annie smooths out her bedcover, picks up her notebook from her bedside table and she starts to write.

CHAPTER TWENTY-TWO

ANNIE

When Annie walks into the café the next Saturday, she feels light-headed, as if she's only half there. She has to stop a couple of times and hold on to a handrail to steady herself. She's been thinking too hard, that's the problem. Remembering too much.

There's Henrietta at her usual table, with all her pens and papers lined up in a neat row, and it's a relief to see her looking so organised and eager. She hopes Henrietta isn't going to start playing detective again, firing off more bullet-pointed questions. She notices that something odd has happened to Henrietta's hair – it's almost doubled in size. Annie narrows her eyes. It needs a bit of taming, but it's a move in the right direction. It's got personality.

'Are you feeling OK to continue, today?' Henrietta asks. 'Did you have something in mind to cover? Because if we have time, I thought I might share a memory too.'

'It's alright, Henrietta,' Annie cuts in. 'I know I look rough today. Bad night. And yes, I know we're running out of time. But I do have something in mind, as it happens.'

She gives Mia a wave, lovely Mia dressed up all nicely today for Stefan, who was looking ever so smart himself on the minibus. He's popped upstairs for an appointment with his physiotherapist, but she knows he'll be back in the café soon enough, so he can see Mia. He doesn't need reminding that life is short and it's best to make the most of it, while you can. Unlike Henrietta, who, Annie fears, is letting life pass her by.

'Henrietta, I need to tell you about Terry's accident. It was a nasty, messy accident for a nasty man. I'm not sure it's the sort of thing you usually put in these Life Story books, but it's part of my story so it needs to be told. It's up to you what you do with this information. I just want rid of it.'

Henrietta glances at the clock, then gives a quick nod. 'Of course, Annie. It's good to get things out.' She presses her red button and says clearly for the microphone: 'Annie Doyle, today is the fourth of December and this is session five of your Life Story.'

Annie looks down at her scribbled notes, but most of what she needs to say is in her head. In fact, it's been in there far too long and today she needs to let go of it.

'Me and Terry never had many holidays,' she begins. 'But a couple of years ago he surprised me, said he'd booked a static caravan for a week in Cornwall. I was so excited. I'd been to Cornwall as a child, you see. I told him the name of the village we'd been to, Porthawan, and asked if this caravan was anywhere near there. He gave a funny smile and said, "Might be, might not be."

I knew better than to ask again, but I was really hoping that it was, because I had happy memories of that place.'

It was where she'd had that family holiday, when she was fourteen and Kath was thirteen and they swam every day and collected stones on the beach, lining them up in two neat rows to see who had found the most perfectly round ones. Their dad had bought fish and chips and for once he hadn't moaned about the cost and their mum hadn't fussed about keeping their dresses clean. It had been a perfect holiday, but that's not really the point, she reminds herself. She's come to tell Henrietta about the messy accident that happened much later, just over two years ago.

'So off we went, him driving, of course. But it was such a long way and I needed the loo before we were even halfway down the M3. Lord, he was cross. There were no services for miles, so he pulled on to the hard shoulder. He said, "Off you go. Fanny Annie can piss in a bush."'

She remembers how she'd sat in the passenger seat, not wanting to get out after all, and the way the car was buffeted every time another car or a lorry went by. How Terry had reached over, opened her door and practically pushed her out. Then the texture of the grey metal barrier, scratchy and dirty with big bolts in it; the lorries and vans still whizzing by, nearly knocking her over with blasts of wind.

'I climbed over the barrier, and it was all rocks and scrubby grass. But I could see a bush further up the bank so I started climbing towards it, like he told me.'

Annie closes her eyes. It's best if she doesn't look

directly at Henrietta for the next bit.

'So I got to this prickly bush and I thought, now or never. But I must have been taking too long because above the roar of the traffic I could hear Terry shouting, "Get a move on." I was trying to push the wee out faster, and I'd just about finished when I heard the most almighty bang. The tearing of metal, brakes screaming, another bang.'

She chances a look up and sees that Henrietta's previous impassive stare has been replaced by something far gentler. So she keeps going.

'Terry must have been getting out of his side of the car; maybe he wanted to hurry me along. The police said he couldn't have even seen the lorry. Later it came out that the driver was on his phone. All I know is that once I stood up, I could see that half of our car was gone, shorn clean away. And our luggage was all over the motorway.'

At the time, her first thought had been, well, that's going to be really difficult to pick up. Then she'd noticed that beside the suitcases, the motorway was streaked with dark tyre tracks. And Terry's checked jacket was in the middle of the road, but his shoes were somewhere else entirely. At that point she'd started to scream. The next thing she remembers is the flash of the ambulance lights, a kind paramedic holding her hand to help her back over the barrier.

'The M3 was shut for hours so I suppose he made quite a mess,' she tells Henrietta. 'The thing was, afterwards, all I felt was relief, which I know is wrong. But that man was gone for good, and it wasn't me or anyone else who did for him in the end. It was his own bloody awful temper.'

She nods towards the recording device to tell Henrietta she's done. There's more, of course, but not for Henrietta's ears. How two nice policewomen had dropped her home and then she'd drawn the curtains and slept on the sofa because she couldn't bear to go back inside the bedroom, where the air was still heavy with the stink of him. It was worked into the sheets, the pillows and the collars of his shirts and she was scared that if she slept in there, she'd wake up and find him lying next to her, not dead at all.

Then the misery of his half-hearted funeral, Nev, Smithy, Wills and the printworks boys filing past, all so much older than she remembered them. Bald heads, paunches straining out of their black suits, tufts of hair in their ears. Smokers, every one of them, and their faces all cast in a similar ash-grey. Eyes downcast as they mumbled, 'Sorry for your loss', because they knew what she'd lived with all those years, what Terry was like. And none of them had done a thing about it.

She can't bring herself to say all of these things out loud. Henrietta doesn't need to know what happened a month after the funeral either, the day when she'd optimistically hired the skip, deciding it was time to move on. It had started out so well – she had felt so strong, loading all his brown furniture and his vile magazines into the wheelbarrow. Steering it up a wobbly plank and then tipping it in. And when the lorry came and hoisted that yellow skip into the air, well, it had felt nothing short of wonderful. Good riddance, she'd thought.

But when she'd turned to walk back up the path, it hit her. She just couldn't go back into that house again, to those rooms where she'd spent so many years in fear. Her body wouldn't let her; all it wanted to do was wail and lie down on the crazy paving, driven crazy herself at the waste of all those years.

She doesn't remember what happened next quite so clearly. But this time the paramedics wrapped her in a crinkly silver cape and whisked her off, like Snow White, for a very long sleep on Briar ward, a place where you had to get washed and dressed each morning but you weren't allowed to go beyond the doors. A few visitors came at 3 p.m., frisked for phones and sharp objects, but Annie didn't have anyone to visit her. Auntie Rita, her parents, they'd been dead for years, and there was no way she was letting anyone from work see her like this. In the end, she never went back to her job, anyway.

She was told she'd been 'sectioned' – and she quite liked the sound of that word, imagining how nice it would be if you could do that, slice the parts of your life into neat portions, trimming off the bad bits. If she could, she would cut out her entire marriage and throw it in the sluice bucket, like something bloated and diseased.

The therapist for Briar ward had an office painted in baby blue and the woman behind the desk dressed very carefully: usually a plain dress or top but then she would add a bright scarf or a brooch to show that she thought about appearances, but not too much.

'This is your time, Annie,' she would say. 'I'm here

to listen, whenever you want to talk.'

So Annie would start by saying how much she liked the therapist's silk scarf and then there would be a long silence so, eventually, Annie let a few things slip, but never too much. The therapist decided it was the trauma of witnessing Terry's accident that had triggered her breakdown in her front garden. What that lady with her nice scarf didn't understand was that it wasn't really about that slow-motion moment, the way Terry was there one minute and, whoosh, gone the next. After all, she'd been through that sort of loss once already.

No, it wasn't grief that brought her to her knees outside 53 Chaucer Drive, but a cold realisation of how pointless her own life had been. All those years in that house with its peeling woodgrain vinyl and the doormat that spelled out 'Welcome' but meant anything but.

So she talked a bit, but she didn't really see how it helped. Yes, my husband was so mean, blah blah, poor me. She quickly saw how the game worked, the therapist's way of repeating what Annie said to trick her into saying more. 'So, going back into your house was difficult for you, Annie?' or 'I'm wondering if losing Terry reminded you of losing your sister?'

Bravo, give the lady in the silk scarf a medal.

The therapist's questions felt like traps laid and Annie had worried that if she let down her guard and fell into them, she'd never leave Briar ward. She'd still be there now, instead of drinking tea and deciding for herself how much to tell Henrietta. Henrietta, who wouldn't know a silk scarf from an acrylic one but is so much easier to talk to because she almost certainly has secrets of her own to hide.

And now, back in the café, the clock must have ticked round to nearly twelve o'clock because Annie can see Stefan heading over towards Mia's counter and Mia has a huge grin on her face. Bossy Bonnie from the minibus is standing at the double doors, waving her arms with wild abandon, which means it's time to go.

Poor Henrietta is sitting and waiting to see if there's more. Or maybe she's on the verge of confessing something herself, because her mouth is opening and shutting like a fish's. But Annie has decided that's quite enough for today. It's a help to talk each week, feeling these words rising up and leaving her body. But even Annie has limits – and there are some places she can't go, not even for Henrietta.

She's come to treasure these weekly talks. Feeling Henrietta's grey eyes on her, the touch of her hand and the way she really listens. But if she tells every last, sordid detail, there's no way this girl will welcome Annie Doyle back to her table next week. She'll see Annie for exactly what she is.

No, it's best if she stops right here. That way, she can keep this unexpected friendship going for a little while longer.

CHAPTER TWENTY-THREE

HENRIETTA

After Annie leaves, Henrietta stays sitting at her table in the Grief Café, gazing into the middle distance. To a casual observer, it might seem as if she's looking at the cake cabinet, trying to decide between Mia's new range of Christmas bakes: mince pies or slices of stollen. But Henrietta doesn't even see the cakes. She's thinking about this morning's session.

She'd secretly hoped for the opportunity to share her own story, but then Annie had surprised her by talking in great detail about her husband's untimely end. And she's still not sure what to make of it.

Unusually for her, Henrietta has a strong impulse to talk this over with someone – someone like Mia, in fact. But Henrietta can see that Mia is sitting at a table in the farthest corner of the café, deep in conversation with Stefan, who must have decided to forgo his minibus ride home.

There's a burst of laughter and she sees Stefan reach

out and tuck a curl of Mia's hair behind her ear. Then, like shy birds, they lean their heads closer to each other until they are almost touching. So, thinks Henrietta to herself, Stefan's visits to the Grief Café are motivated by more than a liking for Tunnock's teacakes.

She turns away, smiling to herself. She's pleased for the two of them but also baffled. When, she wonders, did this romance blossom? What invisible sign did one party give off and how did the other person recognise it and respond in kind? The rules of love remain a mystery to Henrietta.

A sharp voice interrupts her reverie. 'I do hope I'm not disturbing you?' It's Audrey, wearing a trouser suit in salmon pink, with matching heels. 'When you're available, I'm afraid there's another delivery of post upstairs. And several emails. One's a little odd: a complaint that's also a suggestion. You'll see.' She waggles her fingers. 'I'm off now, duty calls – Radio London want to interview me. But we'll reconvene on Tuesday, hmm?'

Henrietta knows her face has slipped back into its mask of indifference, the one she adopts in times of stress or when she simply doesn't have a suitable answer. She can feel it frozen in place. All except that tickle of a twitch in her left eye.

'Appraisal, remember? Our little catch-up.'

Ah, yes. Her impending appraisal, the point at which Audrey will inevitably realise that Henrietta's first Life Story book is in extremely poor shape. Today's session with Annie wasn't much help either: it yielded plenty more material, but not exactly what she'd been hoping for. So many accidents, so little time, Henrietta thinks as she heads upstairs to the office.

When she opens the door, she sees what Audrey was rattling on about because the surface of the desk is piled high with padded envelopes and letters and, on the computer, the inbox is full of new emails. Something unusual has been happening of late in the Life Stories Project office: they have been inundated with post and messages. It's all because, some six weeks ago, Ryan Brooks was interviewed by a popular magazine. Henrietta is not acquainted with a title called *Grazia*, but around the same time that Ryan started waltzing around the *Strictly* dance floor he issued a rallying cry for the Life Stories Project, encouraging more people to come forward and share, share, share.

Mia showed her the magazine in question, with a picture of Ryan in his sparkling blue onesie under a headline that read: 'Turning pain into positives – why Ryan Brooks wants to know your Life Story.' And now, autobiographies have begun to arrive, all from people who can't get to a drop-in centre but still want their words turned into a book. Inevitably, some are in the vein of Kenton Hancock – one even included a mock-up of a front cover, with *Mes Mémoires* in large italics.

She checks the emails first, sending out questionnaires and explaining to a gentleman in Fife that, unfortunately, they are not currently able to make home visits.

At the moment our team is very small, but if someone in your family can record your words and send it to me with some photos, I will do my best to make your Life Story book, she writes.

There's an email from a hospice in Germany wanting to set up a Zoom meeting to discuss 'extending the brand' (she leaves that one for Audrey, far more her thing) and another from closer to home, entitled *Complaint/suggestion*.

Dear Ryan, it starts. *These Life Story books are OK but how about this idea – Memory Books telling the stories of those who died before they had a chance to do their own. They could be written by family or friends afterwards. My mum went very quick last year and, to be honest, it wasn't really the time to sit around chatting and making books. But I would still like to have a book about my mum. It would be good if you could add this to your service. Regards, Cerys Meadows.*

A valid point, thinks Henrietta. She will reply in due course.

Next, she opens a padded envelope, also addressed to Ryan. Honestly, when will people realise that he doesn't exactly pop in to help with the admin? Inside is a thick wodge of typed-up pages, a set of photographs and, at the bottom, several home-made birthday cards that appear to have been drawn by a child.

Dear Life Stories Project, the covering letter reads. *This story was written by my wife, Jackie Taylor, who died recently. She had already decided to write down a few things after she was diagnosed, mostly for our daughter, Chloe, to read when she's older. Then I heard about your project and I thought it would be lovely to have Jackie's words made into a book. Kind regards, Nathalie Mason.*

As soon as Henrietta starts reading Jackie's words,

she realises this story could not be more different to the Kenton Hancock variety.

I have started to write down my memories to help me come to terms with what's going to happen to me – and eventually to us all. Some of us go too soon; some hang on too long. I wish I had longer, but it's been a life well lived and, in the circumstances, I'm making my perfect ending.

Darling Chloe, I'm sorry I won't be there to see you grow up, but I'm picturing the years ahead and how you'll share them with your mum. Just now I went into your bedroom and you were curled up in her arms and you fitted together perfectly. That image is with me as I write this and it always will be.

Nathalie, I know you found it hard to accept I didn't want any more life-prolonging treatment, but in my eyes I have not lost a fight. I hate that kind of talk. I had the bad luck to get an incurable disease; it's as simple as that and there's no winning or losing side. It's about cells, not bravery or battles.

To my friends and my family, when it comes to the end, don't worry if you're not there. No guilt, please. Know that I always felt loved by you all, and by my best friends, Abi, Jacinta and Claire. Girls, you picked

> *me up and made me laugh when I needed*
> *it most.*
>
> *Nathalie, ask about counselling because*
> *you'll be processing this for years. At first,*
> *you'll feel as if a huge hole has opened up*
> *in front of you. But slowly the edges will*
> *soften and the hole will start to fill up. As*
> *time goes on, you won't fall into it quite so*
> *often and eventually you'll be able to stand*
> *on the edge and look into it.*
>
> *Remember, grief is the price we pay for*
> *love. Be kind to yourselves – the first year*
> *will be the hardest – and love yourselves as*
> *much as I love you.*

There is an ache in Henrietta's throat and she needs to set Jackie's story aside for a moment and compose herself. This is what a Life Story should be, she thinks – heartfelt and true. Never mind Audrey and her questionnaire and handbook. She needs to get back to Annie's Life Story and write it in a way that feels heartfelt and true. And she can only do this by finding out what really happened to Kath Doyle.

* * *

It's easy to spot The Bell pub from the top deck of the number 52 bus, with its loops of coloured light bulbs and two potted Christmas trees either side of the main doors. So this is where they went, she thinks, the Doyle Girls, in their matching outfits and their flicky hairdos. And this is the first place Annie came looking that wet December night in 1974, when her sister didn't come

189

home.

Inside, it's dark and smells of spilt beer and the staleness that comes of someone wiping an unwashed cloth over the bar. These days, it's not quite the buzzing, cool hangout that Annie Doyle described.

'An orange juice, please.' Henrietta is not in a profligate mood.

The barman stoops to pick out a mini mixer bottle. He wipes the dust from its neck with a blocky thumb before opening it, then pours it into a glass. They both watch as a dubious sediment floats to the bottom.

'Ice, if I may?' she asks.

Without a word, he takes the lid off a plastic ice bucket, rattles the scoop and gestures for Henrietta to help herself. Were she here for pleasure rather than business, Henrietta would be minded to write a review on Tripadvisor. She's still mentally composing a few pithy phrases ('Juice, warm. Welcome, less so . . .') when she realises he's talking to her.

'It's over there,' he's saying.

For a moment she thinks he means the jukebox, the one that she's been picturing Annie and Kath standing at, choosing their favourite songs. But that must be long gone. 'Sorry?'

'The photo. That's what you're here for, aren't you? All the tourists come here, buy one cheap drink and take selfies beside it.'

'I don't have a clue what you are talking about,' she says.

'Bowie. July 1973,' he says, like she's an imbecile. 'The night he played Hammersmith Odeon and announced it was Ziggy Stardust's last appearance. But it wasn't, was it?'

'Was it not?' Henrietta has no interest in pop trivia.

'No. Because he came on here afterwards, didn't he? There was a lock-in and he gave an acoustic set. Quite a night, by all accounts.'

Of course, Henrietta has heard of David Bowie – there was a documentary about him recently on BBC4 – so she heads over to look at this photo. It's fixed to the wall with screws, and there he is with his spiky hair and a glittery top. There's no sign of his friend Ziggy, though.

She scans the small crowd gathered around Mr Bowie, but knows she won't see Annie or Kath. They didn't start coming here until the year after this was taken, once Kath was eighteen. They were good girls, as Annie keeps saying. But at the back of the photo is a man with long sideburns and shoulder-length hair who looks uncannily similar to the barman.

'My dad,' a voice behind her says. 'That's what everyone asks next – how come I'm in that photo?'

'And your father, is he still alive?' Spending her working days surrounded by people living on borrowed time, Henrietta does not have high hopes.

'Last time I checked he was. He's upstairs watching *Escape To The Chateau*, his favourite programme. He'll be down soon if you want to wait. He loves talking about the old days.'

* * *

The landlord of The Bell is called Reggie Cox and

his son was right, he does like reminiscing. It takes Henrietta a while to move him on from talking about Bowie, Dylan and Van Morrison to the subject of the people who drank in here, circa 1974.

'I would very much like to ask you about two customers from that era, if I may,' she says.

At this, Reggie starts to look shifty and sucks hard on his e-cigarette. 'You said you weren't police, right?'

'No. I'm a transcriber and proofreader. And a failed librarian,' she replies. 'The people I'm interested in are Annie and Kathleen Doyle. Might you remember them?'

At that, he lets out a booming laugh. 'That really is going back in time. But, yeah, of course I do. You don't forget girls like that – gorgeous. Especially Kath. Back then, I was in my prime.' He tries to suck in his stomach and puff out his chest but the effect is not altogether successful. He lets out a wheeze and his belly drops down again. 'As I say, back in the day.'

When he hears about Annie's illness, he looks genuinely sorry. 'Send her my very best,' he says. 'She's had a tough life all round. Losing her sister so young. Then she got married, moved out of the area. Don't think he was the easiest of blokes, either, that Terry . . .' He turns away, flips the top off a second bottle of juice, pours the lurid liquid into a fresh glass and shovels in some ice. 'On the house. Any friend of Annie's is welcome here,' he adds.

Henrietta takes a polite sip. It was an effort finishing the first one; even with ice, this is still not a tipple she would recommend.

'So I'm conducting a little background research on Annie's behalf, in order to write her Life Story,' she says. 'And clearly the death of her sister should be included. I'm wondering if you can remember the night in question, the twenty-first of December 1974?'

'You're joking, aren't you?' Reggie Cox loops a bar towel over one shoulder. 'That's, what, nearly fifty years ago. I was just a lad myself and I would have been rushed off my feet. The twenty-first, you say, so just before Christmas, right?'

'Indeed, the Saturday before. The thing is, Annie remembers coming in here that night, looking for Kath.'

'I honestly can't remember,' he says.

'What about the police? Do you remember them coming in to ask questions, back then?'

'I can assure you that neither me nor my dad heard a peep from them. Pigs were not welcome in our pub.'

'I beg your pardon?'

'Sorry, no offence. You did say you weren't police, didn't you?'

Henrietta nods.

'Back then, there were pubs that police didn't come near, unless they had good reason, like a raid. And others where they conducted their own business.'

Henrietta must have adopted her blank expression again.

'You know, meeting grasses, doing deals. Pubs like The Red Lion – that was their turf. Wall to wall with dealers, dealers turned grasses and bent coppers. Tip-off central, it was. Best thing the council ever did, tearing that place down.'

'The Red Lion, up near the bridge?'

'That's the one. Thought that would have been before your time, though. You *sure* you're not police?'

'Yes, definitely.' Henrietta needs to think. This information feels important, but it worries her too, what it could mean. That a pub by the canal was a place for tip-offs, where the police received information – possibly in exchange for turning a blind eye to other crimes.

'So, The Red Lion,' she says. 'I wonder, would you know if Aidan Doyle ever drank there?'

'The girls' dad?' Reggie shrugs. 'No idea. I was just a lad and he was one of the local old boys. All I know is, my dad told me to steer clear of the place.'

'Yes, this is what I've heard too,' Henrietta replies faintly.

It's later, as Reggie walks with her towards the pub's swing doors, that he says it.

'Such a shame, so sorry to hear about Annie. Back in the day, the Doyle Girls were legendary, and they made quite a pair.' He laughs. 'Yep, thick as thieves they were.' Henrietta smiles back, because that's exactly how she imagines them.

Reggie is holding the door open. 'Course, they fought like cats, too.'

'I'm sorry?'

The taste of all that orange juice turns sour in her mouth.

'Don't look so shocked – everything was a bit less PC back then.' Reggie gestures out at the pavement, now black and slick because while Henrietta has been sitting inside it has started to rain. 'Yeah, right here it was, out in the street. Had a blazing row one night.'

'And I suppose you've no idea when this would have been?' Henrietta hears herself talking, but her mind feels very far away.

Reggie pulls on his plastic cigarette, shakes his head. 'Who do you think I am, Mr Memory?' He turns to go, but then he stops.

'Actually, I do remember, because it was an odd night all round. News came on the radio about a bomb going off up on Oxford Street. No one was hurt, but my mum was up there doing Christmas shopping. There were no mobile phones in those days, so all we could do was sit tight and wait. Half an hour later she walked in safe and sound, no idea what all the fuss was about.

'Still, it left a weird mood in the air. Felt like a close call, I suppose, so my dad decided to shut up a bit early. People didn't want to leave right away so they hung around outside, just chatting, I suppose. And that was when the Doyle Girls had their row. Probably had a few too many. Or just sisters being sisters, eh.'

Henrietta walks away, tapping on her phone, and she finds the date Reggie Cox was talking about before she even gets to her bus stop. He was right: a car bomb had gone off outside Selfridges on Oxford Street on the evening of Thursday 19 December. The night Annie and Kath Doyle had a big argument in the street was just two days before Kath Doyle set down her clothes by the banks of the Grand Union Canal and was never seen again.

CHAPTER TWENTY-FOUR

ANNIE

'You're in luck – we've just had a cancellation,' the salon receptionist says. 'Could be your last chance for a haircut before Christmas.'

Last chance ever, thinks Annie, but she doesn't say it. She woke up this morning and decided she didn't just fancy a haircut, she needed one. Something short and sleek, the kind of look she had longed for in the late seventies, when she saw it in all the magazines and on the TV.

'Can you do a Purdey cut?' she asks the boy, who is lifting up the limp ends of her grey hair, letting them drop back down again as if she's beyond help. He looks blank.

'Like Joanna Lumley, when she was in *The New Avengers*,' she says. 'Or a Vidal Sassoon bob? That would do. Surely you've heard of that.' The lad looks it up on his phone and gets snipping. She can see him cutting and combing from every angle because this place is more like a house of mirrors than a hairdresser's – reflections everywhere.

It's funny, she thinks, as she watches the feathery wisps of her hair fall to the ground, how the smell inside a hairdresser's has barely changed over the years. Every few months she and Kath would treat themselves to a shampoo and set on payday. They sat side by side on red leatherette seats and Pilar, their hairdresser, would lower down two huge helmet dryers, like they were off on a space mission.

When they were done, Pilar yanked up the dryers, took out the rollers and let rip with a giant can of Elnett hairspray like she was chasing a swarm of flies. Those were the best times: paydays, her and Kath getting ready to go out, sisters and the best of friends.

The rush of the hairdryer suddenly stops and Annie is back here again, in this too-clever-for-its-own-good hairdresser's, staring at her worn-out face beneath a brand-new haircut.

'The best I can do,' the lad says, running his hands over her hair, drawing two pointed ends together under her chin. He's looking sceptical, and now she's not too sure, either. It would have suited her much better forty years ago, but she wouldn't have dared try this style back then.

Walking back home, the pain slides back in, a steady twist of nausea that tightens with every step, and she remembers she hasn't eaten anything all day. She might have a new haircut, but this is a reminder that everything below her head is atrophying. She tries to ignore it, to focus instead on the surprise of cold air on the back of her neck, the way her haircut makes her head feel lighter. Yes, that's exactly the feeling she's been longing for.

Once she's home, Annie goes straight to her bedroom. She wants to sleep, but those photo albums are still spread out over her bed. Something snaps inside her. Enough of reminiscing, of looking at lovely Kath and dumpy Annie, and with one brisk swipe she sends the whole lot flying. The loose photos that she's set aside for Henrietta flutter to the ground too, and that's annoying because she has to get down on her hands and knees, and then she curses herself and her temper all over again. What a mess you made of your life, Annie Doyle, she thinks, and then she stops trying to pick up the photos and just stays kneeling down there for a while.

She can almost see it from here, of course. It's been under her bed since she moved to this flat and she still keeps it hidden – force of habit, she supposes. It's the shoe box of Kath's things that she's managed to keep safe for so long now. Back in Chaucer Drive, it lived in a kitchen cupboard, tucked inside a bigger cardboard box with a picture of a Magimix food processor on the side, which meant Terry would never go looking inside it.

She always waited until Terry was out for a good length of time before she let herself look inside the box. Sometimes she'd chance it if he was off for an afternoon of golf, but she was only really safe if he was away on one of his business trips.

Even then, she rationed the time she gave herself with these belongings. Such a paltry haul to show for eighteen years of life. These are the things she'd taken from Dynevor Road, along with some of Kath's clothes, slipping them into the suitcase on the morning of her wedding. Just as well, given what happened to everything that got left behind.

Sometimes it hurt too much to look inside this box. But the main reason why she didn't open the lid too often was because she didn't want to lose its smell. There's barely a trace of it left these days, but if she breathes in deeply and closes her eyes, she can remember it. It's a mixture of Rimmel lipstick, the dregs of a bottle of Charlie perfume and a scent less easy to identify. It's the smell of Kath.

All of the objects in this box are special in their own way. Kath's collection of tiny white china horses that Annie always coveted. A worn-down lipstick and a mascara that's been dry and clogged for decades. A keyring with a plaited leather tail that was a present from Auntie Rita. Older still, an outfit for her Sindy doll: a red sweater, flared jeans and a miniature pair of rubbery shoes. A hairbrush that still has a few strands of Kath's long dark hair caught in it.

She needs to close the box now, to keep it all safe for a little while longer. She can't bear to think that, soon, there will be almost nothing left to remember Kath Doyle by. But then she remembers the book that Henrietta is writing and she's grateful.

Annie crawls over to her bed and climbs under the covers. She needs to save her strength for Saturday so she can see Henrietta and keep talking for as long as possible. There's an odd symmetry to the way that each week her body feels slightly heavier, but her mind feels lighter. This weekly act of talking to Henrietta is helping. But if it's going to work properly, Annie needs to speed up because there's not much time left now.

CHAPTER TWENTY-FIVE

HENRIETTA

If there is a single word in the English language that strikes fear into Henrietta's heart, it is 'appraisal'. That was what the new manager at the library called their first (and final) meeting. When she was dismissed from the petrochemical company, they didn't bother calling it an appraisal, they called it an exit meeting and the head of HR brought along a special crate with Henrietta's belongings (a pair of Crocs, her lunchbox and Thermos) already packed in it. In return for leaving without any fuss, she was assured a good reference, 'to help her move on'.

But today, with her first Life Stories Project appraisal due in just fifteen minutes, Henrietta's heart is thumping and there is a dry feeling in her mouth. Still, this anxiety is almost a welcome distraction, temporarily nudging all thoughts of Annie Doyle to one side. Since her secret visit to The Bell, she can't stop thinking about Reggie Cox's words. And each time she goes over them, she gets a feeling of dread.

When he told her that a rough crowd drank at The

Red Lion, Henrietta had felt the satisfaction of a piece of this jigsaw slotting into place. The pub wasn't far from Dynevor Road and Aidan Doyle and his unsavoury friends might have been regulars there, making them potential suspects.

But then Reggie had talked about Annie arguing with her own sister in the street only two days before she died. Having spent so many lonely years at The Pines, Henrietta is no expert on sibling rivalry, nor how far rivals can go. But she can't reconcile this behaviour with the Annie she knows – or thinks she knows.

An email pings on her work phone: Audrey, reminding Henrietta of the agenda for her appraisal, just twelve minutes away:

> *Time Management, hints and tips*
>
> *Productivity Rate – just checking in <smile emoji>*
>
> *Professionalism and Detachment*

With five minutes to go, another email from Audrey arrives and the subject line alone makes her stomach lurch. It reads: *Your meddling is not appreciated.* It seems an addendum has just been added to today's meeting, with no smiley emoji in sight.

Upstairs in Audrey's office, Henrietta dutifully takes her place on the less comfortable plastic chair and watches as Audrey struggles to readjust the height of her swivel chair, pneumatically zipping up and down until the level is to her liking.

'So, Henrietta!' Audrey exclaims, as if this meeting

is an unexpected pleasure. 'Let's get started.'

Henrietta tries to arrange her face into a pleasing expression. It's the one she thinks of as 'expectantly helpful'.

'First up, following on from my last email . . .' Audrey leans across the table, her eyes alarmingly bulbous in her spectacles.

'I didn't mean to meddle,' Henrietta blurts out. 'It just seemed so wrong, leaving something as big as that unresolved. I thought it merited more on-the-ground research. But I do realise I have fallen behind and I'm trying my best to catch up before Christmas.'

It's only then that she looks down at the desk and sees what Audrey is referring to. Not her internet searches or off-duty dashes halfway across London, but Kenton Hancock's Life Story book.

It lies open at the final page, the one where Henrietta had used her initiative and added another picture before sending it for printing.

Audrey frowns, then goes back to tapping a pink fingernail on the offending photograph. Kenton and his friend look back up, birdwatching binoculars slung around their necks. Both are positively beaming.

'Kenton's widow did not need reminding of her husband's close friendship with Colin,' she says. 'I deliberately left out that photo because it stirred up difficult memories. Hence my addendum to today's agenda. In future, if you wish to make any unauthorised changes to the highly successful Life Story template, just run it by me, would you, hmm?'

Relief washes over Henrietta. Kenton's photograph

is the least of her meddling worries.

Thankfully, Audrey is already moving on, addressing time management and productivity.

'While we value a sensitive, individual approach for each of our clients, when do you estimate your first Life Story will be completed?'

'Annie Doyle's will be completed within seven sessions. Just in time for Christmas. Definitely. It's a fixed deadline.'

'Excellent. And if you could forward me a list of your next books and estimates for completion?'

'Will do. Right on it.' Appraisals are far easier, Henrietta realises, if you just pretend everything is fine, rather than owning up to anything.

'Which brings us to item number three. Professionalism and Detachment.'

Henrietta's stomach gives a lurch. 'Absolutely. That's me. Professional at all times.'

'So you've read the handbook?'

'Well, most of it. I've been quite busy, you see.'

'Because I did notice that the browsing history on my computer was a little . . . wide-ranging. Maybe a little too thorough?'

'Thoroughness is indeed one of my traits,' replies Henrietta.

'We humans are naturally curious beings. But the Life Stories Project has a script to stick to. We use a tried-and-tested questionnaire and then we have pre-set chapters for the book itself. Early Years, Family Times, Achievements, Love & Marriage and Golden Years, remember? So that we don't go off at odd tangents.'

Henrietta thinks about the questionnaire and the chapter format and how they won't work for Annie, or Eric the artist, or Jackie, who wanted her book to be a long goodbye letter. She wants to say that people's lives can't be squeezed so neatly into categories, but Audrey is standing up and it appears that her appraisal is over.

'But that questionnaire,' Henrietta says. 'It's nonsense. I mean, not everyone's life is the same. I don't think we should be using it.'

Audrey's face has turned a peculiar colour that almost matches her pink top. 'I devised that questionnaire myself in careful consultation with our benefactor, Mr Ryan Brooks, who is delighted with the results. In fact, he's just extended our funding for another year.' She gives Henrietta a tight smile. 'So I suggest you stick to the script.'

Now she's holding the door open, waiting for Henrietta to leave. 'Of course, your proofreading is impeccable.'

Henrietta takes the lift back down to the ground floor, where she peels the Life Stories sign from the Grief Café wall and packs it away until next time. She didn't even get a chance to ask Audrey about access to the office laminator. Next, she gathers up a pile of unused questionnaires; useless things, really, not fit for purpose.

Like an old companion, a cloud of gloom settles around Henrietta and her face sets into its familiar mask of indifference. Nobody ever listens to what she has to say. She's clearly being told to stop meddling, to desist from meticulously verifying the details in her books and, instead, to turn out a series of pointless Kenton Hancock-type fictions as swiftly as possible.

Usually, Henrietta has a great deal of time for rules, but only when they keep things in the correct order and, right now, she's finding Audrey's rules a hindrance rather than a help.

The story of how one Doyle sister died and the other survived needs to be told. She may have bent a few rules along the way, but Henrietta feels sure that she's on the verge of finding out what happened to Kathleen Doyle. It's just that she's not so sure she wants to know the answer any more.

CHAPTER TWENTY-SIX

HENRIETTA

It's the Saturday of Annie's sixth session and Henrietta finds herself in a quandary. On the one hand, she's looking forward to seeing Annie – she even found herself smiling on her journey into work this morning and, if she wasn't very much mistaken, the bus driver smiled back. But on the other hand, she needs to ask a difficult question and it's not the easiest one to drop into the conversation. 'By the way, Annie, were you in the habit of acting in a reckless and violent manner towards your sister?' No, that won't work at all. Perhaps once she sees Annie, everything will become much clearer.

At 11 a.m., Bonnie is first through the doors, wearing a bright red Santa hat. Stefan is next, but Mia's not in the café today so he raises a hand to Henrietta and continues through the foyer towards the lifts. Then comes Nora, the lady with the headscarf, who also heads to the lifts.

And then the doors close.

Henrietta tries to steady her breathing. Perhaps Annie paused outside for a moment, to gather her thoughts. The doors slide open again and Henrietta looks up, giving her best 'hello' smile. But it's just one of the nurses back from her break, scooping windblown hair into a ponytail as she walks by.

Henrietta tries to tell herself that there could be any number of good reasons why Annie hasn't come today. She might have overslept or forgotten it was Saturday. Or perhaps she decided to do some Christmas shopping and neglected to notify Henrietta. Yes, she tells herself, there could be any number of good reasons. It's just that she can only think of one. She recalls the painfully slow way Annie walked last Saturday and how she'd barely eaten a thing. A week can be a long time for someone as ill as Annie.

She looks over to the tea counter, but of course there's no Mia, and Morose Mike has a long queue of customers. Henrietta thinks of asking Bonnie, but she and her Santa hat have disappeared up to the second and third floors, where the serious business of treatment, rehabilitation and end-of-life care goes on. That's where the physiotherapists, the doctors, palliative care nurses and counsellors work, a world far removed from the chit-chat that happens at Henrietta's table in the Grief Café.

But Henrietta knows she won't go chasing after Bonnie. As she sits in the fug and the noise of the café, Henrietta can feel that familiar blank expression forming on her face, the one that protected her through her lonely schooldays and then university and jobs where nobody spoke to her. It's the face that hides the rising panic of knowing that she's failed again. Even worse, that she might have lost a friend.

An hour later, Henrietta spots the white pompom of Bonnie's Santa hat bobbing its way back through the foyer. Henrietta has just accepted a walk-in appointment, but she can't help herself, she has to try.

'I'm sorry, I shan't be a minute,' she says, and scrapes back her chair. She runs out to the front steps, just in time to see Bonnie hopping into the passenger seat of the minibus and doing up her seatbelt. It's too late – Bonnie is off and she hasn't even noticed Henrietta, left standing on the top step, where the wind is blowing the dust in tight, angry circles.

Back at her table, Henrietta apologises again and tries to re-assume her efficient persona, as if nothing has happened. The appointment was booked in the name of Elodie, but she's come with her mum and in the end it's the mother who does most of the talking, explaining that Elodie has her own ideas about how she wants her Life Story book to look. 'Like Myspace used to be,' she explains. Henrietta must be looking blank, so she tries again. 'Just lots of pictures and captions, really. That's the sort of thing Elodie loves.'

Then the mum stops speaking because it's become harder for her to get the words out and Elodie, who had been gazing out of the window, takes charge. 'I know I'll leave behind my old Facebook page and Instagram posts and people can write things on there. But it'll be nice for my family to have something a bit retro to look at. A book is something that will last, you know?'

Henrietta does know. Audrey won't like this one bit, but she makes an executive decision to dispense with the standard questionnaire and format. After all, Elodie won't have anything to fill in under what jobs she's had or whether she has children. The poor girl is only fifteen.

So she tells Elodie to email her all the pictures she wants to include and their captions. 'And if you want to write something longer in your own words, you can do that too,' she adds. Elodie and her mum seem quite pleased with this outcome. 'Thank you for being so matter-of-fact. It helps,' says the mum. 'I'm so tired of the head tilt. The sympathy.'

Then Henrietta shows Elodie and her mum some examples of the Life Story books, including Jackie's, which is just back from the printers. As the three of them turn over the shiny pages, Henrietta is overcome with the waste of it all. Jackie, Elodie and Annie, all these lives cut too short.

Audrey can talk all she likes about Professionalism and Detachment, but Henrietta doesn't think she can keep up the pretence much longer. Her lip begins to tremble and she feels as if someone is reaching inside her, grabbing her heart and squeezing it hard. Whatever mistakes Annie Doyle made in the past, she's shown Henrietta nothing but kindness and respect. Supposing Annie did find her sister that night and they argued again and there was some dreadful accident – she's certainly paid for it in spades. And, now, her time is fast running out.

If the truth of what happened to Kath remains buried, is that really so bad? Like Annie said, it's not as if Henrietta is going to get a gold star for solving this mystery. All that Henrietta knows for sure is that right here, right now, she wants Annie to be alright.

As she sits among the empty mugs and plates of the Grief Café, she's not thinking about Kath Doyle any more – she's more worried about Annie. For the first time in twenty-three years, Henrietta Lockwood is crying and her old mask of indifference is nowhere to be seen.

CHAPTER TWENTY-SEVEN

ANNIE

Annie has been dozing on and off all day. The way her mind dips in and out of sleep is half pleasure, half pain, because she's scared of where her dreams will take her. She's talked more about Kath in the past few weeks than she has in decades and this must be why that old dream keeps coming back. The one where she's down by the canal and it's dark and she's trying to blink away the darkness, straining to make out what's in the water, and she can't bear reliving it, not again.

There's that same dank smell of the slippery towpath, but something else too, a rancid tang of too-old rubbish. Or is it the reek of that green-sided goldfish tank, the one that really needed cleaning? Where was that again, the nursery? No, that's not right, she's getting confused. It was before that, a different place, a school with low-down sinks and toilets and sounds that bounced off the walls and music playing in another room along the corridor.

But now someone is playing awful music, with a guitar solo that makes a loud screech of feedback. She wishes they would stop, but it keeps going, on-off, on-off.

Then she surfaces and the noise turns into a doorbell, not a guitar at all. The smell is still here, but it's from her own bedding, which she hasn't changed since God knows when.

Annie is awake now, and someone is definitely ringing her doorbell, very persistently. Surely Bonnie can't have come back?

This morning Annie couldn't get out of bed, so she hid under the duvet, trying to block out the thrum of the minibus engine as it waited for her outside. She'd imagined Bonnie getting agitated, then how a small tailback of SUVs might be building up behind the minibus. Busy mums gripping their steering wheels tightly, fearful of being late for their infant ballet shows, Pilates or coffee dates.

Eventually the sound of the motor eased up a notch then faded and Annie thought she was safe. But then it crept back again, purring like an unwanted cat. The driver had only gone once around the block. She gave in and answered the phone after that, telling Bonnie she was indisposed. 'I'm on the toilet. I may be a while,' she said in the end, which got Bonnie off the phone sharpish. Then the minibus revved up properly and headed off without her.

Since then, Annie has barely moved from her bed. She sat propped up to ease the acidic burn in her throat and the radio sometimes soothed her back to sleep. She's sure she just heard the shipping forecast, but whether that means it's nearly dawn or teatime, she couldn't say.

Fisher, German Bight. North-east four or five, occasionally six, the words unchanged since her childhood.

But now her doorbell is ringing again and it's setting off another tight band of pain, around her head. Annie slides her legs out of the bed, wraps her dressing gown around her and weaves her way towards the intercom phone by her flat door.

'Yes – who is it?'

There is a moment's silence and in the background Annie can hear a taxi passing by, a siren in the distance. Then it comes, that familiar voice, but slightly distorted, as if that person has never used an intercom before and is pressing her lips right up to it.

'Hello, my name is Henrietta Lockwood and I'm with the Life Stories Project.'

This makes no sense. The girl is here – right here on her doorstep. She can't have Henrietta seeing her like this; she's not even dressed. And that musty smell has followed her out to the hallway, which isn't a good sign.

'Oh, Henrietta, I'm sorry. I'm not feeling so good.' Annie leaves the intercom receiver dangling on its twisting cord and hobbles back to her bedroom.

CHAPTER TWENTY-EIGHT

HENRIETTA

Henrietta can see a light on in Annie Doyle's flat. She knows which one it is because a neighbour told her, a man coming down the steps as she was walking up. He'd looked a little surprised when she asked if Annie was still alive.

'Pretty sure she is. Her radio wakes me up every morning.' He gives her a wink. 'When you see her, tell her I'm not a fan of the shipping forecast.'

The relief had been huge and she'd felt an unnatural urge to hug him, this man in his corduroy jacket with his hat pulled down low. Naturally, she resisted. But now there appears to be something wrong with Annie Doyle's doorbell, or perhaps she is hard of hearing.

Henrietta had remembered Annie's address from the first time they met – Ash Tree Court, because she'd misheard what Annie had said in her old-school London accent. Annie had looked a little offended when Henrietta asked if everyone who lived in Ashtray

Court was a smoker. 'Actually, I gave up years ago,' she'd said. 'I was told it wasn't ladylike.'

In reality, Ash Tree Court is squeezed between two far grander Victorian houses, the more modern block lying low, as if embarrassed by its ordinariness. One bell is clearly marked 'A. Doyle' so Henrietta tries a last time. If she holds her breath she can hear the distant ring of the doorbell from inside the building.

When Annie's disembodied voice comes through the intercom box, it makes her jump, but Henrietta regains her composure and introduces herself, pressing her mouth right up to the panel.

It's good to hear Annie's voice, but Annie sounds less glad to hear Henrietta's. In fact, she seems to have wandered off and all Henrietta can hear on the intercom is white noise, the odd distant clank and bang. Perhaps her unscheduled visit has scared Annie off. She decides to change tack.

'I was in the area, just passing. So I thought I'd pop in,' she tries, feeling rather pleased with her improvisation. But there's still no reply. The metal panel on the intercom is cold on her lips and the name plates are getting moist from her breath.

'Annie?'

Minutes pass. Henrietta hears footsteps and a heavy panting behind her and turns, but it's just a woman in gym gear jogging by. A black BMW glides slowly over the speed bumps, smooth as a shark.

Then, without warning, an angry buzz comes from the door, a noise that reverberates into her gut. 'Go on then. Push the door,' says Annie Doyle's voice, and so

Henrietta does.

Inside, the communal hallway smells of pine disinfectant and there is a low table where post is arranged in four piles. She stands and waits, looking at four white doors. Then one on her left opens, just a crack. 'Well, come on then, don't dawdle out there,' comes a voice. The door opens a fraction more, revealing a portion of Annie's pale face.

Henrietta knows this is the moment when she should put her client at ease, make light of this home visit. 'Good evening. I was just passing and thought, "Why don't I pay a visit to Annie Doyle?"' But Annie has already turned away, leaving the door to her flat open. Henrietta follows her into a corridor, then a living room that faces on to the street, with a clear view of the porch where Henrietta has been standing for the past twenty minutes.

'Yes, you said,' Annie mutters. 'I haven't cleared up. I wasn't expecting anyone.'

But to Henrietta, the room looks exceptionally tidy, spartan even. There's a simple scrubbed pine table, a single dining chair and an armchair. A couple of pictures hang on the wall and there is a wooden bookshelf in the corner, its shelves barely half full, as if Annie has only just moved in.

She notices that Annie is leaning against her armchair with an odd kink to her body and that something strange has happened to her hair. It's cut in a style of an inverted pudding bowl, clipped very short at the nape.

Annie winces and lets herself drop down into the

seat. 'I suppose I should offer you a drink, but I don't know what I've got,' she says, sounding even fainter than she did over the intercom. There is a sheen of sweat on her forehead and her silky dressing gown has fallen open at the front, showing a long, baggy T-shirt.

This is it, Henrietta realises, her chance to do a Good Deed, and without giving Annie a chance to disagree, she takes charge. 'Then it will be a pleasure for me to make us both a nice cup of tea,' she says. 'Kitchen, this way?' She points back out to the corridor and Annie raises a hand, a gesture that could mean 'Help yourself, it's that way' or could equally be read as 'Go away and leave me alone.' Henrietta chooses to take it as the former.

'Milk? Sugar?' she calls out, as she picks up one mug from the draining board, finds a second one at the back of a cupboard. She's getting the hang of this, and she can see why Mia enjoys all her busying around in the café. It does make one feel useful.

Unfortunately, Annie doesn't appear to have any milk or sugar, but there are some dusty teabags in a box. Annie hasn't moved from her chair, but she accepts the steaming mug with both hands and nestles it into her stomach.

This doesn't feel like the right time to pull Annie up on missing today's appointment, let alone start asking the questions she has. So Henrietta looks around, searching for something else to chat about, an ornament to admire, perhaps. The painting on the wall is a seascape in broad sweeps of white and steely blue, with a steep cliff behind.

'I've no idea where it is,' says Annie, following her gaze. 'I just liked its . . . mood.' She waves her hand again, her fingers fluttering at some unnamed thought or time that hovers just beyond her reach. Her hand comes to rest again around the mug and she sips from it, gingerly.

Then Annie says, 'I suppose you thought I was dead.' The bitter black tea must have fortified her in some way.

'Of course not.' Henrietta looks down at her work shoes, places her feet more neatly together, so the laces on each shoe line up. 'Well, maybe a bit. I did worry a bit.'

She looks around the room again, at the bookshelves lined with a few Penguin paperbacks, the old-fashioned sort with orange covers. A row of pebbles is arranged on the top shelf, each a perfect orb, and a few small trinkets are laid out on the mantelpiece. Henrietta has never been one for interior design – most of the things in her own flat are cast-offs from her parents or were ordered from Ikea – but as she sits in this room with its white walls and its simple furniture, she feels calmer than she has in a long time. There is something to be said for uncluttered spaces – and she realises that this could be what is referred to as a topic of conversation.

'Annie, you have a very pleasant home. Have you lived here long?'

'Two years,' says Annie. 'And thank you. I like it too because it's all mine and I have all I need. Of course, it's not really mine, I just rent. I got it through the doctor, or the social worker, one of those people.' She's looking beyond Henrietta now, out to the darkness beyond the window.

'Social worker?' Henrietta asks cautiously, thinking back to when Annie had let loose the stream of words about her late husband and fear and blood and lost babies and she thinks she understands, but she's not sure.

'Is it like a women's refuge then, Ash Tree Court?'

'Eh?' Annie peers at her, frowning. 'What you on about? No, although I could have done with one of those all those years ago. No, I got it after Terry's accident. When I couldn't bear to go back to that house in Dollis Hill. All that brown . . .' She trails off.

Henrietta has never been to Dollis Hill, but presumes it must be a rural location, a brownfield site, perhaps.

'I threw all his stuff out,' Annie is saying, gripping her mug so tightly that her knuckles shine. 'I didn't want a stick of it. Or my old clothes. I didn't want any reminders of that time.'

Then she stops, looks straight at Henrietta. 'You haven't brought that recording thing, have you? This is just between me and you.'

'Of course not. I'm visiting as a friend.' Henrietta feels her face go hot as the word 'friend' slips out, but Annie doesn't seem to mind; she's talking again, faster and angrier than she ever has before. Her tea sloshes around in its mug, but she doesn't notice.

'I put it all in that big yellow skip, but then I had a funny turn, as my mum would call it. But when I got taken to hospital, they didn't call it a funny turn, they called it a breakdown.'

Henrietta is having trouble following this. 'The Rosendale, you mean?'

'No, no, pay attention. This was a couple of years ago. A different sort of hospital altogether, when I was sectioned. They thought I'd gone doolally, but it was the sanest I'd been for years, if you ask me. Anyway, they put me on Briar ward and later they took pity on me, said I didn't need to go back to Chaucer Drive. The social worker showed me this place instead, and it was love at first sight. Just wish I'd had it sooner. Would have saved a lot of bother.'

'Well, you're very lucky,' says Henrietta, relieved that they both agree.

All at once, Annie leans towards her, bangs her empty mug down on the table. 'Lucky? You think I'm lucky? You sound like that woman from the housing. Yes, for the past two years of my life I've been able to wake up without feeling like a bag of nerves. But what about the rest of my life – why couldn't I have had it sooner?'

'I'm sorry,' stumbles Henrietta. This is not how she envisaged a conversation about home decor panning out. She realises that her tea is almost cold and, actually, it's cold in this room, full stop. She watches as Annie runs her hand over the back of her neck, where the skin is so very bare, and she wants to wrap this woman in something warm and comforting.

Whatever happened on that night in 1974, Annie lost the most important person in her life and it's clear that she has been grieving ever since. Her sense of loss is everywhere in this bare flat: in the spaces between that row of carefully placed pebbles and that single mug on the draining board. And it's been threaded through the stories that Annie has been telling her each week. Annie has been telling the Life Story that she needs to be heard and it didn't stop with the mystery of her sister's death. It's also everything that Annie endured afterwards: her loneliness, her grief and her abusive marriage. Annie has been talking; it's just that Henrietta hasn't been listening properly.

And, in talking about it, she's been a braver woman than Henrietta, who has never been able to share anything with anyone. She almost did, last week, but then it stayed stuck inside her. There is a fluttering feeling at her throat because Henrietta has just made a decision. Annie has told her so much and now she will return the favour. She wants Annie to know that she's not alone in her loss.

So she starts to explain that she's been thinking about Annie and her sister a lot, perhaps a little too much, because Kath's death reminds her of something in her own past. Of a picnic when Henrietta and her friend Esther were nine and little Christopher was just four. Of how the three children ran and climbed into the back of the red car and slid about on the hot back seat, with Christopher sitting in the middle.

'When we got to the beach, we ate our sandwiches and then my parents lay in the shade of a *haus win*, that's a rickety bamboo shelter that fishermen used for overnight stays. But us children, we all wanted to swim.

'I'd brought my mask and snorkel and this orange

rubber ring that meant you could float on the surface and gaze down at all the fish under the sea. Annie, it was like another world under the water. There was coral, tiny slivers of electric blue fish darting here and there, orange starfish clinging to the rocks.'

She, Esther and Christopher had each taken turns with the mask and the snorkel. Christopher hadn't used one before and he was so excited he kept jerking up out of the water when he saw something. 'Look!' he was trying to say, but it got muffled by the snorkel and came out like a hollow mooing sound. The girls laughed at him and he laughed back, swallowing gulps of sea water, which made them laugh even more.

'Then me and Esther decided to practise our breaststroke and I let Christopher carry on using my mask and the orange rubber ring to show I was good at sharing.' She needs to explain this next bit carefully because she wants Annie to understand that, in truth, she had started to feel a bit cross because Christopher was hogging the mask and it was beginning to annoy her. She swam past him a few times and he was still staring down at all the sea-life below, bent at the waist, the shiny rubber ring bobbing and winking in the hot sun.

'Then I swam past again and something made me stop and give him a push, just a little one, for fun,' she says. 'But all that happened was that Christopher and the rubber ring began to drift away. He wasn't moving his arms or his legs at all, so then I grabbed him, shook his shoulder and I started shouting, really loudly.

'My dad woke up first and came splashing into the

water. He pulled Christopher out and on to the hard pebbles and started pressing his chest. It took longer for my mum to come down. She had loosened the halter neck of her swimming costume, you see.'

Even now, Henrietta can see her mother sliding her feet into her flip-flops, tying the strings of her costume in a bow behind her neck before she walked down to the small, lifeless body that her father was shaking, pummelling, trying to wake up.

'In the end, the doctor said that he'd been in the water too long for us to help him. About five minutes too long, he said. Those five minutes that I'd been swimming back and forth, thinking how kind I was to lend Christopher the mask, then getting a bit cross because he was hogging it.'

All this time, Henrietta has been twisting the toggle on her coat one way, then the other. She can't bear to look up at Annie, because she's afraid she'll see disgust in the old woman's face. But then she does look up and Annie doesn't seem angry or disgusted. Instead, she looks puzzled.

'So, let me get this straight,' she says. 'Esther and Christopher. Who exactly were they?'

'Esther was my best friend,' she tells Annie.

'And Christopher was . . . ?'

'Christopher was my little brother.'

Saying those words out loud, Henrietta feels herself pulled back in time to that house in Masura, the one on stilts with a concrete car port underneath, where Christopher used to ride his little red fire truck round and round in circles. The house where she could look over and wave at Esther's window, always lit up in the evenings. But that night, when they came back from the hospital, the windows all around them were dark, even Esther's.

'Nobody came to our house all night and they didn't come the next day either. Eventually, the priest who ran the mission station knocked on our door. He said it was all arranged. He'd booked us three seats on a mission plane and the coffin was being sent straight from the hospital to the airstrip. It was only right, he said, that the Lockwoods should take their little boy home and bury him in British soil.

'But my dad didn't want to leave. He kept saying his job there was his "calling" and he didn't have to go. Then the priest got very angry. He said, "What is wrong with you? We are all sorry for your loss, but you need to go home and go today. The plane is waiting. You need to bury your son. And take your daughter home."

'At that, my father understood. We all understood.'

As their car sped out of the mission gates towards the airstrip, her parents stared straight ahead. They couldn't even bear to look at Henrietta, and that was when she had realised the incontrovertible truth of the matter. The responsibility rested with her alone. After all, her parents had been sleeping.

'It was my fault, you see. I was the one who had showed Christopher how to use my too-big mask and snorkel and I gave him the orange rubber ring, which must have kept his face down while the seawater leaked in. I was meant to be looking after him.'

She remembers that hot dash across the runway,

her mother pulling her in a grip full of hate. A small coffin already loaded into the dark hold. Her parents had lost their only son and the blame lay squarely with Henrietta, their lumpen, inept daughter. The child murderer, who the priest said must be sent home.

'Back in England, we never spoke of it again,' she says. 'My father got bits of work as a supply teacher. My mother volunteered and baked an awful lot of cakes. We all lived in silence in our cold, miserable house in Kent. And every time I go back there, it reminds me of my little brother dying and how it was all my fault.'

Annie sits forward in her chair. 'What a terrible thing.'

Henrietta braces herself, waiting to be told how very stupid she was.

But Annie doesn't say that. She doesn't say anything for a while. Then, very slowly, she starts to shake her head. 'But you do realise, Henrietta, that none of that was your fault.'

Has Annie even listened to a word she's been saying? 'Well, of course it was. I was in charge, I gave him the mask and I swam past him. I didn't do anything to save him.'

Then it's Annie's turn to look cross, furious in fact. 'Henrietta, you were nine years old. Your parents were in charge – or they should have been.'

'But they were sleeping.' Henrietta's answer comes out almost as a whisper and a thin thread of fear begins to wrap around her gut.

'My point exactly. As you know, I never had children, but I've looked after plenty of them. And I know that that's what parents should do: look after you. And when something goes wrong, as it often does in life, your parents' job is to comfort you, make you feel better. If there's an accident, for instance. Because that's what it was with your poor brother, it was an accident. Surely that was what the priest was telling them to do – go home and look after your daughter.'

The way Annie puts it sounds so convincing, and she feels the thread of fear tighten. But why would her parents let her believe she was to blame, for so long?

Annie is gripping the arms of the chair, ready to push herself up. 'Hen, it's too late for me. I'll never find out what happened to my sister. But sometimes you just have to let go of things, for your own sake. I think it's time for you to stop feeling guilty about an accident that happened a long time ago and that was never your fault. You need to get on with your own life.'

Now Annie is standing, but Henrietta can't bear to say goodbye, not now all these muddled secrets have spilled out. It's too soon. Then she has an idea.

'Annie, I can't leave you here, not now. There isn't even any food in your cupboards. How about I take you out for a cup of tea, to a café perhaps?'

Annie raises her eyebrows and then she smiles. 'I think I know just the place. Just wait a sec while I make myself respectable.'

CHAPTER TWENTY-NINE

HENRIETTA

It turns out that Annie's idea of making herself respectable is quite different from Henrietta's. Instead of changing out of what look very much like a bed T-shirt and leggings, Annie just adds a bulky sweater dress to her ensemble. Then she puts on her ankle boots with pointed toes and buckles and, finally, a military-style jacket that has innumerable flaps and pockets. She glances at herself in the hallway mirror and stands a little taller. 'Right then, Henrietta Lockwood. Shall we go?'

As they walk down the front path of Ash Tree Court, Annie reaches out for her arm and Henrietta slows her pace so they can walk together. She can't help thinking Annie would benefit from purchasing some more appropriate footwear, but at least some of her old strength is returning.

Apparently, they are going to Emir's Café, which, Annie explains in an exasperated tone, is nothing like Nando's or McDonald's, and no, not a bit like Greggs, either. She's right – it's a tiny place round the corner from Annie that looks very much like a run-down workman's caff. But when Annie pushes open the door, the air is full of wonderful smells, a mixture of hot spices, fresh herbs and a cinnamon sweetness, and Henrietta realises she's very hungry.

Hanging back, she is surprised to see this oddly clad woman being greeted like an old friend. They are shown to the best table, right by the window, and a tall silver pot of tea is conjured up. Emir himself, a twinkly man with a moustache and a quick smile, pours it, holding it high above their two glasses. Henrietta worries it will splatter or scald, but he fills them without spilling a drop. 'Always a pleasure to see our Annie,' he says, with a slight bow.

A constant flow of dishes appears without either of them even looking at a menu: neat pastries containing crumbly cheese and herbs; spoonfuls of garlicky yoghurt and grainy hummus; a salad dotted with jewel-like pomegranate seeds and tiny chopped leaves. This version of salad bears little resemblance to the lumps of iceberg lettuce that Henrietta buys to accompany her tins of tuna or slices of boiled egg.

'Mint tea – that's the business,' says Annie, who does little more than nibble at each of Emir's fresh offerings but does drink plenty of the tea, which also keeps coming. 'Settles the stomach.'

Henrietta can't imagine ever having the gall to walk into a café like this, but Annie says she makes a point of trying out new places. 'When I moved back to this area, I tried to visit a new shop or café every day, even the really snooty ones,' she says. 'I found a deli that does delicious olives and a haberdashery shop that sells lovely trims by the yard.' She stirs more sugar into the already achingly sweet tea. 'Then, of course, there's the market.' Annie tells Henrietta about her shopping trips there and how she's trying to make up for her 'bad clothes years'.

'There's a woman who runs a stall near the flyover, Chantal, she puts things aside for me if she sees something in my size. That's where I got my pixie boots.' Annie points one foot out from under the table, wiggles her ankle a bit to show it off. 'People call it vintage now – but to me, it's all the stuff I saw on other people but never bought. Like I say, making up for all my lost years.'

This market sounds very different to the handful of stalls outside Henrietta's local Poundland, where she buys cut-price dog treats and, every now and then, a new sweatshirt.

Fridays, Annie is telling her, are when you get the best stuff. That's when she found her 'proper French beret' and a flowery Courrèges sundress that she wears with a black polo neck underneath. 'No point in me waiting for summer, is there?' she says, bitterness creeping into her voice.

Emir brings over a final plate of delicacies, studded with sesame seeds and thick with honey. Henrietta worries she'll get sticky fingers, but Annie pushes the plate of pastries across the table. 'Go on – just lick your fingers after!' They are stuffed with a thick wodge of green paste – pistachios, apparently – and absolutely delicious.

'So you live on your own, too?' Annie asks, when at

last the meal seems to draw to a close.

'Well, me and Dave. He's my dog,' Henrietta explains, then gasps as she remembers it's way past Dave's tea time. She gets out her phone and uses her honey-coated fingers to jab out a message to her upstairs neighbour: *Dear Melissa, I am visiting a friend. Would you be so kind as to feed Dave and let him into the backyard to do his business? Henrietta Lockwood.*

There's a row of tiny dots under her words, which shows her that the message is being read. A reply comes back almost immediately: *Sure, no probs. Will do it now. Always nice to see Dave. M x*

First Melissa became Mel and now she's just 'M' – Henrietta is delighted that this friendship is becoming more informal by the day.

Emir brings over the bill, which seems improbably small for everything they have had, but he won't accept a penny more. 'My pleasure, ladies. An early Christmas present,' he says, holding his hands together.

It seems a shame to leave the warmth of Emir's Café, which has got noisier and busier as they've been sitting there. It's only when they go outside and Henrietta sees the long queue of people waiting for a table that she realises it must be quite the place to be.

A group of women in the queue are swigging from bottles of lager and Henrietta can see that they have taken great care to look unkempt yet also chic. Two have hair tied up in complicated arrangements; a third has a sharp black bob and is wearing a coat in a brilliant blue.

Henrietta offers her arm for Annie but realises she's

no longer beside her. Instead, Annie has stopped to chat to these flamboyant creatures who, in turn, have taken a shine to Annie. 'Ohmygod, your jacket, it's insane!' says one, reaching out to stroke her glittery cuffs. 'So vintage. So cool,' she adds. Then she looks at Henrietta, who is struggling to get her arms into the sleeves of her duffle coat. 'Ohmygod!' she says, now pointing at Henrietta's polar bear sweatshirt. 'Pure kitsch. Love it!' And with that they disappear into Emir's before Henrietta can even tell them where she bought it, should they wish to purchase a similar style. That, she reflects, has to be the best £19.99 she has ever spent on a garment.

Annie insists on waiting with Henrietta at her bus stop, stamping her boots now and then to keep warm, the buckles making a rather festive jingling sound. Henrietta wills the bus to come – surely standing in the cold night air can't be good for the old woman's health – but Annie doesn't seem in any hurry to get home.

'Those girls, all dressed up, that would have been me and Kath, back in the day,' Annie says.

'The fashion thing, you mean?' Henrietta squints at a bus that's just come into view, but it's the wrong number.

'Yes, the fashion, the music. The nights out.' Annie is talking more softly now, as if the walk and the meal have drained her. 'When I think of what I would do differently, if I had my time over . . .'

The bus stop is outside a huge double-fronted Victorian house and Annie is looking up at the white facade. 'These places,' she says, 'they all used to be bedsits – families, artists, musicians, all sorts crammed in there. Mick Jagger made a film round the corner and that painter, what's his name, Hockney, he was here, too.'

To Henrietta, this sort of set-up sounds horrific, like the worst student house-share ever. She visited one for an end-of-year party, once, by mistake. She thought it was going to be a sit-down meal with congratulatory speeches, but as she walked up the front steps a girl was being sick out of a window, and it only got worse inside. Some men from the rowing club were taking turns to drink something called a yard of ale and a couple on the sofa appeared to be attempting intercourse while still clothed. She had left pretty sharpish.

'I used to think how, if things had been different, me and Kath could have shared a flat together. I didn't know that at the time – I thought the only way to leave home was to get married. Stupid, I know. But that's what girls like us did. Waited to be rescued by a man. For better or for worse.'

Annie pulls out a huge purple silk handkerchief, like something Oscar Wilde might carry, and wipes her nose.

Another bus comes into view, then a second behind it, and Annie waves her handkerchief to make sure it stops. 'Here we go; they always come in twos.'

'Thank you, Annie. I have had a most convivial evening and I look forward to seeing you in the café next Saturday.'

'A pleasure. Good to see you out and about, Hen. Don't hide yourself away – it can become a habit. I reckon it's time for you to live a little.'

And with that, the bus doors judder shut, Henrietta taps her card on the machine and walks to the back of the bus, where, if she hurries, she can catch a last glimpse of her friend, an elderly woman with a lopsided walk heading home on her own in the dark.

CHAPTER THIRTY

Henrietta

Over the next week, Henrietta pays particular attention to her routines because what she craves right now is stability. She did it – she told Annie about Christopher and nothing dreadful happened. There was no thunderbolt, no finger of God came down from the heavens and pointed at evil Henrietta, the child murderer and wrecker of lives. But it was Annie's response, those four little words, that really threw her: 'It wasn't your fault.'

Everything in her flat looks exactly the same, but she has the unnerving feeling that some vital axis in her worldview has slipped and everything is in danger of sliding off course. If she gets up from her sofa too fast, the floor rises up at an odd angle, and as she walks around her flat, her steps thud in a way that feels far too loud. I'm all at sea, she thinks to herself as she tips Dave's food into his bowl, just missing the edge. Quite anchorless, as she stumbles, holds tight to a door handle.

On Sunday, she wasn't sure she could stomach lunch at The Pines, but she went anyway. She sat and dutifully chewed the slices of meat and the over-boiled carrots, and she tasted nothing because all she could think about was the overwhelming hum of silence in the air. At one point she had to put down her cutlery and place her hands over her ears, but it made no difference. Nothing could cut through it, not the scrape of her father's knife on his smeared plate nor the tiny chink as her mother put down her glass of sherry. No one else seemed to notice it, but to Henrietta it was deafening.

She wanted to push away her apple crumble and ask, how come there are no pictures of Christopher in the house? Why are there blank spaces in the photo album upstairs? And why did you go for a nap and leave your four-year-old son in the water when he couldn't swim?

Henrietta was five when Christopher was born, so she must have built up plenty of memories of him. But it's as if they've faded, the years of silence leaching them of colour and sound. But now, if she tries very hard, things come back to her, but as sensations rather than images.

The softness of his hair. A small, sticky hand, holding tight to hers. His red ride-on fire truck that he rode in circles, laughing as he pressed the horn, beep, beep! Turning the pages of a book, reading him a story in the heat of the afternoon. Not the Bible stories her parents favoured, but one about a dog called Hairy Maclary and another about a Rainbow Fish that shared its brightly coloured scales with all its friends until it had none. 'Rainbow Fish – again!' he'd say. As she read, he drank his milk and she'd feel his head getting heavy.

And then, at last, she remembers his voice. Etta, that's what he called her – Etta. Because when he started talking, her name was too long for him to manage.

But last Sunday, Henrietta knew better than to say any of this. Instead, she announced she needed to leave The Pines early. 'Before tea?' Her mother looked at her askance. 'You must be sickening. Off you trot then. We don't want London germs down here.'

Monday and Tuesday pass in a fog. She barely even thinks of the mystery of Kath Doyle: even Henrietta Lockwood can only concentrate on one watery death at a time.

Her parents ring on the Wednesday.

Wherever possible, Henrietta tries to take calls from her parents while she is completing a household task such as washing up, wiping the insides of her kitchen cupboards or making a sandwich. That way, her mind can skim over the surface of the conversation and is less likely to snag on their inevitable criticisms. Her mother wants to remind Henrietta how thoughtless she was for not coming to help to make Christingles for next week's service. 'Poor Mrs Battersby's fingers were raw – raw – from pushing in all those cloves on her own,' she shouts down the line.

When her parents use the phone, they don't bother putting it on speaker – Edmund and Virginia Lockwood stand very close together and her mother bellows out her opinions.

In the end, Henrietta does something rather bold. She holds her phone close to the washing up bowl, swishes the water around and shouts into it, 'Sorry, you're breaking up, breaking up.' It does the trick. Then she sits with Dave for a very long time, stroking his head until she feels calmer.

* * *

By Thursday, Henrietta's world is feeling slightly less swimmy, but she decides it's best if she keeps a low profile during her shift at the Rosendale Drop-In Centre. It's Audrey that she'd quite like to avoid. First, she's pretty sure that last week's visit to Emir's Café with Annie contravenes all the advice on Maintaining Professional Detachment in the Life Stories Handbook and, secondly, she knows that Audrey will be expecting an update on the progress of Annie's book.

With only one Saturday left before Christmas, there is no earthly way that Henrietta can meet the deadline. To be honest, she doesn't know what to do with Annie's collection of sad stories, let alone the huge unresolved question at its core. She wishes someone could tell her how this story ends, because she still doesn't have a clue.

Audrey, however, is not that person. She would have moved things on far more briskly, ignoring the gaps and ensuring everything was tied up neatly in time for Christmas. But from her hours in the Grief Café, Henrietta is beginning to understand that the gaps in conversation, the moments when people fall silent, are just as important as the words they say.

As she arrives at work, Henrietta finds the route to her table is blocked by two cardboard boxes, full to the brim with tinsel garlands and sparkling baubles. The reason for these boxes (which surely break several health and safety rules) is the huge Christmas tree that has appeared in the corner of the café, ready for decorating.

This is all Mia's doing, and she's also placed a special cardboard box on her counter. It's covered in Christmas wrapping paper and a label on the front reads 'Memory Tree Baubles – Help Yourself'. Henrietta peers inside. The box contains many pieces of paper, each cut into the shape of a Christmas bauble with a loop of ribbon at the top.

'It's a tradition here, Hen,' Mia explains. 'Visitors can write a memory about their loved ones and hang it on the tree. It can be for someone alive or dead, whichever you like.' To get the ball rolling, Mia chooses a pink one and Henrietta watches as she writes, *Brice, the night we met. Miss you always, Mia xxx*

Then Mia reaches into the box and chooses another paper bauble, green this time, and she writes: *Stefan, you're my teatime treat. Mia x*

'Perk of the job,' Mia says, with a wink. 'I get to do two. One for you, Hen? Go on.'

It would be rude to refuse, so Henrietta chooses a blue paper bauble and takes it back to her corner table. She has to keep her writing small to fit it all in: *Dave, I was secretly pleased when you dug up Mummy's lobelias. Thanks for keeping me company.*

Then, when Mia's not looking, she goes back to the box and picks a second paper bauble, red this time, a nice bright colour. And on it she writes: *Christopher. Reading you stories. Love always, H x.* She knows she has to do this quickly, before she can change her mind, so she walks over to Mia's counter again, and puts both in Mia's 'done' pile, with Dave's one on top.

Her first appointment this morning is Garry, 'That's Garry with two Rs', who wears a navy polo neck and trousers with creases so sharp they stand proud of his legs, even while he's sitting down. Garry made his fortune as a life coach and has been having chemo treatment during the past year. 'I'm keeping everything crossed, but you never know what's around the corner,' he says. 'I thought I'd do my Life Story now, while I'm feeling OK. Then, when my time comes, it'll be all lined up, ready to go – boom.' He bangs his fist on his thigh.

Garry has even conscientiously filled out the Life Story questionnaire. 'Here's all the stuff about school, marriage and family,' he says, as he hands it over in a clear plastic wallet. His eyes are an improbably bright green, almost certainly contact lenses, but engaging nonetheless. 'There are things I need to say in this book that I should have said long ago. Mostly, that I'm sorry. To a lot of people.'

'Wouldn't it be better to do that in person?' Henrietta picks up Garry's plastic folder and sees that, unlike Annie, he's brought in plenty of photographs. They slide from one end of the folder to the other and she glimpses a football team; a wedding photo; two children playing in a blue swimming pool.

'I wouldn't know where to start,' Garry replies. 'They aren't family, they're strangers. I ran scams, have done for years. Started off selling insurance policies that didn't exist, back in the seventies. Then I got into the double-glazing game. We'd sit in people's living rooms all night if we had to, just to close a deal.

'Then in the nineties it was all about timeshares – spent a lot of time in Spain, Portugal, it was a good life. I changed my company's name so many times I lost track – had to check my business card each morning to remind myself.

'Then came the internet and I thought I'd had it; nobody needed face-to-face sales any more. But then I saw my chance to diversify and I set myself up as an online life coach.'

Henrietta can feel her mask of indifference taking over, her lips set in their customary thin line, her eyes wide and blank. 'I'm not here to judge, Garry. We have all made questionable decisions in our pasts.'

'People signed up thinking I could change their lives. All they got was a series of inspirational quotes, one a day for a month. They were things like "Go For It", "You Got This" and "Today Is A New Day". I bought a book of quotes in a service station for 99p and charged people a grand for that course. By the time they wised up, I'd changed the company name, deleted the website and moved on.'

Regardless of Garry's shady past, as his session draws to a close, Henrietta shakes his hand.

'I'll be back in January to talk some more,' he says, 'but don't go publishing my book till I'm six feet under, will you, love?'

Henrietta gives him her word.

'You got this!' Garry says, nimbly sidestepping a box of tinsel garlands.

After Garry, her appointment book is free so she

wanders over to watch Mia decorating the tree. Mia takes the task very seriously, standing back each time she adds a new item to make sure she's getting the effect right. Finally, she hangs her baubles and Henrietta's on the top branches of the tree.

Henrietta clears her throat. 'Brice was your fiancé, wasn't he?'

'Yes, three years he's been gone.' Mia adjusts one of the silver garlands. 'Some people say it gets easier, but I think you just adapt. The grief doesn't go; you just mould yourself around it. But I won't lie, Christmases are hard.'

'It is a time of year when emotions are likely to run high,' Henrietta agrees.

'How about you, Hen? You lost someone?'

Henrietta thinks about everything that Mia has been through and how she came to work here because 'people here get it', and then Henrietta thinks about how nice it would be if people 'got' her, too. She takes a deep breath, counts to ten and then she says it.

'Yes, my brother died when he was very young,' she replies.

'I'm so sorry.'

'It was twenty-three years ago, when he was four and I was nine. But I think of him every day.'

'Of course you do,' Mia says. 'It's good that you talk about him, though. Keep his memory alive. It'll be nice to remember him this Christmas, with your parents.'

This is so far from the truth of life at The Pines that Henrietta can't think of a reply, but then she's saved because she can see that Stefan has arrived and is heading over towards them.

'My two favourite ladies!' he says.

Henrietta frowns because today isn't Saturday and Stefan only comes in on Saturdays, but he seems to understand her confusion. 'Yeah, I know it's not my usual day, Hen,' he says. 'I'm here to take Mia out for lunch. She works too hard, never gets a break.'

'Very thoughtful,' says Henrietta. If she could wink, this would be the time to do it, but the last time she tried someone asked if she had something in her eye.

Now she's got used to his gold tooth, his shiny head and his over-familiar manner, she finds Stefan surprisingly good company. He tells her he's considering doing a Life Story book, but he won't be needing a questionnaire. He says he has a headful of stories and if he wants to do a book, he'll come over and just talk – that's what works for him.

'The questionnaire does feel a little impersonal,' Henrietta concedes. 'But Audrey says it provides a useful chronological framework.'

At that, Stefan takes off his beanie hat, runs his hand over his bald head and grins at her. 'Ah, Hen, I reckon chronology is overrated. If I've learned anything from the past few years, it's this: what matters most is the here and now, not what happened before.'

But now the lift doors are opening and Audrey steps out, resplendent in a coat the shade of candyfloss. Mia and Stefan exchange a quick look and simultaneously move off. The centre's glass doors glide shut behind them just as Audrey reaches Henrietta, now alone by the Christmas tree.

'Oh. Where's Mia off to in such a hurry?' Audrey asks.

'Um, early lunch?'

'Hmm. Anyway, I just came to say, it's all confirmed. My course is on for next week.'

Henrietta sifts through her mind for a clue, trying to recall a memo or email or conversation about this, but draws a complete blank.

'The one about how to make a podcast,' says Audrey. 'So we can launch our own one in the new year. I'm thinking of calling it Grief Café Conversations.'

Henrietta nods enthusiastically. The more projects Audrey has on the go, the less likely she is to remember Henrietta's fast-approaching deadline.

'Oh, and another thing . . .'

Henrietta's heart gives an uncomfortable leap.

'Love to have a quick skim through your first Life Story book before it goes to the printers. Must be nearly ready now?'

'No problem. This Saturday is my seventh and final session with Annie. Just a few last details to confirm, then I'll email you a link,' says Henrietta.

She won't, though. And come the new year, she knows she won't be sitting at this table in the Grief Café. A shame, because she rather likes this job. But once Audrey discovers Henrietta can't stick to a simple timetable, her contract will be terminated. Already, she can imagine her drive of shame back to Tunbridge Wells to break the news to her parents. And how her father will shake his head in disappointment at his foolish daughter who never could avert a disaster unfolding in front of her eyes, whether she was nine or thirty-two.

Audrey turns to go.

'Don't forget your bauble,' says Henrietta.

'Sorry?'

'Mia's baubles. We're all doing it, writing down a happy memory of a loved one.'

Audrey fiddles with the clasp on her handbag and looks distracted.

'You could laminate it if you like?'

Audrey gives Henrietta a sharp look and click-clacks her way out of the double doors.

CHAPTER THIRTY-ONE

Annie

The thought began as an intermittent buzz around the edges of her mind, but now it's stuck in her head, like a fly caught in a jar. It's only going to get louder and angrier, and the only way to lift the lid and let it fly away is to talk to Henrietta.

She'd tried to get ready in time to catch Bonnie's Saturday minibus this morning, she really had, but everything was too complicated and heavy and she couldn't manage it. Even answering the phone to Bonnie had felt like an effort, and now the minibus is long gone. And with it, possibly her last chance to see Henrietta.

Last Saturday, when the girl turned up on her doorstep, it had taken Annie by surprise. Henrietta had talked about going on a picnic in some faraway country, where her little brother had drowned. All because her parents – who sound like terrible people – hadn't looked after him.

All week, Annie has thought of Henrietta confiding in her, and now she feels rotten to the core because she hasn't been entirely honest in return. She needs to find Henrietta and tell her the final bit of information about the accident, how it really happened. Then Henrietta can put it in the book or she can keep it to herself, Annie really doesn't care. All she wants is to be rid of it.

Henrietta's sad story about her brother was a reminder of what happens when you bottle something up: it doesn't go away, it just seeps into everything, taints your whole life.

She's not even sure Henrietta will still be at the Rosendale on a Saturday afternoon, but she needs to see her. There's nothing for it. She'll just have to make her own way to the centre. She'll wear her favourite coat this time, the orange bouclé one with chunky buttons and a collar that keeps her neck nice and warm. She gets out her best, brightest lipstick and tries to make a nice shape around her mouth, but it keeps going lopsided. Not to worry; at least she's making an effort.

All those buckles on her boots are too fussy for today, her hands just aren't doing what they are supposed to, so she makes do with her Moroccan slippers, the ones with sewn-on sequins that are comfortable, if a bit flappy.

At the top of the road she looks left, the way that leads to that iron bridge over the canal, where she used to go walking on her afternoons off from the nursery. Just to look, she told herself, to keep the faith. That summer of '76, the hot one, the canal level dropped so low that the outlines of all sorts of junk emerged on the surface – pram wheels, car exhaust pipes. The long back of a white leather sofa that, for one horrible moment, Annie thought was something else.

She didn't tell Terry about those afternoon trips; it was her private pain. She tended to walk along the towpath from Ladbroke Grove to Wormwood Scrubs, or sometimes she headed the other way, towards Paddington. In one direction it skirted Kensal Green Cemetery and then ran alongside the railway tracks, the prison in the distance. In the other direction was the robot-like shadow of the new high-rise block of flats, Trellick Tower, then St Mary's Hospital, with its twisting incinerator chimney. Either way, it seemed like there was death everywhere she looked. She almost envied the families she saw in the cemetery, heads bowed down. She and her parents hadn't had a coffin to throw dirt on, or a headstone to visit.

Today, instead of turning left she turns right, towards the Tube station. Her sequinned slippers are making it hard to walk and she has to scrunch her toes as she takes each step. But of course the real problem isn't her shoes, it's that sharp scissor of pain, reminding her that something has gone terribly wrong inside her.

By the time she gets on the train she's finding it hard to take in proper lungfuls of air, so she shames a long-legged youth into giving her a seat. He's spread himself across two of the fold-down seats, flicking through pictures of girls on his phone, swiping right, right, right every time until Annie decides she's had enough. 'Young man, I am terminally ill and on my way to my cancer centre. Let me sit down.' The boy leaps up as if he's been burned and a stunned silence descends on the carriage.

As the train rattles along, Annie looks down at her twinkly slippers with their pointed toes that have gone raggedy at the ends. It's unfair that just as Annie is getting her life straight, she's hurtling to the end of the line, heading for the last stop.

She registers that she's glad she decided to wear this coat, the one she splashed out on because she loved the colour, a burnt orange. It makes her think of all the nice bits of autumn and winter that are nothing to do with the guilt and sadness that come with Christmas.

She likes how it makes her stand out from the crowd – something she hasn't done since before Terry, before she lost Kath. 'Good for her age,' she hopes people might say about her. Or 'a little eccentric', but there's nothing wrong with that – it balances out all those years of being invisible.

The train is slowing down so she gets ready to step as elegantly as possible on to the platform, ignoring the tight ache in her spine that's spreading down the backs of her legs like treacle, like the blood when she was reading *The Very Hungry Caterpillar* in the nursery, all those years ago.

There's a small jolt as the train comes to a stop and Annie realises that, now she thinks about it, she can't feel her legs any more. Instead, everything is focused on her head, where a band of pressure is gathering, as if someone is turning a screw tighter and tighter.

She puts a foot on the platform and looks towards the stairs, wondering how many there are and why they can't put the signs for the lift somewhere sensible. And then both of her ears go muffled, her legs bend like wet cardboard and there is nothing to see but a soft blackness.

CHAPTER THIRTY-TWO

HENRIETTA

It's Saturday afternoon and Henrietta is sitting at Audrey's computer, picking at a mince pie in a desultory way. There's a scattering of crumbs on the keyboard but she can't be bothered to brush them away. In fact, she doesn't really want this pie at all – Mia brought it over to her this morning, when she saw her sitting all alone at her table in the Grief Café.

Because, at 11 a.m., there had been an awful inevitability to the way that the double doors had opened and only Bonnie had walked in. No Stefan, no Nora and definitely no Annie.

'I bring sad tidings,' Bonnie had said, her face shiny and round. Then she'd quickly added, 'Don't worry, Annie's OK. She just wasn't feeling well. Sends her apologies.' Then Bonnie had taken off her Santa hat, toyed with the white pompom. 'I'm sure she'll be back in the new year, hey?'

Henrietta had felt something cave away inside her. She could picture Annie in her living room, with her row of perfect pebbles and her painting, wearing that impractical silky dressing gown or one of her ludicrous dresses. Then she tried to imagine her sitting there for two more weeks until the new year, and she couldn't, in all honesty, see that happening.

So now she's come upstairs, hiding from the endless loop of Christmas carols playing in the café, and is sitting at Audrey's computer. She's reminded of her blundering enthusiasm a few short weeks ago when she sat here looking up newspaper reports about Kathleen Doyle's disappearance, fancying herself some sort of sleuth, and she feels ashamed.

When she told Annie about Christopher, Annie gave her nothing but sympathy and support. And in return, what has Henrietta done? She's sneaked around behind Annie's back, fossicking for details of a sad death that's none of her business.

Six weeks ago, Henrietta had heard that one word – 'drowned' – and she'd run with it, letting herself imagine all sorts of dreadful things, telling herself she was being superbly efficient, when all she was doing was meddling. And trying to lay a different death to rest.

She nudges the mouse and the screen wakes up. There's a whole slew of new emails she should be going through: people who want to send in their Life Stories or add extra material to reprints. There's a woman who represents a community group in Birmingham suggesting that books should be printed in languages other than English and a man in Manchester offering to make Life Story videos, which might suit some people better. Both good ideas, and she will reply in due course.

Then she notices a rather cluttered row of bookmarks running along the top of the internet browser window: clearly Audrey has been doing some Christmas shopping from the comfort of her swivel chair. Henrietta clicks on each of them, observing that someone on Audrey's list is in line for a pair of thermal socks, while another relative can expect what looks like a pink neck massager in the shape of a rabbit.

The next bookmarks, however, aren't Audrey's. They are for the British Newspaper Archive, the Canal & River Trust and an HSE report on survival times in open water. A wave of shame washes over Henrietta. Audrey hadn't been spying on her – Henrietta had left the evidence of her meddling in plain sight.

She's about to delete each of them when a pretty picture on the screen catches her eye. It's of a family enjoying a day out on their narrowboat, navigating an impressive sequence of locks. When Henrietta had first asked Annie about dredging operations, what she'd had in mind were the Scandi TV dramas she watches, where divers are forever throwing nets into lakes in search of rubbery bodies. Once found, these bodies are winched out of the water, inevitably trussed up in wire or with a limb or two missing.

But now she thinks about it, a canal as shallow as the Grand Union wouldn't really need much dredging. A body would eventually drift towards a lock, where the police would be alerted – and even an officer as lackadaisical as DCI Williams would have had to take action.

Henrietta's fingers move swiftly and efficiently over

the keyboard as she goes back and forth, looking things up, searching for information. The fact that no body had ever been found suddenly seems far more significant than Aidan Doyle's dubious character, Annie's argument with her sister and those unaccounted-for hours on the night of 21 December.

Again, she goes back to the chart showing survival times. If the temperature of the water had been freezing, Kath's chances would have been very slim – her heart would have stopped after around twenty minutes. But if the water wasn't quite so cold, the chart estimates that a person could survive for up to thirty minutes before their internal organs began to shut down.

A crucial factor, she realises, would have been the weather on that night in December 1974. The Met Office has a useful FAQ section that says: *Did you know? . . . We hold records of the weather for every month of every year, stretching back several decades.*

No, Henrietta did not know this. A few clicks later, she discovers that there was no chance of a white Christmas in 1974. In fact, that December was an exceptionally wet month, with inch upon inch of rain. But, most interestingly, it was also unusually mild. The average temperature in London was a positively balmy 12–16°C, the warmest since 1934. 'Roses were still blooming over Christmas,' the Met Office official had felt moved to add. All of which means that while the water in the Grand Union Canal would have been far from pleasant, it was not freezing. Against her better judgement, Henrietta feels a small spark of hope.

Her theory might take a while to follow through,

but that's fine. Henrietta is well aware of her failings, but nobody could say that she is not methodical. She returns to the newspaper archive and begins to tap in various combinations of names – Kath Doyle, Kathleen Doyle and K Doyle – and then different combinations of dates – all of them *after* December 1974.

She remains at Audrey's desk, typing, retyping and cross-checking, and by the time she's reached 1977, she has found fifty-two references to Kathleens, Kaths and female K Doyles in the British press. There are numerous records of gravestones in Ireland and several obituaries, but none are relevant. There's a story about an American actress seen out and about in London and a notice about a schoolgirl in Scarborough who won a poetry competition. There was a Kathleen Doyle on trial for fraud in Durham in 1978, but she is too old to be of interest, so Henrietta keeps looking.

By 4 p.m. she's flagging but decides to give it one last try. And then she finds a small article from 1979 in the *South Wales Guardian* about a planning application to turn an arable field into a campsite. One of the two applicants was a Kathleen Doyle. By now, she's well aware this is a very common name, but it's the other name that jumps out from the pages of tight, grey type, because it's an unusual one. She stares at the dates, does a quick calculation. It's unlikely, but possible. And isn't this what detectives do – follow a hunch because it might lead somewhere?

She puts another search for the two names into the archives of the *South Wales Guardian* and finds a follow-up story with the applicants, a Jeronimo Jones and a Kathleen Doyle, pictured standing in the middle of their field.

Henrietta goes back to Sharon Sharpe's first story in the *Kensington News & Post*, flicks between the two pictures, peering, wondering. The Welsh Kathleen has longer hair and she's wearing bellbottoms and a tie-dye T-shirt, while her friend Jeronimo sports dungarees and a smile that suggests he has been imbibing large quantities of marijuana.

She squints, looks again from one report to the other. These two women don't look exactly the same. But, then again, they don't look entirely different. She searches the two names again in Google, adding 'Brecon' and 'farm' – and page after page of far more recent results spool down her screen. Except these newer ones concern only Jeronimo Jones – there is no further mention of Kathleen Doyle.

But for Mr Jones, that initial planning application was the start of something much bigger because these days he runs his own limited company called Sanctuary Inc., offering holidays and spiritual retreats in the Welsh hills. The Sanctuary website is full of sepia-tinted photographs of people doing soul-enriching activities: gathering around campfires and hiking over hillsides. Yoga and meditation classes are offered in his extended farmhouse and visitors can stay in rustic cabins, a barn, or yurts pitched in a meadow.

On the home page there is a moody shot of this Jeronimo, dressed in white and standing on a rock, silhouetted against a sunset. Underneath, it reads: *Come and be calm with us. Discover Sanctuary – a place, simply, to be.*

It's worth a try. Henrietta reaches for her mobile and taps in the number.

A woman with a whispery voice answers. 'Hi, Willow is taking your call. How may we offer you Sanctuary?'

'Please may I speak with Mr Jones?'

'Ahh, yeah. Actually, maybe no, not really. He's about to welcome guests to our Evergreen winter retreat . . .' The woman's voice tails off, as if she's losing interest.

Henrietta uses her firmest voice. 'It's essential I speak to him. I'll hold.' She starts doodling on Audrey's pink phone pad: manic, sharp shapes that are not at all calm, because she's never felt less relaxed. She feels on the brink of something exciting and hopeful.

'Hi.' Finally, a man's voice comes on the line. 'This is Jeronimo. How may I offer you Sanctuary?'

'Mr Jones? Hello, my name is Henrietta Lockwood and I'm with the Life Stories Project in London. We tell people's life stories, because everyone has one.'

'OK, cool. You need to call back in the new year and ask for Events . . .' he starts. But Henrietta isn't done yet.

'Mr Jones, I'm not interested in booking an event. It's you I need to speak to. It's about someone who may have been known to you in late 1974, perhaps early 1975. I'm enquiring about a Ms Kathleen Doyle. Mr Jones, hello?' But the line has gone dead.

Henrietta rubs her eyes, looks back at the blurry picture from the *South Wales Guardian*. She's still staring at the computer when a knock on the door makes her jump. It's Mia from the café.

'There you are, Hen, I've been looking all over for you,' she says. 'I'm sorry, but it's Annie, she's been brought in. And she's asking for you.'

CHAPTER THIRTY-THREE

ANNIE

As she comes to, it's the familiar beep-beep, beep-beep that tells Annie where she is. There's a drip attached to her arm and a dark blot of blood has soaked through the big square plaster in the crook of her elbow. She's in a different room from before, a smaller one, but she's got a garden view. Is that a good sign or a bad one? Annie's not sure. Either way, she can see a canopy of bare branches reaching into the flat, grey sky.

She realises that the pain is gone – which must be something to do with the drip – but all her limbs feel weighed down, like she might never be able to move them again. Then the bed gyrates, a subtle grinding of gears that comes from under her, deep within the mattress. She asked about it last time and she knows it's to stop bedsores developing.

Annie can't help letting her eyes close again. For once, someone else is looking after her and she feels the warm pleasure of giving in to that. Someone got her ready for bed too because she can see she's wearing a hospital gown with all the shapeliness of a winded balloon. She almost laughs: at least Terry would approve.

Nurses come and go. One wakes her up to show her how to operate the dial on a little box that delivers pain relief through one of the many tubes that seem to run into and out of her body. But every time her eyes close, it's back, closing in all around her. The silt, the stench of sour mud. The thought of the wormy creatures and broken things that must have lain at the bottom of the canal with Kath for so many years now.

The next time she wakes, she hears a sound that makes her want to weep with joy. The rattle of the tea trolley. Mia rounds the corner, parks her trolley and comes straight over to help Annie sit up against her mountain of pillows. Her hands are cool and gentle and Annie realises that no one has touched her like this in a very long time.

'I've told Henrietta you're here, like you asked,' she says.

And then Annie remembers. That is what she was doing, all dressed up in her orange coat that's been put away God knows where. She was coming here for one last session, before it's too late. She realised she couldn't leave it like that with Henrietta, without telling her this last gruesome detail. She's come so far, telling Henrietta so many secrets, why not confess it all – the whole truth and nothing but the truth.

When Annie met Henrietta six weeks ago, she saw the girl as a cypher, a way to leave this world feeling less burdened by her past. But then, week by week, things changed. Henrietta listened and she made notes, but she never passed judgement. She made Annie feel that her words mattered – that Annie's life had mattered.

Henrietta even came to visit her at home, when it was plain that Henrietta Lockwood rarely went anywhere apart from work. And in her own inappropriate, over-enthusiastic way, she had tried to get to the bottom of what had really happened to Kath.

She doesn't think of Henrietta as the Life Story transcriber any more. She thinks of her as her friend. And it's important to be honest with your friends.

'Ah, that's good,' she says, breathing out. 'I need to set the record straight.'

* * *

It's almost dark when Annie wakes again, and she feels sure she had something to say to Henrietta, who is here now, beside her bed. But Annie can't find the right words; they are running away from her, scampering down over the hospital bedcover, across the white mountains of sheets. These sheets that look so much like white cliffs, with rugged, pointed bits and dips and shallows where the sea rushes in, and then her mind loops back from this seaside scene she can see so clearly, as she remembers what she came here to talk about. Why she set off this morning in those silly shiny slipper shoes.

'Henrietta,' she says. 'I need to tell you. About the accident.'

'Annie, none of that matters now. I'm not a hundred per cent sure, but I'm beginning to wonder if there even was an accident . . .' Henrietta says. 'And, if there was, it might not have been fatal.'

Annie doesn't need Henrietta's obtuseness right now – of course it was fatal.

'Come,' she says, and Henrietta leans forward, puts her ear so close that her fluffy hair tickles Annie's nose. She can smell the girl's shampoo, something wholesome and no-nonsense, and it reminds her of the lemon soap their mum always bought, pungent yellow blocks. So hard to work up into a lather first thing in the morning.

But now she's drifting away again and she needs to steer back to shore and say what she came here to say. Get it out, once and for all. The accident.

'When I told you how Terry died, it wasn't quite like that,' she says. 'I saw it coming.'

'Don't worry, Annie. It sounds like his accident was a long time coming.'

'No, I mean the lorry. I saw it. Terry had stepped out of his car. He was looking up at me shouting, always shouting. Always so angry. And I opened my mouth to tell him, "Move, get out of the way", and there would have been time. But then . . . no words came out and I just watched. I watched as the lorry hit. And then it was too late to say anything. Henrietta, I killed him.'

There's a long silence, or maybe she just nodded off again, because Henrietta's voice jolts her awake.

'You didn't kill him,' she says very slowly. 'You just decided not to save him.'

'Yes.'

'And I'm glad of that. Because you saved yourself.'

Then Annie feels the strangest thing, the flutter of a kiss on her forehead. And this time she knows it's safe to let the tiredness sweep back in.

The last thing Annie sees before she plummets down again is Henrietta hunched over a stack of notes written on small pieces of pink paper. She's muttering names and words, as if she's looking for something specific, a piece in a never-ending puzzle.

Minutes later, or it could be days, Henrietta's voice drags her back up from this black, heavy sleep.

'Annie, there's no way to say this without sounding melodramatic. There's something I need to find out. But I'm coming back, so you must wait for me. Please.'

Annie wonders if Henrietta is off to the drinks machine or somewhere further afield. Either way, it's nice, this feeling that someone is looking after her. She reaches out her hand and, to her surprise, Henrietta grasps it tightly.

CHAPTER THIRTY-FOUR

Henrietta

When Henrietta gets home, she finds a Christmas card has been pushed under her flat door. It's from her neighbour Melissa and it has a picture of a snowy country scene. Inside, it reads: *To Henrietta and Dave, Happy Christmas. I'm away until the new year, but let's catch up for a drink soon? Love, Melissa x*

This feels like a message from another world, one where people aren't dying in hospital beds and describing fatal car crashes. Still, it gives Henrietta a warm feeling and she will respond in kind as soon as she can.

But first, she has to finish what she started on Audrey's computer. After seeing Annie lying there, listening to her confess her last dark secret, it's more important than ever to follow this idea through. She opens her laptop and types in the website address for Sanctuary Inc. in Brecon.

She has to send two strongly worded emails and then leave three messages for Jeronimo Jones before he finally calls her back, and it turns out that he is rather less Zen than his website makes out. In Henrietta's opinion, he is verging on paranoid and keeps talking about how he can't allow 'bad vibes' from that time back into his life, and asks several times if she's been a Hells Angel, of all things. It's only when Henrietta reassures him that she wasn't even born in the 1970s and has no desire to ride a motorbike that he agrees to answer her questions. Henrietta is ready, pen in hand, so she can take notes.

'The roots of Sanctuary date back to January 1975, when I and a group of fellow creatives decided to step back from mainstream society and form our own community,' Jeronimo starts.

Henrietta has the distinct impression that this is a story Mr Jones has told many times to far larger crowds. But she's not interested in the earliest campers who arrived or the bands that played in the meadow for free on one 'legendary weekender'. She's only interested in one person.

'I'm sorry to interrupt you, Mr Jones,' she says. 'But please could you confirm if you ever knew a Kathleen Doyle from London?'

The line goes silent and Henrietta is worried that he's put down the phone on her again. But then Jeronimo begins to speak, softly at first.

'Kathleen was a sweet soul,' he says.

Henrietta gasps, presses the phone harder to her ear to make sure she doesn't miss a thing.

'She came to us fortuitously,' continues Jeronimo. 'Guided to us, if you like.'

This is all too nebulous, and Henrietta has no time

for it. 'Could you be a little more precise?' she asks testily.

And so Jeronimo begins to tell Henrietta everything he remembers, right from the first time he set eyes on Kathleen Doyle.

'We had a gig on the Fulham Palace Road in December 1974, the Saturday before Christmas. I say "we", but I wasn't in the band as such. I just drove the van.

'Anyway, the gig was a disaster. The London music scene had changed since the guys last played at The Greyhound and a gang of yobs stormed the stage. Mitch's drum kit got kicked in and they spat and chanted, "Hippies out." It's fair to say there wasn't much peace, love or understanding on the Fulham Palace Road that night.'

Henrietta bites her lip, willing him to get to the point.

'We were meant to stay in a squat in Earls Court,' says Jeronimo. 'But it was rank, so we decided to drive through the night. I'd invited the band back to crash at my place in Wales for Christmas. I said they could stay as long as they wanted, work out some more songs, then hit the festival circuit in the summer.

'The rain was slashing down and I took a wrong turn at a big roundabout. We should have been heading west towards the M4, but we found ourselves going north. I reckoned if I just kept driving I'd see another sign.

'It was Andy who spotted her first. We'd just crossed over some bridge and there she was, by the side of the road, just standing there, like she was stunned or in shock or something.

'I mean, we'd all seen our fair share of stoned, zoned-out and smashed people, but this was something different. It was dark, but Pam noticed that she was wet through, only wearing a thin slip and tights, no shoes or coat.

'So we called out to her, asked if she was OK. She looked over, but it was like a part of her was missing. There was an emptiness, you know? She was just . . . broken.'

'So what did you do?' asks Henrietta.

'I pulled over and Pam wrapped a poncho round her and we sat with her for a bit. She was as cold as stone, shaking and in a bad way. She was soaked, but it wasn't just the rain. There was an odd smell about her, something earthy, and she had mud in her hair.

'She wouldn't – or couldn't – even tell us her name. Andy was keen to get back on the road. We couldn't leave her there – she would have frozen to death. And we didn't know where else to take her: no one trusted the pigs in those days. So she came along. We reckoned that once she'd come down from her trip she could tell us what she wanted to do.'

'And did she?'

'Well, it took a while,' says Jeronimo. 'And she never did tell me how she ended up standing by the side of the road that night, all wet and frozen like she'd come back from the dead. But that was how Kath came to live with me in Wales.

'She came for Christmas and then she stayed on for

five wonderful years. She was my love, my muse. But then things got hairy, when her past caught up with her.'

'So this is definitely a Kathleen Doyle who was born in west London?' Henrietta needs to be sure.

'She never told me about her people. But later some bikers turned up and they were definitely from that part of London: Shepherd's Bush, I think. They kind of took over my place and one of them kept asking questions about Kath. I was weak then, I didn't know how to get rid of them, so Kath just took off one night. Her and her little girl.'

Henrietta has been scribbling down notes, but at this she stops.

'Little girl?' she repeats faintly.

'Yes, I loved them both. I even wrote a song about them: "The Image Of Her Mother". Quite a hit on the folk music circuit.'

'So does that mean . . .'

'Well, yes.' He gives a fake modest laugh. 'I do still play it, on request.'

'No, no,' Henrietta cuts off his nonsense. 'Kath had a baby?'

'Ah, right. Yes, beautiful little girl, she was. We had a naming ceremony for her. And a re-naming ceremony for Kath in our meadow. Kath wanted to be reborn, so she called herself Clover. Clover Meadows.'

'But then she "took off", you say. Did you stay in touch?'

'As my old friend Sting would counsel, setting someone free is a sign of love.'

But perhaps Jeronimo can sense her mounting frustration, because then he tells her something more useful. 'Actually, the word was that she went to Cornwall.'

When Henrietta finally finishes talking to him and puts down her pen, she realises two things. One, she has accidentally stolen Audrey's pink phone pad from her office. And, two, whatever did happen on that mild December night in 1974, Kath Doyle survived.

Dave is lying on the sofa, regarding her with suspicion, but he's going to have to wait a little bit longer for his walk. Henrietta goes back to her laptop and types in the name Jeronimo gave her, Clover Meadows, and then 'Cornwall'. At first, all she finds is a campsite near Newquay by that name and a garden centre, just over the border in Devon. But then she goes on the Companies House website and finds a C Meadows who runs a retail business in a village called Porthawan. This sounds remarkably similar to the place that Annie had talked about visiting as a child. That can't be a coincidence, can it?

There's no website for this shop, only a landline number and, when she rings it, a robotic voice tells her it's no longer in service. Henrietta opens up Street View. After a few dizzying false starts, where she ends up staring at blank sky or down at the gutter, she finds herself navigating the streets of Porthawan, a small, pretty harbour town. And then she finds it: a shabby-looking shop with 'Seachange' spelt out in faded letters. In the window hang several objects fashioned from twigs and feathers, which she believes are called dreamcatchers.

She can't get the image of Annie lying in her hospital bed out of her mind. It's all such a fix and Henrietta badly wants to make it alright, to bring Annie's drowned sister back from the dead, while there's still time. It's a ridiculous idea, perhaps the most ridiculous she's ever had. But if she hurries, she can make the night train from Paddington to Penzance.

Henrietta gets out her backpack and puts in a pair of comfortable slacks, a change of underwear (big pants, for warmth) and her second-favourite sweatshirt (with a penguin on the front). With Melissa away for Christmas, there is no question of leaving Dave behind, so she adds his water bowl, food bowl, his favourite liver snacks and some dog food. Then she puts on his neon dog coat, the one with the least ambiguous message on the side: KEEP AWAY – NOT FRIENDLY.

Logically, she knows it's a very sad situation, but she can't help feeling excited because, for once in her life, Henrietta Lockwood is being adventurous. She's definitely about to contravene several more rules in the Life Stories Handbook, but she wouldn't have it any other way. She is about to do something important, for someone she is very fond of.

* * *

As it's the weekend before Christmas, the ticket price is astronomical and there are no sleeper berths left. She can purchase a seat reservation, though. 'Some people say it's alright for a bit of kip. If you've drunk enough . . .' the man in the ticket office informs her laconically.

However, as they pull out of Paddington, it becomes clear that nobody else on this train has any intention of sleeping. Every single person in her train carriage except Henrietta is determined to get as drunk as they can, pulling slabs of cans out of supermarket carrier bags, ripping open gift-wrapped bottles, popping corks. A woman with flashing fairy lights and a purple feather boa looped around her neck is drinking prosecco straight from the bottle and a group of blokes on the next table are singing football songs. Every few minutes one of them opens a can with a wet 'pfftt' noise. There is belching and laughing and swearing. Someone has brought a music speaker and, by the time the train pulls into Reading, Henrietta is well apprised of what Mariah Carey wants for Christmas.

Henrietta sighs. This will teach her to be impulsive, she thinks, holding Dave close to her and preparing to endure the rest of this long, ill-advised journey. But by Exeter, the carriage thins out. The football boys change trains and the fairy-lights woman has nodded off, the feathers of her boa trembling each time she breathes out.

Henrietta still doesn't dare move, but not because of the sleeping drunks around her. Instead, she is trying very hard not to disturb Dave's unexpected state of calm. Bizarrely, she hasn't heard a peep out of him since they got on the train. She had been so busy rushing to the station, then finding the platform and locating her seat, that she clean forgot about his reactive, antisocial nature.

Thankfully, there are no dogs, bicycles or joggers in this carriage and a short while ago, of his own accord, Dave slid down off her lap and spread himself out in the middle of the aisle, tummy down, grey muzzle resting on his paws. The rocking motion and the heat rising up from the floor seem to soothe him. In fact, Henrietta has never seen him so calm. Perhaps Dave, too, has his own secret backstory, a life before he arrived at Last Chance Dog Rescue that involved many happy hours of travel on an intercity train.

In the end, Henrietta sleeps a bit too, which is just as well because this Cornish Night Riviera service doesn't exactly go like the clappers. At some point it shunts into a railway siding, which was not part of Henrietta's romantic-train-dash-through-the-frosty-night scenario. She wakes to a view of dark freight wagons outlined against the sky, while all around her strangers sleep on, contorted into a variety of uncomfortable positions.

When the train at last creaks into motion, Henrietta has an ache in her neck and can taste the sourness of her breath. She is still unsure about the wisdom of her trip and yet Dave has never looked happier. Life is full of surprises, she reflects as she steps down from the train on to the empty, windswept platform of St Austell Station.

CHAPTER THIRTY-FIVE

Henrietta

Dave is not best pleased at being hustled out of his warm train carriage and into the cold outside world. He gives his ears a good shake, pees up against a lamp post and looks at Henrietta as if to say, what now? Good question, she thinks. It's barely 7 a.m. and the station car park is empty except for a single taxi, with the shape of a large man at the wheel, his chin resting on his round chest. Henrietta raps on the window and steps back smartly when he winds it down. A solid wall of smell wafts out: sweat, cigarettes and old farts.

'Are you available for hire?' she asks, covering her mouth.

The driver shifts in his seat, easing from one buttock to the other. He takes off his glasses and rubs his eyes. 'Can be,' he says at last.

'I would like to go to Porthawan, some six miles from here,' says Henrietta. 'I assume from the state of your vehicle that you will not mind conveying a dog.'

She and Dave sit on the back seat as the taxi glides past the closed shop fronts of St Austell in the gloom.

It's a while later that the car reaches the crest of a hill and the sea appears, a steely grey ribbed with white waves. Above it, the sky is lightening, turning a deep, luminous blue.

'But it's beautiful,' says Henrietta. The cab driver isn't the chatty sort, but she doesn't let that put her off. 'I have never visited this area before. I am more familiar with the coastline of Kent. And of Papua New Guinea.' She regards the thick folds on the back of the driver's neck and realises that this is not one of her better conversational gambits.

'I'm looking for a shop called Seachange,' she says as a last try, and only then does the driver half turn his head.

'Ah. She's a good sort, is Cerys,' he says. 'Used to work on the minicabs, till Clover got cancer. Terrible to lose her mum so quick. Must be a year ago now.'

The car veers left then right, following the weave of the high-hedged road, and Henrietta considers this information. It feels like a physical thing that she needs to examine, something hard and weighty.

She thinks of Annie lying between starched sheets waiting for news, and she needs to cover her mouth again. Not because of the taxi's smell but because she has to choke back a sob at the shame of it, the waste.

She's too late, and Kath Doyle, the woman she's been chasing, is already dead. The lost woman with long dark hair, who she has been imagining ever since she first heard her name, is gone. Over the past six weeks, Henrietta has built up a whole personality for this woman. She knows it's stupid, but she felt as if she knew her.

Then, after talking to Jeronimo, Henrietta had pictured meeting this woman, taking her back to London so she could be reunited with Annie.

And now, none of that is going to happen. She's missed Kath not even by a whisker, but by a whole year.

As the taxi driver changes gear to start his descent down a steep hill, she forces herself to think about the other thing he said – that the daughter is still here. There is a niece, at least, for Annie. Something else about the taxi driver's words is troubling Henrietta, hovering on the edge of her consciousness, but she's foggy with fatigue and it spins away again, out of reach.

* * *

The driver lets them out at the harbour, but points out the lane where they will find Seachange. She decides it's best if she and Dave sit on a bench outside a fish and chip shop until 8 a.m., which feels like a more respectable time to go knocking on someone's door delivering life-changing news.

The shop is set between white-painted cottages, but Henrietta isn't sure if she's got the right address because the shop doesn't look like it did on Street View: it's more dilapidated and the shop sign says 'Seacha'. At first she wonders if this is a Cornish word, but then realises it's just that someone has let the painted letters flake away. The dreamcatchers are still in the window, but they look faded and dusty. Seachange does not appear to be a thriving business.

Dave shakes his ears again and yawns and Henrietta

knows she can't put this off any longer. There's nothing as useful as a doorbell, so she raps on the door with her cold knuckles. She can see a shadow moving around inside, a slight figure.

Then the door opens and she finds herself facing a small woman with cropped hair, wrapped in what looks very much like a horse blanket. Henrietta hasn't worked out what she's going to say, but the woman in the doorway doesn't seem in the least bit surprised by her arrival.

'If you're owed money, there's none left,' she says, pulling the blanket tighter around her. 'You're not the first and you won't be the last, but my mum's gone. The shop is about to go under and I've got nothing. So you may as well sod off.'

Not the welcome she was expecting.

'Hello, I am Henrietta Lockwood and I am with the Life Stories Project in London,' Henrietta says.

'Wow,' says the woman in the horse blanket, her eyes widening. 'Talk about personal service. You must really like my idea.'

And then, through her tiredness, Henrietta feels the distant clunk of something dropping into place. This is the woman who sent an email about doing Memory Books. The one who lost her mother a year ago.

'Ah. You must be Cerys. Cerys Meadows. Perhaps I can come in and explain?'

Cerys sighs, opens the shop door wider. 'Be my guest.'

* * *

Cerys is a chatty sort, which is just as well because Henrietta is still gathering her thoughts. Unfortunately, Cerys doesn't have any coffee, just raspberry tea, and Henrietta perches on the edge of a beanbag while Cerys boils the kettle. This is an unconventional seating option, but as she looks around she can see that nothing about this place is conventional. The walls of the flat above the shop are hung with Indian throws, there are piles of cushions embroidered with shiny mirrors and every flat surface is covered with battered paperback books, chipped cups or smeared plates. Dave is happy because he's discovered a rich seam of crumbs buried deep within the folds of a rag rug.

'So, I'm glad you liked my idea. But I'm afraid I haven't even started my mum's Memory Book,' Cerys calls out from the kitchen. 'It's not the easiest time, after you've lost someone. No one tells you, do they? How grief is a sort of madness. One minute you're firing off emails to someone in London about this great idea, the next you can't even get out of bed.'

Henrietta is trying to work out how to tell Cerys that although her Memory Book idea is a good one, it does not merit a 300-mile journey to meet her in person, six days before Christmas. 'Actually, this isn't about the Memory Book. I have come to notify you of a relative who may be unknown to you. As a matter of some urgency.'

Cerys comes and stands in the doorway of the kitchen, with her hands on her hips. When she speaks, her voice is cold and flat. 'No, that's wrong. I don't have any family. You've got your facts wrong.'

She is talking fast and hard and, sensing a change in the atmosphere, Dave starts building up to one of his deep, throaty growls.

'Sorry, bit of a sore point,' Cerys says. 'But, as I say, you've got it all wrong. My dad is out of the picture and my mum lost touch with her family when she was young. She grew up in care in Wales.'

Henrietta knows diplomacy is not her forte. So she decides to just say it.

'Cerys, your mum didn't grow up in care. Or in Wales. She grew up in Dynevor Road in west London and she had a mother, a father and a sister. Her sister, Annie, was eleven months older than her and they were very close. In 1974, your mother had some kind of accident and ended up travelling to Wales. With a man called Jeronimo.'

'Jeronimo,' Cerys echoes, as if that name makes some sense to her.

'Then your mother brought you to Cornwall. All this time, your mother's family thought she was dead. Your grandparents died a while ago, but your aunt, Annie, is still alive. She never stopped thinking about your mum. And I think she would love to meet you.'

Cerys is running her hands over her short, spikey hair, walking up and down this small room.

Henrietta keeps going. 'But Annie is very ill. If you want to meet her, we need to go back to London as soon as possible. Today, in fact.'

At this, Cerys stops pacing. 'I don't even know who you are. You could be making all this up. You could be a complete nutter, you and your dog.'

She takes a step towards Henrietta, who is gradually losing her purchase on the slippery beanbag, her bottom sliding closer to the floor.

'If you know so much, what's my mum's name then, eh? Tell me that.'

Henrietta's bottom has now reached the floor and she lands on it with a soft thud. 'Your mother changed her name to Clover Meadows when she lived in Wales. In a naming ceremony. It took place in a meadow, clearly. But the name she was born with was Kathleen Doyle. Everyone called her Kath.'

Cerys turns, walks out of the room and slams the bedroom door. Dave and Henrietta look at each other, neither sure what to do next.

Eventually, Henrietta gets to her feet. She shouldn't be surprised, really, that she's messed this up, like everything else. She will have to go and see if there is anywhere in this town to buy a coffee and then she will set about finding a taxi to take her back to the station.

Then the bedroom door opens and Cerys walks out. She's wearing a tracksuit and carrying a sports bag.

'Right, best get going. I've called Clive the cabby, he's picking us up outside in five.'

CHAPTER THIRTY-SIX

HENRIETTA

Back at St Austell Station, Henrietta taps her credit card code into the ticket machine and notes that Great Western Railway is doing rather well from this turn of events. She's spotted an overweight Labrador slumped on the floor nearby, so she's keeping a tight hold on Dave's lead, ready for the usual barrage of barking and snarling to start. But Dave barely seems to notice the dog. Instead, he's got his nose in the air, as if trying to sniff out the approaching train.

Sitting either side of a table in Quiet Carriage A, Henrietta supposes she and Cerys might make an unusual-looking pair. One is a solid and broad woman in easy-fit slacks and her second-favourite sweatshirt, depicting a penguin. The other looks more like a gangly child with cropped hair, huge eyes and skinny arms sticking out of a vintage Nike tracksuit top. Only the most astute observer (Henrietta) would spot the neat bulge of pregnancy hidden under Cerys's baggy top. On the floor between them, Dave is already fast asleep, soothed by the rocking motion of the train.

Because she left in a rush, Henrietta hasn't brought anything to read, but Cerys seems better prepared. She's had her earbuds in ever since they left Porthawan but she's also brought a well-thumbed crime novel with a huge shiny dagger on the front. 'You're never alone with a book, as my mum would say,' she explains. It's not long, though, before she pulls out her earbuds and puts her book face down on the table.

'This is doing my head in,' Cerys says. 'Like really doing my head in. My whole life, my mum said she was born in Wales, then her dad kicked her out when she was a teenager. She was in care for a bit then met Jeronimo and lived on his commune. Then there were some bad vibes on the commune so we came here, to Cornwall. Whenever I asked my mum about her family, she always fobbed me off. My mum was . . . vulnerable, I suppose you could call it, so after a while, I stopped asking. I didn't want to make things any harder for her.'

Henrietta thinks about how Jeronimo described Kath rising from the dead covered in silt and weeds, teeth chattering, cold to her bones. Then she thinks back to what she knows about Kath's home life and the possible reasons why she might have decided to keep running on that night in December. How those reasons might have depended on who she met down by the canal and how she ended up in the water.

'Maybe your mum found it hard to talk about the past. It takes time for things to come out.'

Cerys pouts like a sulky boy. 'Yeah, well, clearly nothing did come out, did it? Not ever. My mum's gone now and she left me thinking I had no one.'

Henrietta can't think of an answer to that so she keeps quiet. But Cerys is just getting into her stride.

'And what about this long-lost family, too? What was to stop them coming to find me?'

Henrietta considers what happened to the Doyle family after Kath disappeared. Annie, who rushed into an abusive marriage. Their mother, Deidre, who took to her bed and never recovered, and their father, Aidan, so broken that he cut every reminder of Kath out of his life, including Annie.

'When your mum went missing, it was the undoing of them, that's what Annie said. They thought she was dead and, in their own ways, each of them gave up on life.'

Cerys turns her head away and they both look out of the window at the dank landscape of ploughed fields, a low-lying fog blanking out the hills beyond. Gradually, the fog clears and the fields give way to marshy sandbanks. On one bleak stretch, the silhouette of a stranded boat stands out, its hull exposed like bare ribs.

'So, what's she like then, my Aunt Annie?' asks Cerys.

Henrietta chooses her words with care. 'Annie is a remarkable woman. She was dealt a very poor hand in life but coped with it admirably. I am proud to be helping Annie tell her story. Actually' – she pauses – 'I am proud to think of her as my friend.'

'She sounds a bit like my mum, then – shit life, strong woman. My mum had it hard and she made some mistakes. She didn't have the best taste in men, for a start.'

Henrietta nods. Somehow this is not surprising. 'And your father? You mentioned you weren't in contact.'

'Ha.' Cerys's laugh sounds more like a bark and Dave looks up briefly before flopping back down on to the floor. 'Least said about him the better. Jeronimo Jones never bothered to keep in touch with me or my mum. "Jeronimo was only interested in Jeronimo," that's what my mum used to say.

'He didn't want to see me when I was little, so I didn't try to find him when my mum died. I didn't look up many of her old friends, actually . . .' She trails off. 'It wasn't the easiest time. Organising her funeral.'

'I can imagine it would be a time of great stress,' Henrietta says. She decides not to mention that she spoke to Jeronimo Jones only yesterday and he had, indeed, sounded like a remarkably self-absorbed man.

Cerys is looking at her in an odd way. 'Do you realise, you talk like you're reading from a leaflet?'

'It has been commented upon,' says Henrietta with a sniff.

'Anyway, I decided to skip a heart-to-heart with Jeronimo,' says Cerys, pulling her tracksuit zip up to the very top, tucking her chin inside. 'I've had enough of people's empty words. Everyone around town saying sorry for my loss. Then asking if I have plans for the shop, when what they mean is what will I do about it because I'm up to my eyes in debt.'

Henrietta had noticed that Seachange looked a little forlorn.

'So, your mum ran her own business?' Henrietta says instead.

'She did. She opened the shop when I was ten and it always did OK, although I've no idea how. But there's not a big market for loon pants and bongs these days, even in Cornwall. For the past few years, the shop's been haemorrhaging. I can't find any accounts books and I never got a chance to ask my mum about the money side before she died. It happened so fast . . .'

Henrietta looks in her bag for a tissue.

'Sorry, I'm a bit hormonal,' Cerys says. 'Plus, I just miss her. It still hurts so much.'

It's a relief to see the refreshment trolley trundling its way along the aisle, so Henrietta busies herself shifting Dave's tail from its path, finding her purse and, finally, purchasing a cup of coffee and a snack. She's about to say grief is the price we pay for love but, although it's true, it does sound like something from a Life Stories leaflet, so she resists. Instead, she opens her KitKat, snaps it and slides half across the table.

'Ah, top choice. Thanks,' says Cerys. 'And thanks for coming all this way. Annie must mean a lot to you.'

CHAPTER THIRTY-SEVEN

CERYS

Henrietta has promised to give her a call as soon as they are allowed to go on to the ward and see Annie again. Cerys waited with her in the corridor for as long as she could bear it, but then she had to get up and start moving. It's barely a year since her mother died and somehow she's ended up in yet another hospital, breathing in the same antiseptic air, about to see the same thing happen all over again. And she couldn't take it. 'Just taking a break. Back soon,' she told Henrietta.

So now Cerys is doing what she always does when life gets too much, she's walking. She doesn't want to stray too far from the hospital, so she's walking round and round the same block, her trainers slapping on the dark, wet pavement. It's not like at home, where the air holds the tang of briny sea or the earthy loam of the hills. Here, it's all hard surfaces and blank-faced people going about their ordinary lives on the Monday before Christmas.

When she was younger, the idea of going on a country walk never entered Cerys's head. It was what tourists did, those silver-haired couples in bright jackets who clattered past the shop with walking poles, peering at plastic-covered maps.

But from the day she found out that she was pregnant, Cerys felt an urgent need to keep moving, fuelled by a nervous energy. So each day she headed out on the coastal path, almost enjoying the ache in her legs because it showed that her body was working, doing its job and sending oxygen-rich blood to the small cluster of cells that was taking shape inside her. She liked to imagine the twin hearts in her body: her own steady thud and then its tiny companion, a faster, frantic beat, determined to stay alive.

Once she was up on the cliff path, walking helped her think – or not think, depending on her mood. She liked the way that the sounds around her changed according to whether the path faced the sea or dipped down into a hollow. At exposed points, the drag of the shingle stones on the beach became a roar in her ears and the wind blasted her face, drowning out everything. But then she would turn a corner and the world would go quiet, like the volume dial had been flicked to zero.

On those near-silent stretches, she let herself go back into her head, testing how she felt about the baby growing inside her and the decision she still had time to make. She's pretty sure she's made the right choice – after all, it was the one her mum made, and she coped. Most of the time. And her mum had been a hell of a lot younger than Cerys when she got pregnant. She'd been eighteen.

But Cerys isn't in Porthawan any more, she's in the

middle of London, and there's nowhere to go when you want to be on your own and let the thoughts rise up and then, gradually, dampen down. There are people everywhere, and if you dare to slow the pace they keep coming behind you, tut-tutting or swearing at you for getting in their way.

Yesterday already feels unreal: stepping on to the platform at Paddington Station, the rush and noise, then taking the Tube straight to the hospital. It was past visiting hours, but Henrietta managed to sneak them in, just for a few minutes.

And there she was, this thin little woman called Annie, who was family, proper family at last. She was sleeping, but seeing her face was a punch to the gut, because she looked so much like Cerys's mum.

It was nice of this Henrietta to let her crash on her sofa last night, but she barely slept because her head was a mad jumble of thoughts. Plus, the sofa cushions smelled of meaty dog treats, which didn't help.

So now Cerys is just going to keep walking around the streets of this insanely rich part of London, waiting until 2 p.m., when visitors are allowed in. She passes the gate to a small park, but it's all black railings and tarmac paths, with kids on scooters zooming from all directions, and she can see there's no space in there to just sit and think. She keeps going, passing a huge branch of Marks & Spencer, once, twice, then three times, hearing a blast of Christmas music each time. And each time, it makes her more furious.

She can't deal with another death now, especially when it's a person she's only just met but who should have been part of her life since she was a baby. She's angry at her mum for letting all this happen, for lying about her past and cutting Cerys off from the family she could have known all along.

Cerys has always thought of Wales as her roots. She's lost count of the number of times people have asked, 'How come you're Cornish but you've got a Welsh name?' Was it really so hard to figure out? She and her mum had lived in Wales until Cerys was five and her memories of the commune are sketchy, like a video with jumpy edits. Jeronimo with his long hair and blue dungarees, a droopy roll-up always hanging off his bottom lip. She remembers his pet sheep better – it followed him everywhere he went, even into the farmhouse, barging the toddler Cerys out of the way and leaving neat piles of droppings on the stone floors.

'Jeronimo gave me sanctuary,' her mum always used to say. 'When I had nowhere to go.'

But now it turns out she did have people, parents and a sister called Annie. It hurts so much that Cerys will never get to know her aunt, who sounds pretty cool, truth be told. What had happened that was so terrible that her mum couldn't go home, even years later? None of it makes any sense.

And right now, the thought of going back into that hospital room to watch as death creeps closer is one thing too many to bear. Almost a year ago, in the hospital in Cornwall, she kept asking the nurses, 'How long? Just tell me how long before she dies.' They wouldn't be drawn, they said everyone's time was different. But now she's seen it happen once, Cerys is pretty sure she can recognise the signs for herself. She knows that Annie is on her way.

She'd stayed with her mum through that long night, holding her hand and trying to block out the sound of her breathing as it got more laboured. After a few hours, it became hypnotic: the sound of air being sucked in, then an awful rasping as it came out again. At one point, her breathing became more like a bellowing. It was a sound Cerys had never heard before, an animal keening, something primal and basic. It was as if, once Clover had gone beyond words, it was her only way to say, 'I'm here, I'm still here.'

Cerys had panicked, run out to ask for help. 'I think she's in pain. She's trying to shout – can't you give her something?'

But the nurse was unfazed. 'She's on morphine, my lovely. Don't worry, she can't feel anything.' She stood next to Cerys at the end of the bed and nodded towards Clover. 'If you look at your mum's face, it's very calm. She looks peaceful.'

Cerys wasn't so sure, because that deep, lowing noise was still coming and it didn't sound remotely peaceful, but she wanted to believe it was true. In that stuffy room, as she carried on watching her mum's chest rising and falling, it was as if Cerys, too, was trapped between two worlds. Wanting her mum to keep breathing and simultaneously, guiltily, willing her to slow down and just stop, because the end had to come. It was just a matter of time.

The clock hands moved round. Two different nurses came to 'make Clover more comfortable'. They sent Cerys out of the room for that bit, and she had an inkling that it was something to do with bodily fluids. Then, as the weak winter sun came up, they left Cerys alone with her mum and there was a terrible kind of relief when, finally, Clover's breathing began to ease. The cries faded into sighs. The gaps between them became longer. And then there were no more breaths.

Cerys had leaned forward to stroke her mum's hair and kiss her cheek. She was shocked to discover that, already, Clover's skin was cooling. She noticed that her mum's jaw had dropped wide open, showing her bottom row of teeth. And in that moment she realised that it wasn't Clover lying there any more. All that remained in that hospital bed was a small, narrow body made of bones, teeth and cooling blood.

She hasn't shared that memory with anyone and she doesn't know if she ever will. All this dying is making her heart ache and it's not right. She can feel the grief gathering inside her again and it's not fair on her unborn baby, who doesn't deserve all this pain seeping through, before she's even taken her first breath.

She walks past Marks & Spencer for the fourth time and hears a blast of music that's unavoidable at this time of year – George Michael is singing about last year's Christmas and he's hitting her where it really hurts. She doesn't want to start crying out here on the street where everyone can see, so she looks at the window display very hard, waiting for the moment to pass.

There's a stack of fake presents in the shop window, boxes piled high and tied up with ribbons, and the glass itself is covered in huge white decals in the shape of snowflakes. She and her mum used to make snowflake decorations, but they never looked as perfect as these ones. They used to cut them out from the pages of the free local paper and stick them up in the front window at Bessie's. Bessie was their landlady and they lived in a bedsit at the top of her house until her mum got the shop.

Even when they had no money, her mum always made sure Cerys had a stocking at the end of her bed. It might be filled with junk her mum had found in the charity shops – soft toys with missing eyes, once a tiny white china horse – or useful things, like a new tin opener.

Cerys knows she had what her teachers called 'a chaotic childhood'. There wasn't always food in the cupboards and, when there was, her mum hadn't always paid for it. Then there were her poor boyfriend choices. Jeronimo, the dad who was never there for her. Later came Vic ('Call me Uncle Vic'), a flash bloke with a flash car. He'd helped set her mum up with the shop, but never let her forget it. He always popped up when you least expected him and set her mum's nerves jangling, so she was all hard edges and tight smiles.

Then Roy came on the scene and things felt easier, like everyone stopped holding their breath. But then, without any warning, he took off and it was back to Vic, with his sideburns and his cold blue eyes that followed her mum's every move. Yes, her mum had made some bad choices, but Cerys had always known she wasn't one of them. 'You and me, Cerys, we're a team,' her mum would say. 'Like sisters.'

CHAPTER THIRTY-EIGHT

ANNIE

She had what the nurses are calling 'a good night', which must mean she slept for parts of it. And when Mia brings her a cup of tea first thing, she almost believes that this soft, hazy time can go on forever, this limbo of waking up to try a sip of tea or a spoonful of ice cream and then nodding off again. But then she lifts the sheet up and sees how her limbs have ballooned up and her skin has turned an almost luminous yellow. That's her liver packing up, then.

The next time she wakes, Henrietta is here, lovely Henrietta, who has come back from the drinks machine. And she's telling her the oddest story. Annie tries very hard to listen, but the names and the years are all wrong, the now and the then sliding into each other. She's talking about someone called Jeronimo, a silly name if ever there was one and not someone she would ever know, and Annie is about to let herself sink down deeper into the velvety warmth when she hears Kath's name.

She needs to focus, to listen harder, but these words

don't make any sense.

'Kath didn't die in 1974. She got herself out of the water just in time. Then a folk band in a camper van picked her up and she hitched a ride to Wales. She was soaked through – even her hair was clogged with mud.'

Annie can taste the mud; she can smell it. It's been with her ever since that night, an echo of what she has always known, deep in her bones, that her sister struggled against. 'Silt,' she wants to say, but all that comes out is a 'Sss . . .' noise.

'The commune was run by Jeronimo, and he loved your sister. They had a baby and Kath gave herself a new name and everything. Then she left him and started over again in Cornwall.'

The drugs are making everything so soft and easy, but she's finding it hard to catch these words as they drift by.

'New name,' she tries to say, but she can't get further than 'Nnn . . .'

She needs Henrietta to slow down, to start again, because she's hearing the words 'Kath' and 'baby' and 'Cornwall' and she wants to hang on to them. Annie struggles to open her eyes.

'And that's where I've been, Annie. I'm so sorry, I was too late for Kath. But I've found her daughter.'

Oh, bless this Henrietta with her doggedness, her strange way of showing love, the way she never lets go of an idea. She's telling her such a wonderful story, about Kath running away to live in Cornwall, and it makes perfect sense because she can imagine her there. It would be like their very best holiday together.

Rubbing cream into Kath's shoulders, freckled and turning brown. Kath's warm hands doing the same for her.

Finding pebbles on the beach, lining up two matching rows of stones. How, like the two of them, these stones looked identical from afar, but up close they were quite different. The taste of salt. Sun too bright. Seagulls wheeling. The sky an impossible blue. And as Annie thinks of Kath living that life every day for all these years, she smiles and closes her eyes.

When she next wakes, Mia is there and she's saying something about a special visitor who will be here at 2 p.m. so Annie should try to stay awake for that. But then Mia says a Welsh name that means nothing, so she lets that one float off, surrenders to the drowsiness.

The sleep she's getting right now is the best ever: it's as blank and clean as the sheets that someone tucks around her and just as smooth. Because Annie has had enough bad dreams to last her a lifetime. Often they start with her walking along a dark towpath, knowing that she has to watch out for the slimy, mossy patches underfoot. No matter how careful she is, she knows that sooner or later she'll slip, then wake with a jolt before she hits the water.

In another dream, she's already in the water and something is tangled in her hair, dragging her down fast and hard, and her mouth is stopped up with mud. Because that's what she imagined happened to Kath all those years ago and she's never been able to get those thoughts out of her head, awake or asleep. Thinking of how Kath would have struggled as the mud sucked her down and the black waters closed over her head.

But no, now she remembers that Henrietta told her it didn't happen that way. That Kath didn't end up at the bottom of a canal, a bloated jumble of bones and bleached skin, sinking deeper into the silt. Yes, she went into the water at some point, and nobody knows why. But the important thing is that Kath had the sense to pull herself out and give herself another chance. She escaped. And, for that, Annie is glad.

When Annie next wakes, the air feels different: denser yet softer around her. She gets it now, why people take drugs – it makes everything so easy. She would love a sip of juice, but she can't form the right words.

She hears the shush-shush of a nurse's tights, the creak of the door, voices as someone writes notes on her chart. She hears them say it's the twenty-first of December and she thinks, of course it is. It's the solstice, the darkest day, but also the turning point because from now on the days get lighter and longer. Although not for her.

A while later – it could be minutes or hours – she opens her eyes and Kath is sitting beside her bed, which is a nice surprise. 'You've come to wave me off, then,' Annie tries to say, but all that comes out is the 'w' of wave. She tries again. She wants to say, 'Come to the edge of the water with me, come down to the sand.' Because now it feels like she's taking slow steps into the sea. The warm water is lapping at her tummy and soon it'll be up to her chest, when she'll have to make a little jump and start swimming properly.

But the funny thing is that this person looks like Kath but also she doesn't, which is confusing but also fine. She's cut her hair very short – it suits her – and she's crying. Annie wishes she wouldn't, because she's glad that this Kath-but-not-Kath person is here and that she can carry on living even if Annie can't on this, the darkest day. She never stopped thinking about Kath, missing her, and now, at last, she's come back.

Then Annie lets herself slip under, beneath the waves. Because this water isn't like the sort that's haunted her dreams for years. It's not dark and foul, like the canal. This time, it's the sea and the water is warm and blue and it sparkles. So she's swimming, panting, trying to keep breathing so that she can reach a resting place. But there isn't one in sight so she just keeps going, keeps breathing in and out, trying to keep her head above water.

But then she realises that it doesn't matter because she can breathe fine underwater – why didn't she know this before? So she lets herself sink down through the clear water to the sandy bottom and then she realises that down here you don't need to breathe at all and so she stops.

CHAPTER THIRTY-NINE

HENRIETTA

Audrey has told her to take some extra time off if she needs to. She sent Henrietta an email saying that grief is an inevitable part of the job and that the Life Stories Project prides itself on being an understanding employer. She also congratulated Henrietta on locating Annie's long-lost relative in time to say goodbye: 'Just the kind of thoughtful touch we like to encourage,' she said.

Henrietta decided not to mention that tracking down Annie's niece had involved several hours of research, a tense telephone conversation with a man in Wales and a 600-mile round trip to Cornwall. 'Oh, it was nothing. I just looked her up on the internet,' she told Audrey.

It is two days since that awful afternoon when Henrietta and Cerys sat and watched the life drain from Annie. She'd read up on it beforehand – she likes to be prepared – and had been expecting to witness something significant and spiritual. A change in room temperature, or a hovering light above Annie's bed to signify her soul leaving, perhaps. But she must have been reading some fanciful websites because, when it came, the end of Annie's life was the opposite of momentous. There was no crescendo of music, no harps or angels. One minute Annie was there, fading but definitely still a person. And then, with the next out-breath, all her Annie-ness simply evaporated. And Henrietta didn't feel a moment of spiritual understanding, just a heart-crushing absence.

She wishes she could say she'd maintained her professional decorum, but she hadn't. She'd cried big, mouth-open sobs and Cerys had been the one to take control, guiding her into the family room. Then she'd brought her up some tea and cake and when Henrietta saw the slice of Bakewell tart, it set her off all over again because she knew Annie was never coming back.

Since then, Cerys has been staying with Henrietta, but this morning they're back at the Rosendale, waiting in the Grief Café, of all places. They have a midday appointment upstairs with the ward sister, where they will pick up the medical certificate and a bag of Annie's belongings.

There's no sign of Mia today – she must be off for Christmas – so it's Morose Mike on duty.

'Funny seeing you here without your forms and your Thermos flask,' he says to Henrietta.

She tries to raise a smile. But he's right, she does feel quite lost here without her paperwork and her laminated sign. And without Annie.

'Heard about Mia and Stefan, I suppose?' Mike has a big grin on his face – in fact he's looking the opposite of morose. 'Having Christmas away together. A romantic break in Scotland, apparently. Then meeting Stefan's folks for New Year.'

'That's nice,' says Henrietta vaguely. For an instant she thinks, I must tell Annie, before she remembers. Instead, she says to Cerys, 'Annie got on very well with Mia. She was a good friend.'

Cerys nods. She's wearing a baggy football top today, sitting with her legs apart and cleaning her nails with a leaflet about Writing Your Will. Her top makes it harder to spot her rounded tummy, which Henrietta supposes Cerys will talk about when the time is right.

'Shall we get this over and done with, then?' Henrietta stands first and then the two of them head towards the lifts.

The official stuff is straightforward and when the ward sister gives them a booklet about arranging a funeral, Cerys pockets it quickly. 'I'm a dab hand these days,' she says. It's the big plastic bag of Annie's belongings that's harder to deal with.

There isn't much in there – Mia said that Annie had only intended to pop into the centre to see Henrietta. Inside the bag is the dress she was wearing and a woollen coat. There's an old leather purse, her travel pass and the keys to her flat. Finally, there's a pair of sequinned slippers, the soles quite worn away and still damp from the London pavements. 'Size five,' says Cerys, holding them tenderly, turning them over and touching the parts that have moulded to the shape of Annie's feet. 'Same as my mum.'

Outside the Rosendale, they stand on the steps and

Cerys lifts the set of keys out of the plastic bag. 'Come on. Can't do any harm, can it?' she says. So instead of turning left for the bus back to Henrietta's they turn right and take the Tube to Annie's flat.

On the train, the deep rumble and the clatter of the train carriages is so loud there's no chance of talking. Not for the first time, Henrietta realises that Cerys is, to all intents and purposes, a perfect stranger, yet they've been in each other's company for the best part of four days now and seem to rub along OK. She likes how Cerys is matter-of-fact about things: she says what she means, which takes the guesswork out of human interactions. Henrietta feels relaxed around her. Well, she is Annie's niece, after all.

The rocking of the train carriage puts her in mind of how Dave has been easier company since their return from Cornwall. It's as if he's been reminded of another life, with a different way of behaving. Yesterday, Henrietta looked on a local map and found a new dog walk, a footpath that runs alongside the railway line where the overground trains going into London Bridge slow down and wait for the signals to change. She and Dave stood there for a good hour, trainspotting through a chain-link fence. Dave was entranced; he even wagged his tail. Henrietta was so cheered by this that when she saw a fellow dog walker in the distance, she waved and called out, 'Hello! This is Dave! He adores trains!' She'll get the hang of dog walkers' etiquette yet.

As she and Cerys walk towards Annie's flat, Henrietta finds she is in an odd position of knowing where they are going, while Cerys, whose family is actually from these streets, has never been here before. 'Annie told me this is an area that was once very poor and is now very rich,' she says as they pass a row of pastel-coloured townhouses.

Cerys is unusually quiet, as if she's taking it all in. When at last she speaks, she says, 'So I guess my mum would have walked this way lots of times. And Annie. And my grandparents.'

'Yes, your mum grew up nearby in a terraced house in Dynevor Road. Sadly, it's no longer here. I looked it up and the entire road was bulldozed in the 1980s. There's a private gym there now. With spa treatments.'

They turn a corner and arrive at Ash Tree Court. Cerys gets the keys out, but neither of them wants to make the first move.

'This is going to be strange,' says Henrietta. 'I still can't believe she's gone.'

'I'm afraid your mind plays tricks on you for quite a while,' Cerys replies.

Henrietta decides it's time to be strong for them both. 'It's the front ground-floor flat. I'll lead the way.'

CHAPTER FORTY

CERYS

She'd thought that nothing could top the events of the past few days, but standing in her aunt's flat is the weirdest experience. She's never set foot in this place and yet everything about it is familiar. There's a painting on the wall of a beach, not unusual in itself, but something about the colour of the cliffs and their angle reminds Cerys of home.

Then there's a sparse array of objects arranged on the mantelpiece, the kind of things that her mum used to collect, too. A tiny toy figure, waving; a broken fragment of a willow pattern plate, its edges smoothed and worn; a pill box painted with golden marigolds. Then she turns and sees the row of pebbles, arranged in order from a pea-sized orb to a stone the size of a golf ball. Each one is perfectly round and grey and they make total sense to Cerys because her mum had some exactly like that in her bedroom.

There's a ringing in her ears and a floaty feeling that means she needs to sit down and soon, so she drops into the only armchair. When she turns her head, even the cushion by her cheek smells familiar.

'This is a bit like my mum's place,' she manages. 'But about a hundred times tidier.'

Henrietta doesn't say anything; she just waits. Cerys likes this about her, the way Henrietta doesn't natter away making pretend conversation; she can't stand that.

She gets up again, peers into the corridor and goes into the kitchen. 'Wow. Everything is so clean and neat. I wonder if Annie and my mum shared a room when they were younger? If they did, I bet it drove Annie mad. My mum was so messy.'

'Annie moved here two years ago. I get the feeling she wanted this to be a fresh start.'

Since Henrietta arrived in Porthawan with her penguin sweatshirt, her deranged dog and her dogged manner, Cerys has barely thought about her Memory Book idea. But looking around, she senses that there will be plenty of clues to her mum's backstory right here in this flat.

What she's not ready to think about right now are the gaps – why her mother never introduced her to the family Cerys deserved to know and why she lied about where she was from. Every time she starts to pull at these loose strands, her heart beats faster and her throat closes up. She wants to magic her mum back to life so she can rage at her and shout, 'How could you? You kept so much from me. And then you left me.'

It's later that she and Henrietta find the notebooks and the photos. On the floor next to Annie's bed is a small notepad that Henrietta says she recognises from the Life Story sessions. There is a stack of photo albums on the bedside table and, on top of them, a small pile of pictures has been set aside.

'So she did find some after all,' Henrietta says quietly.

Cerys starts with the loose photos that her aunt must have picked out. She's never seen pictures of her mum when she was young, but here she is, living a whole life Cerys knew nothing about. Her mum had always let her imagine that she'd grown up in Wales, but instead, here she is aged fourteen outside a grey London church in a white confirmation dress with her mum, her dad and a sister who looks just like her.

Another, tucked in an envelope, shows her mum standing beside her bike, holding the handlebars and smiling. Then there are some photos of the two sisters sitting on a beach and Cerys instantly recognises it. It's the one near Porthawan and must be the whole reason why Clover moved them there. A place that must have reminded her mum of happy times.

Henrietta finds another album full of photos taken at the nursery where Annie worked. There are some sweet ones where she's surrounded by kids who clearly adored her and together they choose some of the nicest ones for the Life Story book.

Underneath those, they find a couple of smaller plastic books, more like flimsy wallets, the sort that chemists used to give away free with each order of photos. Cerys opens one, sees a blur of a too-blue sky, then a face that makes her heart lurch. She snaps it shut because it makes no sense, none at all.

She opens it again, in case she imagined it. The photo is of a car, the same one that used to pull up outside the shop on a Friday night with a low, steady purr. When the engine cut and the car door slammed, that was Cerys's signal to kiss her mum goodnight and go to her room. In this photo, leaning over the bonnet of this car and polishing it, is Vic.

She keeps going. On the next page is a photo of Annie on Brighton Pier, shielding her eyes from the sun and, again, there's Vic, standing next to her. He's even wearing his leather coat, the one that smelt of smoke and creaked at the elbows, and Cerys's breathing speeds up because she can almost feel him in this room, a charge of dark energy.

She stays sitting on the bed, unable to move, and after a while Henrietta comes over and gently takes the plastic book from her hands.

'It's Vic,' is all Cerys can say.

'Vic?' Henrietta frowns, looks down at the picture. She begins to flick through the book. 'Ah. You must mean Terry.' She continues turning the pages, talking more to herself now, as if she's forgotten Cerys is there. 'Although, come to think of it, Annie did say that's what all the printing works lads did. Used their surnames as nicknames. So Brian Neville was Nev, Ian Smith was Smithy . . .'

Slowly, she closes the book. 'So, I guess you're right. Terry Vickerson would have been Vic.'

Then she falls silent. 'But I don't understand. How did you know Terry?'

'I knew Vic,' Cerys replies. 'He was my mum's boyfriend. She called him her "forever man". Because she could never get rid of him.'

CHAPTER FORTY-ONE

HENRIETTA

Henrietta usually spends Christmas Day in the bosom of her family, but this year is different. Instead of a morning of attending church and exchanging disappointing presents, she's been sitting on her sofa with Dave, thinking over all the things that she knows about Terry Vickerson. How he'd spent decades making Annie's life a misery and then, when he'd somehow discovered that her sister was alive, he'd kept that information from her, too, and stolen away her last chance of happiness.

He'd been a printing rep – Annie had told her that – and Cerys said that was what had brought him to Cornwall. 'He first came down our way to do business with St Austell printworks when I was about ten,' she said. 'And then he just kept coming. At first he'd visit my mum every month, then it slowed to once or twice a year. He liked to keep her on her toes. But the visits stopped a couple of years ago.'

As for Henrietta's parents, she rang them yesterday to tell them she wouldn't be home for Christmas this year. Initially, her announcement was greeted with a stony silence. Then, down the phone line she heard her mother hiss, 'Tell her she has to. I've already bought the bird.'

Henrietta had tried to explain about losing her friend Annie and how Cerys was alone in London for Christmas, but her father had cut her off. 'I fail to see why that sordid family drama precludes you from your own obligations.'

Henrietta considered saying that in the short time she'd known Annie Doyle, this woman had shown her more warmth than she'd felt from her parents in thirty-two years but, on balance, she decides that's a conversation for another time. When her father rings off without saying goodbye, the silence on the line feels like a release.

After their visit to Annie's, Cerys decided to stay on in her aunt's flat for a few days. She said she wanted time to think things through. 'It's not spooky being here,' she told Henrietta over the phone. 'It feels like a way for me to get to know Annie a little. And in a funny way, my mum, too – Annie was a part of her life I never knew existed.'

But today Cerys is getting a taxi over to Henrietta's so they can have Christmas dinner together. As Cerys does not strike her as someone who stands on tradition, she decides on a simple repast for the two of them: baked beans on toast and then a tin of Ambrosia rice pudding.

'Delicious,' says Cerys, when they get to dessert. 'I haven't had this in years.'

Henrietta agrees it does taste wonderful. But that may be because she's already drunk the best part of the bottle of red wine that Cerys brought over.

Given the circumstances, they agreed not to exchange gifts, but Henrietta makes an exception for Dave and hides an extra liver sausage under the sofa cushions for him to snuffle out. 'He's glad to have his bed back then,' observes Cerys.

Henrietta also plans to buy a gift for Melissa upstairs, to say thank you for the times she's looked in on Dave. The market stall outside Poundland won't be back until January, so she still has time to make her final decision, but she is leaning towards the sweatshirt with a panda on the front. She can't wait to see Melissa's face when she unwraps it.

After they've finished their Christmas dinner, Henrietta and Cerys take Dave for a walk. There are no trains today, but Dave seems happy enough to stand and gaze out towards the railway tracks, which glint in the crisp winter sunlight.

'Evil, that's all I keep thinking. Just evil,' says Cerys, and Henrietta knows who she's talking about. 'Vic must have played them both along, kept them both in the dark. He's definitely dead, you say?'

'Yes, I'm afraid Terry Vickerson came to a rather messy end on the M3 two years ago. All his own fault, I might add. Oddly enough, he was taking Annie away for a week in a caravan in Cornwall. It would be nice to think he was finally going to reunite Annie with your mum. But we'll never know.'

Cerys rubs her hand over her belly in small circles,

as if to soothe her baby and herself. 'That's a nice idea, but you didn't know Vic. He was the sort of person who would have left his wife stuck in a caravan up the road, nipped over to see my mum a few times and then driven home again, without either of them having a clue. He'd have got a kick out of that. Control, that was his thing.'

'And you never had any idea about who he was?'

'None at all. I didn't even know he was from London. I assumed Bristol, because he had contacts there. I mean, I guessed he had a wife, that my mum was his bit on the side. But I had no idea who she was . . .' Her voice turns harder. 'But of course my mum did. What a thing to do – to your own sister.'

Henrietta is beginning to realise that when it came to Terry Vickerson, things were rarely how they seemed from the outside.

'Try not to judge your mother too hastily. It might not have been so simple.'

'Believe me, my mum didn't do simple – her life was always messy. What I can't work out is, how did they meet again and why did she get together with him?' Cerys shoves her hands into her tracksuit pockets.

'Like I said, it happened when I was about ten. My mum was going through a rough patch and we had no money. And then suddenly there was this Vic coming every weekend, taking us out for lunches, buying my mum presents. On the face of it, our life got easier. We moved out of our bedsit at Bessie's, got the shop and the flat over it. But why him? It was never what you could call a happy relationship.'

Henrietta, too, has unanswered questions. She's puzzled as to why Kath didn't find a way of letting Annie know she was still alive. And while Kath clearly went into the canal at some point on that night in 1974, Henrietta is still none the wiser about exactly how or why that happened. She still hasn't laid this particular ghost to rest.

'I don't suppose any of your mum's old friends might be able to help answer these questions?' she says. 'There might be a perfectly innocent explanation – that your mum and Terry Vickerson met by chance all those years later and love took its course.'

Cerys rubs her hand over her spiky hair, which Henrietta can now see is threaded with grey at the roots. 'My mum and Vic – I don't know what you'd call it, but it was never love. He was more like an illness. An infection that kept coming back.'

The two of them turn and start walking back to Henrietta's flat.

'Maybe there are a few people I could look up,' Cerys says, after a while. 'I mean, some of my mum's friends were just drifters and freeloaders, but a few were OK. I wouldn't have a clue where to start looking, though. Some, I didn't even know their surnames. Not going to get very far googling "Bessie, retired sex worker" or "Bristol Roy, part-time dealer", am I?'

Henrietta can't help but feel a flutter of excitement. 'Those might not be the best starting points,' she says slowly, 'but there are ways and means of finding out such things.'

Cerys raises an eyebrow.

'I don't like to boast,' Henrietta says, 'but I do have some experience in background research.'

An hour later, the two women are sitting side by side on the rug in front of Henrietta's gas fire, looking at Henrietta's laptop. Dave, sated on an excess of Christmas liver treats, is spreadeagled on the sofa in a most indecorous pose.

'Everyone called him Bristol Roy, but I have a feeling he was Roy Something-beginning-with-D,' Cerys says. 'He brought stock for the shop. I think he did a bit of dealing too, but he always said he wanted to give it up and become a potter. I bet he never did. Probably been dead for years.'

Henrietta tries searching for 'Roy', 'potter' and 'Bristol', but Cerys is right, nothing comes up. Then she tries with Royston, Leroy, Elroy and Delroy, but still doesn't have any luck. Cerys yawns, stretches out on the floor. 'Not everyone's idea of a Christmas Day quiz,' she says. But Henrietta isn't listening. She's found the membership pages of the Craft Potters Association and is trawling through all the surnames beginning with D.

Cerys is lying on her back now, hands cupping her still-small belly. 'When Roy brought stock for the shop, he'd always leave us a few of his own pots, too, but they never sold. Poor Roy, he tried hard, but he could never get the handles right. "Anyone can make a mug, it's the handle that's the tricky part," he used to tell me.'

Henrietta passes the laptop over. 'Might this be him?' The listing is for a Roy Dovey, who runs a shop called The Potter's Wheel in Bristol, with a photograph of his work. Cerys peers at the picture of two mugs and a teapot. 'I'd recognise those chunky handles anywhere.' She gives a big smile. 'Henrietta, you are nothing short of brilliant.'

Cerys has booked a taxi to take her back to Annie's flat, so they go outside to wait for it. Her plan is to head back to Cornwall in a couple of days, then return to London in time for Annie's funeral. 'I'm thinking I might take the long route home,' she tells Henrietta on the doorstep. 'Swing by Bristol. See what I find.' She taps her phone in her pocket. 'I'll keep you in the loop.'

Ah, yes, Henrietta thinks, Annie's funeral. She has been making a list of people from the Grief Café who will want to come: Mia and Stefan, of course, then Nora and Bonnie, Morose Mike and Audrey. She might make another journey to west London to tell Reggie at the pub and Emir at the café. Then, if she's feeling brave, she'll venture up to Portobello Road and find someone called Chantal, who runs a clothes stall near the flyover.

'You could bring someone to the funeral, too,' she says to Cerys. 'Your boyfriend, maybe?'

Cerys is looking away, studying the row of houses opposite as if she's just developed an avid interest in 1930s suburban architecture. 'Yeah,' she says. 'That's a bit complicated. But, you're right. I need to sort it out.'

'When are you due?' Henrietta asks.

'Wow, nothing gets past you, does it?' Cerys laughs. 'Bit of a surprise at my age, and it wasn't exactly planned. So, yeah, I'm due in the spring.'

They stand together in companionable silence,

their breath fogging in the winter air. Cerys turns to Henrietta. 'So you'll have to come down and visit. How about we make that a deadline for finishing the books? Your Life Story book for Annie and, depending on how I get on with Roy, I might make a start on this Memory Book for my mum. I need to get a few things straight in my head, but a book will still be something nice to show the baby when she's older. Not as good as a real grandma, but better than nothing.'

Henrietta is emphatically not a hugger, never has been. But today, as the taxi chugs up the road towards them, she reaches out and draws Cerys to her. And as the taxi drives off, despite the coldness of the day, Henrietta feels a warmth bloom inside her. Cornwall in the spring: something to look forward to.

CHAPTER FORTY-TWO

CERYS

The train journey out of London feels far longer and duller than it did six days ago when Cerys was travelling in the opposite direction with Henrietta. In a funny way, she misses her already, this stout woman from another age with her forthright manner, her odd clothes and her cantankerous dog. She has a lot to learn about fashion and healthy eating, but Henrietta was clearly a good friend to Annie.

At Paddington Station, she exchanged her ticket for a less direct route, one that means she can break the journey in Bristol. 'Change of plan,' she said to the man in the ticket office. 'Ooh, that's going to cost you extra,' he'd said, with relish. She was so not going to miss this London attitude.

Cerys's sports bag is on the seat next to her and she's taken the liberty of bringing a few clothes that she found in Annie's wardrobe. She doesn't think her aunt would mind. In fact, it sounds as if Annie would have loved to know someone was enjoying them. There's a comfort too, in slipping her arms into the sleeves, feeling the fabric on her skin in the same way that Annie did.

The boiler suit is beyond cool and she can wear the stripey shirt-dress with the floppy sleeves as maternity wear. But her favourite is a short yellow dress that she found hidden at the very back of Annie's wardrobe, pristine and barely worn. She can't work out why, because it's not really her thing and it bunches up a bit around her newly rounded tummy. But she just loves it.

* * *

The Potter's Wheel is down a Bristol side street, next to a falafel café and opposite a vintage clothes shop. A bell dings over the door when she opens it. It's so similar to the sound that used to ring out every now and then in Seachange that it throws Cerys a bit, and she's still slightly flustered when a stooped man emerges from a basement at the back of the shop. He's rubbing his hands together because it's freezing in here.

'Sorry, it's a bit chilly,' says Roy, because she knows it's him before he says a word. It's something about his manner, the way he bends forward slightly like a serf from olden times. She guesses that he stores his clay down in the basement: she can smell the earthy boskiness of it.

'It's for the clay,' he says, echoing her thoughts.

'Keeps it nice and cool,' she says, finally turning to face him. His smile stays frozen on his face just a beat too long. 'Sorry,' he stumbles. 'You're the spit of someone I used to know.' He keeps looking at her, taking her in.

Cerys takes her hands out of her pockets and rubs

her face.

'I'm Cerys,' she says. 'Clover's daughter.'

Roy doesn't say anything, he just reaches out for her hands and holds them tight in his, which are so much bigger and rougher, dry with red clay dust that is embedded into the creases of his palms, the edges of his fingernails. Cerys is horrified to see that his eyes are filling up with tears. 'So you are. How's your mum? And how are you?'

Cerys is starting to get that floaty feeling, the one that means she needs to eat and soon, so she sits down in a saggy chair and watches as Roy slops thin-looking soya milk into two teas. He hands Cerys one and her middle finger slips between the handle and the side of the mug, but only just. They both smile, thinking the same thing. 'Still tricky, those handles,' he says.

Then Cerys has to tell him about Clover dying.

'Oh no, oh no,' says Roy, rocking slightly in his seat. 'So fast, so terrible.'

'Yes. It was. It still is,' Cerys says, grateful at last to say this to someone who doesn't try to wish her pain away with platitudes. Then she tells him why she's here. 'Thing is, Roy, I've just discovered some stuff about my mum. That she had a family in London. And that Vic was . . . well, he knew them.'

'Jeez – Vic. It's been a while since I heard his name,' says Roy, chewing his lip. 'Is he still around?'

'Nope, died a couple of years ago. Nasty accident, apparently.'

Roy's shoulders seem to drop and he lets out a puff of air. 'Well, I can't say I'm sorry. If it hadn't been for him, I think your mum and me would have made a go of it.'

Cerys can feel herself welling up, imagining how life might have been if Roy hadn't disappeared so suddenly, leaving them with nothing but a few wonky pots. Leaving them to Vic.

Then that woolly, woozy feeling is back – low blood pressure, the midwife tells her – and she knows she has to put her head between her legs. When she looks up again, Roy is putting on some music and Cerys feels herself sucked back in time, to all those old songs by Simon & Garfunkel, Roy Harper and Bob Dylan.

'Your mum loved Dylan,' he says, doing a head-bob thing that must have passed for dancing in his day. 'She was going to come to Glastonbury with me in '87. Your old landlady, Bessie, was going to babysit you. But then Vic paid your mum one of his surprise visits.' He stops head bobbing and looks oddly sombre. 'Yes, he gave us a surprise alright.'

A dark memory comes back to Cerys: glass breaking. The sound of shouting, her mum crying. And she waits for Roy to continue.

'I met your mum when I was working for Vic and I fell for her. But then Vic found out we'd got close. I should have stuck by your mum, but I'd been a gofer for Vic long enough to know what happened to people who got in his way. I'm ashamed to say, I legged it back to Bristol, like he told me to.'

Cerys remembers Roy bringing the first stock for Seachange when she was ten years old and the idea of her mum opening a real-live shop was beyond exciting.

He set down a big bag of beads on the counter with a metallic thud, handed them boxes of incense, all done up in twists of green paper. Vic was there too, watching, smoking cigarette after cigarette. 'Roy's in the import–export business,' he kept saying, and then laughing like it was a big joke.

'I just thought you were a mate of Vic's who brought stock for my mum's shop. I didn't know you worked for him.'

'I'm afraid so. My job was running speed and hash down through Devon and Cornwall for Vic, and I'd bring a few boxes of hippy stuff too, to make it all look legit. I was just his man out west and I did what I was told.'

Cerys had always suspected Roy had a sideline going, but not that Vic ran things – she'd always been told he worked in printing.

Roy continues: 'The thing was, when Vic expanded out west, he needed a business where the accounts wouldn't be too carefully scrutinised so he could launder his cash. He couldn't believe his luck when he bumped into your mum, already living in Porthawan.'

'Was that all Seachange ever was, a cover?' Cerys thinks of how her mum would hang a new batch of floaty tops on the rail every summer and then put them away again at the end of the season, sun-bleached and unsold. Yet, somehow, the shop had always turned a profit.

When Cerys leaves, Roy makes her promise to keep in touch, but when she opens the shop door and hears the same ding-dong sound of the bell, this time it just makes her feel angry. And so stupid.

Her mum had made a lot of mistakes in her life, but Cerys had always admired her for running the shop. But all this time, it had been nothing but a front for Vic's dirty business. But why would she do that, for Vic, of all people? Once she'd been spotted by him and the game was up, why didn't she just pack in all her hippy nonsense and go home?

Cerys needs to delve even further back into her mum's life, to find out how Vic 'bumped into' her mum in Porthawan and why she went along with his plan. And she knows exactly who she needs to talk to.

Back on the train, Cerys sends a text to Henrietta: *Can you do me another favour? I need to find our old landlady, if she's still alive. All I know is that she went by the name of Bessie Hardy and she left Porthawan in about 1985.*

Henrietta gets back to Cerys within the hour with the information she needs: *Bessie now goes by the name Liz Hardy and is a respected breeder of miniature schnauzers. Naturally, the Kennel Club does not give out her address, but take a look at this.*

Next, Henrietta sends her a link to a newsletter published by a Cornish branch of the Women's Institute, where, a few years ago, Bessie/Liz gave a talk to the ladies of St Agnes village on the ins and outs of pedigree breeding. There's a photo of her in her front garden surrounded by local ladies and Cerys instantly recognises Bessie: she's the one with a twinkly look in her eye, as if she's just about to tell the punchline to a joke. More importantly, a plaque bearing her house name peeps out from behind her left shoulder.

Henrietta, you are a genius, she texts back.

Cerys brings up a map on her phone. If she gets off at the next station and catches a local bus, she can be in St Agnes before nightfall.

* * *

Bessie aka Liz Hardy lives on the outskirts of St Agnes in a house that is as unremarkable as every other fifties bungalow on her road. It is called Eventide – again, utterly bland – and a sticker in the swirly glass of the front door reads 'No Unsolicited Mail'. A nice touch, thinks Cerys, given Bessie's former career.

When Cerys and her mum lived on the top floor of Bessie's tall, wonky house, Bessie spent her evenings playing soft rock, wearing a satin robe and entertaining regulars who clomped up the steps in big boots to do things to the thump, thump of the music. 'Is it a party?' Cerys used to ask her mum. 'Not our sort, love,' her mum would reply, stroking her hair until she went back to sleep.

Today, when Bessie opens the door, she looks smaller than Cerys remembers and her hair has turned an unlikely shade of deep plum. She scowls and looks Cerys up and down. 'If you're the one who rang about the puppy, you need to go on the waiting list.'

Right on cue, two grey muzzles poke out from behind Bessie's beige slacks and snuffle and snort through lavish salt-and-pepper moustaches. Bessie shushes them back indoors and it's only when she turns back that her expression melts in recognition. 'Well, bugger me. If it isn't Clover's girl. Am I right?'

Bessie opens the door to let her in, simultaneously shouting, 'Bed!' This confuses Cerys until she realises it's aimed at the two dogs, who hunker down briefly, then follow the two women into the kitchen. For once, Cerys can see why people have pets, because they provide something to talk about.

Bessie reaches down to stroke the wider one, who is heavily pregnant. Cerys gives the leaner one, a male, a pat on the head. 'Good dog,' she tries.

'You never were one for small talk.' Bessie laughs, which turns into a fruity cough, and holds her hand to her chest. 'Have a cuppa, shall we?' She fills the kettle and picks two identical beige mugs off something that Cerys believes is called a mug tree.

Cerys is not usually prone to nerves, but this house is making her nervous. Everything is in shades of cream or taupe, from the hallway carpet to the paint on the walls, the floor tiles to the kitchen cabinets.

'Nice home you have here, Bessie,' she says. 'I hope you don't mind me just turning up.'

Bessie probably does mind, but not enough to turf her out. 'Bit different from the old place,' she says and her wheezy laugh starts up again. 'Best forgotten, that house and its comings and goings. Although it would be worth a fortune now. I see what holiday homes round the harbour go for in the summer.'

As they move into the lounge, Bessie sits on the velour sofa (in a shade some might call champagne) and points Cerys towards an armchair (in a tone closer to shandy). All around, dust-free surfaces gleam as if Mr

Sheen has only just left the building.

Douglas and Darcy, for those are the dogs' names, have slumped into their faux fur dog beds, Darcy beached on her side so that her distended belly looms above her. Something stirs under Darcy's skin – a paw or the tip of a small muzzle perhaps – and Cerys looks away quickly.

Bessie smooths down the collar of her blouse, touches a gold pendant. 'So. I was sorry to hear about your mum. Lady who cleans over your way told me.'

Cerys blows on her tea, which she can tell is going to be scalding hot. 'Thanks, Bessie. Sorry I didn't get in touch about my mum's funeral. We kept it small.'

She says 'we', but really it was just her who arranged it, hastily and in a blur of grief, with a celebrant who let her play her mum's favourite Bob Dylan CD at the end. Cerys had held it together pretty well until she walked past that oh-so-slight wicker coffin with Bob asking over and over about how it felt to be left on your own.

Bessie leans back in her chair, her halo of plum hair fanning out against the velour. 'That's alright. The past is the past and I reckon none of us want to dwell on that time.'

But this isn't what Cerys wants to hear. 'Thing is,' she begins, 'I kind of do. I've just found out some things about my mum. I met her sister. My aunt . . .' She can hear her voice starting to crack. 'In London.'

She waits for this to sink in. 'Bessie, I need to know how we ended up here and why my mum ended up with him. With Vic.' Even saying his name leaves a foul taste in her mouth.

'Ah, Cerys.' Bessie shakes her head. 'That's all going back a while. I'm not sure I can . . .'

Cerys knows that in a minute Bessie will stand up and show Cerys out of her sparkling clean bungalow because she doesn't want it sullied by a past she's worked hard to leave behind. So she tries a different tack. 'Hey, Bessie. Remember when you met my mum?' This is a favourite story, one she's heard many times, from her mum and from Bessie.

'Oh, I do!' Bessie claps her hands down on her beige slacks. 'First time I set eyes on your mum was in the laundrette. She was keeping warm, watching someone else's stuff tumbling round in the big dryers. Me, I was doing my sheets.' Bessie breaks into a throaty cackle and this time Cerys joins in too.

'It was sad,' she goes on, 'seeing her sitting there wrapped in some old horse blanket. And you, a scrap of a thing, snuggled inside it too.'

Cerys feels a sting of shame. 'Poncho,' she says. 'Not a horse blanket. A poncho.'

'Yeah, that's what Clover used to say, too. It stank like a horse anyway.'

'Probably sheep,' says Cerys. 'Singular. It was Jeronimo's pet.' She blows on her tea. 'We must have just arrived from Wales. It was good of you to take us in.'

'What else was I going to do? Your mum had no money, no family she could turn to.'

'Except she did, Bessie, but one night she ran off to become a hippy and live on a commune. Then, when I was five she got bored of that, so she came here. And when I was ten, instead of behaving like a grown-up and going back to her family – *my* family – she hooked up with her sister's husband. I mean, what was that all about?'

'Your mum didn't exactly "hook up" with Vic,' Bessie says slowly. 'It wasn't like that.'

'Well, it sounds like she quite liked the arrangement. She got a shop out of it. And she let him visit for years – for decades.'

Bessie won't meet her eye. She's looking down at the velour of the sofa arm, running her hand over it back and forth, watching as it turns from light to dark. Finally, she looks up.

'Cerys, love, you've got it wrong. There are things your mum told me in confidence. Things she didn't want you to ever know.'

'I know about the money laundering, if that's what you mean.'

'That came later. When your mum first crossed paths with Vic down here, it wasn't intentional,' Bessie says carefully. 'He found her.'

Bessie takes a deep breath before she continues. 'Your mum came here from Wales to disappear – she didn't want to be found. But she blew her cover, after she got nicked for shoplifting.'

Cerys can still remember the shame of it. How her mum made her sit in the buggy when she was far too old because the buggy's hood concertinaed back to make a secret hidey place. On their trips to the supermarket, Cerys would eye the bright packets of biscuits, noodles and spaghetti and then, magically, some would reappear

– 'Ta-da!' – from the hood when they got home.

The magic buggy lost its powers one fateful afternoon in Tesco when a woman store detective ran after them, huffing and puffing as she grabbed the buggy's handle to pull them up short. Cerys doesn't recall going to the Fore Street Police Station afterwards, but she must have been there. Maybe someone took her to another room and gave her some toys, or maybe she was left jammed into the too-small buggy. It was a piece of evidence, after all.

'But she got let off with a fine,' Cerys says faintly.

'That wasn't the issue. When your mum tried to give her name to the police, they weren't having any of it. Said what sort of hippy made-up name was Clover Meadows and demanded to know her real name. She had no option but to give the name she hadn't used in years – Kathleen Doyle.

'So, you're right, she got off with a fine, but her case was in the paper. Only a tiny mention in the court reports, but it was enough. Vic was down in Cornwall on his proper business for once, visiting the printworks at St Austell, and he picked up the local paper. Vic liked to read the court cases, it was his way to scope out a new area for his other work – the dealing. It was just very bad luck that your mum's name was in it that Friday. After that, it didn't take him long to track her down to my place.'

A sharp memory comes to Cerys. 'There was a night, wasn't there, when Vic found us?' she says. She can almost feel it: a hammering on the front door, her mum scooping her up and running to the bathroom.

The two of them watching as the key rattled in the door.

'But once her cover was blown, why didn't she just go home?'

'I wouldn't like to say,' says Bessie, more vaguely now. 'I know her dad was a tricky character. But you'd have to ask Vic.'

Cerys wraps her arms around herself, suddenly very tired. 'Well, it's too late for that. Vic's dead and now so is my aunt. There's no one left to ask.'

At that, Bessie gets to her feet and Cerys worries her time is up. But instead Bessie heads for the sideboard, where she rattles around until she finds a packet of cigarettes.

'I know I shouldn't. But every now and then, I give in.' She jimmies the handle of her uPVC patio door until it gives way, lights up and lets out a stream of smoke. There is little to admire in Bessie's back garden, just an expanse of concrete slabs, a few straggly pot plants and some neatly coiled dog turds.

Bessie stands in the doorway, takes several deep drags before she turns around and gives Cerys a stern look. 'You said Vic is dead. Are you certain?'

'He is – car crash a couple of years ago.'

Bessie takes a final drag on her cigarette and drops it into a plant pot. No wonder her garden isn't thriving, thinks Cerys.

There's another brief tussle with the patio door before Bessie returns to the sofa. She clears her throat. 'Cerys, your mum didn't want you to know certain things, not while Vic was still alive. But if he's gone . . . it's time to tell you the truth.'

Cerys feels a prickle of unease and she has a sudden urge to walk out of Bessie's cream-and-taupe bungalow and never come back. But she knows she has to keep listening.

'When your mum was eighteen and ran off to Wales, she wasn't trying to become a hippy. She wasn't even trying to get away from her family. She was running from Vic.'

'But why?' This is getting Cerys all riled up. 'Are you saying she was already having an affair with him back then? Her own sister's boyfriend?'

Now there's anger in Bessie's voice too. 'No, Cerys, it wasn't an affair. It wasn't even a fling. He came round to their house one Sunday morning and found your mum in on her own. Raped her on her parents' sofa, then sat smiling and laughing, having Sunday lunch with them all. She was eighteen and she'd never been with a bloke before. And she fell pregnant.'

Cerys swallows down the wave of nausea that has nothing to do with her own pregnancy. She has a horrible feeling she already knows the answer to this question, but she has to ask.

'With me.'

'Yes, with you. She arranged to meet Vic the Saturday before Christmas so she could tell him. At a pub called The Red Lion, I think. After she broke the news, he suggested they take a walk along the nearby canal. You know Clover, she was always a dreamer. She thought he was being romantic, that he wanted to make amends by proposing to her. That was her best bet, she thought, to fix things.

'But the mood changed once they got down to the water. He told her to turn around and start taking her clothes off. She was scared, so she did as she was told, folding her clothes as slowly as possible. She thought he wanted sex, but it felt all wrong, so she stopped. But it was too late. She was still facing the water when he kicked the backs of her legs hard and she went in.'

Cerys covers her face with both hands. She can picture it all too vividly.

'Your mum still thought it was some kind of sick joke, so she tried to wade back to him. He got down really low, almost lying on the ground, and reached out his hand. She thought he was going to help her out, but all he did was push her head back down.

'Oh, but she was smart, your mum, and she was fit. So she didn't try coming back up for air again, she ducked as deep as she could and stayed down there in the mud. She held on to bits of old rubbish – a pram, I think she said. She crawled along the muddy bottom of the canal as far as possible before finally coming up for air.

'It was raining heavily so she was hard to spot, and she carried on doing that, holding on to the weeds and the junk, staying low in the water until she reached the other side.'

Cerys thinks of sunny days when her mum took her to the beach. How she'd sit on a towel, her back a rigid line as she watched Cerys splash about in the waves, but her mum never went in herself, not even to paddle.

'She did well to survive,' Cerys says.

'She did. The rain and the dark were her cover and she crawled up some steps, found somewhere dry to hide. A place used by rough sleepers, she said. After a bit, she knew she had to move to get warm and she ended up by the side of the road. And that was where Jeronimo picked her up.'

'She was pregnant, so couldn't go home to her parents.' Cerys is starting to understand.

'More to the point, Vic would have been waiting, too. So she ran. She laid low in Wales for years, until some bikers from London turned up. One of them was asking too many questions and she reckoned he knew Vic. So she ran again and came here. Had an idea it would be nice for you to grow up by the sea.'

Cerys rubs her eyes hard.

'When Vic found your mum, she was terrified. But he was all smiles. Said he'd forgive her for disappearing with his unborn child if she did him some favours. He got her sorted with false papers so she could manage the shop – and its accounts – in the name of Clover Meadows. And after that, your mum never dared leave town again.

'Vic told her there was no point. He said her family in London had guessed she'd got herself pregnant and disowned her long ago. These days, he and Annie were happily married, so if she ever thought about contacting her sister, well . . . he wouldn't advise that. The betrayal, he said, would destroy Annie. That and the thought of her having his baby, because all Annie seemed to do was miscarry babies.

'Even if your mum had decided to take her chances,

she knew Vic would find her as soon as she set foot in west London. He'd let her slip away once, but he wouldn't make that mistake again. Next time he'd sort her – and you – for good.

'So Clover reckoned letting Vic visit every now and then was the best way to keep him sweet and keep you both safe. She did it all – the shop, the laundering – to protect you, Cerys. And she stayed in Porthawan to protect her sister from the truth.'

When Bessie shows Cerys out, they both stand in the porch, unsure how to leave things. 'Well, if you ever want a mini schnauzer pup I have quite a reputation as a breeder,' Bessie says without a hint of irony.

'You're alright, Bessie, I'm not really a dog person,' says Cerys, starting to back away. 'But thanks, you know. For taking us in, back in the day.'

Bessie stands at the front door of her cream bungalow, cradling Darcy in her arms like an enormous moustachioed baby. 'Someone had to, my love. I know you probably think it was all a bit shit back then. But Clover, she did her best, in the circumstances.'

Cerys walks away fast, before the tears come.

All the way home on the bus she thinks about Vic helping to permanently change her mum's name to Clover Meadows and how he would have pretended he was being kind, when really it was his masterstroke. It was his way to finally erase every trace of Kathleen Doyle, so that no one else could ever come looking for her.

Then she thinks of Henrietta, that most unlikely of detectives, who turned up on her doorstep the week before Christmas in her duffle coat and her penguin sweatshirt, on a mission to find Kathleen Doyle, almost fifty years after she'd disappeared. It had taken a while to happen, but Vic hadn't reckoned on someone like Henrietta Lockwood.

CHAPTER FORTY-THREE

HENRIETTA

Henrietta is rather proud of how she helped track down Bessie Hardy for Cerys, although she didn't let on that she'd had to comb her way through several Betties, Elizabeths and Liz Hardys in different parts of the country before she found the right one. Thank goodness for the diligence of the St Agnes branch of the Women's Institute, is all she can say.

Coming back to the Grief Café after the Christmas break wasn't as bad as she'd expected. Mia and Morose Mike and even Audrey have been wonderful since she came back to work: she'd never imagined it was possible to consume so many cups of tea and slices of Bakewell tart. Still, at 11 a.m. on her first Saturday shift, she couldn't help looking up and expecting to see Annie walking through the doors.

It has felt sad, too, to finally be finishing Annie's Life Story book on her own. As she listened to Annie's voice on the recordings, so clear and true, Henrietta would close her eyes. Because then it was almost as if Annie was right there beside her, about to dunk another biscuit into her tea, wearing something wonderfully impractical with flapping cuffs or jangling buckles. When Henrietta opened her eyes, it hurt all over again to realise that Annie really was gone for good. Yet, in a strange way, she's never felt closer to her.

One thing that is making work a bit easier is that she has a companion by her side – Dave. For now, he's just getting used to the daily routines of the Rosendale Drop-In Centre, but soon he will begin his official training as a therapy dog. All Henrietta did was drop a few hints here and there and asked Mia to do the same. When Audrey announced she was thinking about introducing an in-house companion dog, they both congratulated her on her brilliant idea and then Mia mentioned in passing that Henrietta had an elderly dog that might fit the bill. The fact that Dave will no longer be left home alone on Tuesdays, Thursdays and Saturdays is neither here nor there.

So far, away from the bustle of the outside world, Dave is taking to his new role surprisingly well. He's unlikely to meet any other dogs in here and, bar Stefan when he's in an energetic mood, patients at the Rosendale rarely move fast enough to alarm him. Yes, Dave has career prospects – especially now his odour issues (ears and glands, it turned out) have been remedied.

Henrietta, too, intends to turn over a new leaf for the new year. She is going to start by doing something she's been putting off for a long time – twenty-three years, to be precise – and that is to write a letter to Ms Esther Wame of Masura, Papua New Guinea. These days, Henrietta has discovered, Esther is headteacher of Masura High School and is evidently doing an excellent job – she's often quoted in the national newspaper and her paper 'Emerging from the Shadow of Colonialism' was lauded at the last Pacific Education Forum.

Henrietta wants to write and say how sorry she is for what Esther saw that afternoon, when the two of them were only nine years old. She wants to tell her that she never forgot Esther's friendship and she tries to remember the good times before that terrible day when Christopher died. All because his parents chose to take a nap instead of watching over their four-year-old son, who wanted to see the rainbow fish of the Solomon Sea.

Now it's midday and time for Henrietta to pack up her pencil case, her notebook and her phone and take down her laminated sign. And tonight, when she gets home, she will start writing that letter.

CHAPTER FORTY-FOUR

CERYS

There's a January sale on at the DIY store in St Austell, so all week Cerys has been going back and forth to get the supplies she needs to start doing up the shop. She's got big plans for Seachange, including a new, altogether more wholesome source of income.

Today, she's walking past the harbour with a tin of paint in each hand when she sees him. Her stomach registers him before her brain does and gives a quick, sickening flip. Laurence Hughes is outside his café, stacking sandbags against the doorway in preparation for the storm that's about to blow in. Laurence used to be in accounting in Wilmslow but wanted a life change, so he bought the Beachside Café at the start of last summer, when the queue for crab rolls, ice creams and cream teas stretched out the door.

Laurence hasn't seen her yet, but he's stopped hefting the sandbags to take a call on his mobile. The wind carries his voice and it's clear that he's talking to Samantha, his wife. Samantha wears well-cut jeans with a crisp white shirt, gets her blonde highlights done in Falmouth and on Fridays she goes to Pilates in the Methodist hall to show she's integrating into the local community.

'The fish stall's not even here, Sam. I told you, it's a summer thing. Yeah, OK. I'll go to the Asda on the way back,' Laurence says. 'And dill if they've got it, I know.' His sigh carries on the wind.

'Getting ready for the easterly then, Laurie?' she calls out.

Laurence Hughes wheels around, as if he's been caught in the act of something far more nefarious. 'Ah, Cerys, indeed I am,' he says. 'Don't want to get flooded out.'

There's something so reassuringly normal about Laurence, with his neat haircut, his Barbour jacket and his polo shirt, always done up to the top button. He's a world away from all the things that are still swirling around in Cerys's head: meeting then losing Annie, her visits to Roy and Bessie. She bets that Laurence Hughes didn't spend his childhood keeping warm in launderettes, being an accessory to shoplifting or accidentally laundering drug money.

'So, Laurie,' she says, finally. 'Fancy a coffee when you're finished?'

'Um, sure.' Laurence is looking more nervous than ever, and pushes his glasses back up his nose with his finger.

Cerys keeps walking, swinging her pots of paint. 'No stress, Laurie,' she calls back. 'Just a coffee.'

Laurence Hughes never wanted to be an accountant, or so he kept telling Cerys the first time they met. That was back in August, when they were on the same team for the bank holiday pub quiz at The Ship, when Cerys's knowledge of 1980s pop trivia proved invaluable. Tina Turner's real name? Anna Mae Bullock. Madonna's first UK number-one hit? 'Into The Groove', 1985.

Things got messy after they opened the winners' bottle of champagne and then someone got in rounds of tequila slammers. Cerys and Laurence ended up back at her place, in the double bed that still smelt of her mum, but having someone else beside her helped Cerys forget the pain of missing her, just for a short while.

Laurence must still be keen, though, because he turns up on her doorstep fifteen minutes later, proudly presenting two coffees in matching recyclable bamboo cups. 'So, long time no see,' he says.

'Yeah. I had to go up country.' She opens the lid to hers, sniffs it and puts it to one side; pregnancy has turned her right off the stuff. Then she tells him about her Christmas, how she met her aunt for the first time – 'She was family, real family, Laurence' – and about Vic and the warped hold he had over her mum and over Annie.

'He died a couple of years ago. Funnily enough, he was bringing Annie down to Cornwall for a holiday. But we'll never know what he had in mind, if anything.'

Laurence is sitting on the slippery beanbag, trying not to lose his purchase on it. 'What a terrible shame. He had the power to reunite your mum and her sister.'

Cerys considers this for a moment, imagining how the last year of her mum's life could have been so different. Then she shakes her head.

'He had the power alright. But reuniting? That wasn't in his interests.' She thinks of Vic telling her mum she'd been disowned by her family. Of how Roy had been warned off, and the way Bessie had left town pretty sharpish too, just when Clover could have done with a friend. 'He was better at keeping people apart than bringing them together.'

'And such a shame for you, too. I mean, my family drive me mad at times, but I wouldn't be without them. That's why I'd love to have children. But Samantha won't change her mind.' Laurence is doing that nervous thing again with his glasses.

Cerys clears her throat. She realises she's been rubbing her belly in a soft, circular motion again. She's wearing that funny yellow dress she found at Annie's and, underneath its silky lining, that fluttering feeling is back. A feathering, as if her baby is waving hello.

'Actually, that's another thing,' she says. 'The past couple of weeks have made me realise it's important for people to know where they are from.'

Laurence is nodding politely, like she's delivering a TED Talk. She'd better get on with this.

'You see, I can't give my baby a big extended family, but I'd like her to know who her dad is, even if he's not around all the time.'

Something strange is happening to Laurence Hughes's face, as if it's frozen and yet melting at the same time. But she has to keep going.

'Laurie, I'm pregnant.'

Laurence stares at Cerys, then down at her belly. Slowly, she rolls up the hem of her dress to show him the neat, rounded shape and the faint brown line that is just starting to form, running down from her navel.

Laurence still hasn't said anything, so Cerys just keeps talking.

'Anyway, it's not like I want us to be a couple or anything, but I'm not having her growing up feeling like she's someone's guilty secret. Or guessing who her dad is and getting it wrong, like I did.' Cerys can hear her voice hardening. 'She deserves better.'

'OK,' says Laurence, at last. 'I mean, it's not exactly ideal, vis-à-vis Samantha, but that's my problem to sort out.' He casts around for the right thing to say. 'I'll support you. It'll be all right.'

Cerys breathes out. This will do her just fine for now.

Laurence stays the rest of the afternoon and then the evening, before preparing to head home to talk to Samantha. 'We haven't been right for a long time, and moving to Cornwall never solved anyone's problems,' he says.

'You can say that again,' Cerys says with a soft smile.

'I'll ring you first thing tomorrow.' Laurence turns to go, then stops. 'Um, Cerys. The baby – you said "she". Is it a girl, then?'

'Not officially.' Cerys looks down at her tight bump again. 'But I've just got this feeling. After all, I do come from a family of girls.'

Then she watches as he slopes off down the cobbled street. It's nice, she thinks, the way he looks back, once, twice, then raises a hand to wave as he turns the corner. Laurence Hughes is a good man.

CHAPTER FORTY-FIVE

HENRIETTA

Four months later

It's clear that someone at Bodmin Parkway Station takes their job of planting the spring flower displays very seriously. Through the train window, Henrietta can see all manner of yellow blooms in pots and dotted along the grassy verge by the platform. She can't name any of them but she knows that not so long ago she would have barely noticed them. Or, if she had, she would have scoffed at someone wasting their time on such a pointless, indulgent exercise because anything that came with a hint of joy or a whisper of risk would have been anathema to the old Henrietta Lockwood.

Yet here she is, on board the 10.04 from London Paddington to Penzance, looking forward to her next adventure. Also breaking with tradition, she didn't bring her Thermos flask, but splashed out on a large Earl Grey tea from the buffet car. 'Would you like a KitKat with your tea, madam?' She certainly would. And a bag of cheese and onion crisps, which she will share with Dave, who is currently happily spreadeagled on the floor of the carriage, blissfully soaking up every vibration of the train into his old dog bones. His new dog coat suits him: it reads THERAPY DOG IN TRAINING and is in a calming shade of blue.

There are only two more stops before Henrietta reaches St Austell Station and she feels quite giddy with excitement. On the floor next to Dave is a large rucksack. Along with some tiny baby clothes that she just couldn't resist buying, it contains a long cardboard tube containing Annie's ashes – even urns have moved with the times, it seems.

She and Cerys haven't quite decided where to scatter the sisters' ashes, but there's no rush. Cerys says her mum's ashes have been sitting on the kitchen shelf for over a year because she couldn't think what to do with them. But Henrietta suspects that, one evening, when it feels right, the two of them will walk down to the nearby beach, the one with the round pebbles, and scatter them together.

Her rucksack also contains two large hardback books, one dark green, one ochre yellow. The green one is Annie's Life Story, and she's rather pleased with how it turned out. Even Audrey was impressed: 'One's first is always special,' she'd said, in a condescending way that might have made Henrietta bristle back in November.

The yellow Memory Book for Clover is quite different. Through January and February, Cerys went looking for people who had met her mum over the years and rounded up lots of stories and photos. She talked some more to Roy and to Bessie and even had a heart-to-heart with Jeronimo, who dug out some great photos of Cerys and her mum, taken in the commune's early days. Then they added in some from her mum's London childhood, and the finished book is like a lovely, colourful scrapbook. It will be perfect for Cerys to show to her baby when she's old enough.

Terry Vickerson is referred to obliquely in both books, but not by name. He doesn't deserve that privilege.

Everyone who came to Annie's funeral was sent a copy of her Life Story, while Bessie, Roy and Jeronimo have all put in orders for the Memory Book about Clover. Jeronimo is proving to be quite the canny businessman: he's already talking to Audrey about linking up with the Life Stories Project to hold some grief healing workshops in his yurts. There is even talk of Ryan Brooks coming along to play a gig in Jeronimo's meadow, which has sent Audrey into quite a tailspin.

The best news of all is that Cerys's baby is due next month. 'So you'll have to make yourself useful while you're down here. Help out in the shop if you like,' Cerys told her over the phone. They talk once or twice a week now and Henrietta enjoys their chats immensely. She keeps Cerys up to date on all Dave's health issues, Audrey's outfits and how Mia and Stefan's romance has 'gone exclusive', whatever that means. 'You are funny,' Cerys says, and Henrietta doesn't always understand why, but she knows Cerys means it in a nice way, so it barely matters.

Seachange is doing very well since Cerys relaunched it as a shop specialising in handmade Cornish goods.

She worked up a watertight business plan with someone called Laurie and now sells blankets woven in Portscatho, pottery made in Fowey and spoons whittled in Newlyn. There's already been an article in a Sunday newspaper about Cerys and her shop, heralding her as a champion of the new wave of Cornish crafters. Privately, Cerys plays down this success: 'I just looked on Etsy and worked out what sells. Out with the dreamcatchers, in with the carved spoons, Ettie,' she'd said with a laugh.

That's what Cerys calls her now, Ettie. Cerys said she always found Henrietta a bit of a mouthful and reckoned that the change might do her good. 'Be an Ettie. It's a lovely name,' she suggested.

Henrietta hasn't mentioned this idea to her parents yet, and she's not sure she ever will. Officially, she and Dave are down here on holiday, but the Life Stories Project is expanding. So when Audrey renewed Henrietta's contract (and Dave's), she also lined her up with a few meetings with a view to opening an outpost of the Life Stories Project in Cornwall. So, if that works out, she won't be driving to The Pines to endure Sunday lunch for quite some time.

Now the train is pulling into her station and Dave is already panting with excitement. With her rucksack in one hand and Dave's lead in the other, Ettie Lockwood steps down from the carriage and into the spring sunshine.

ACKNOWLEDGEMENTS

Some words of thanks

First of all, love and thanks to Alastair for believing in me and for reading innumerable drafts of this book. And to Tom and Martha – love you lots!

At Madeleine Milburn Literary Agency, I can't thank my agent Hayley Steed enough. None of this would have happened without you. I've learned so much and I feel incredibly lucky to have you in my corner. Thank you to Liane-Louise Smith, Georgina Simmonds and Valentina Paulmichl for introducing Henrietta and Annie to overseas readers, and to Madeleine Milburn, Giles Milburn, Georgia McVeigh and Elinor Davies for their kind help at various stages.

At Amazon Publishing, eternal thanks to editor Leodora Darlington, who brought me on board and had such a clear vision for this book, and to Victoria Oundjian and the rest of the team. I was lucky enough to have a US editor too, so thank you David Downing for your skill, encouragement and good humour. I am also indebted to copyeditor Sadie Mayne, cultural research reader Freya Ward-Lowery and proofreader Sarah Day.

Emma Rogers, you have created an amazing cover – thank you so much.

At my German publishers, Droemer, I'm hugely grateful to editor Julia Cremer, and to Maria Hochsieder for her sensitive translation.

A big thank you to my friends, in particular Jane Cussen and Caroline Smith, who read early drafts, and to my equally excellent friends Alison, Susy, Rachael, Sharon and my brother, Nick, and his partner, Sarah.

To the fellow writers that I've met on Twitter, especially the @debuts23 group – here's to us all. I'm so glad we have each other.

Priscilla Winfrey, thank you for advising me on era-appropriate Papua New Guinean Tok Pisin!

Some words on starting to write

OK, so by now you'll have guessed that I'm on first-name terms with grief. I lost my mum in 2014 and a close friend in 2018. If you are grieving, I send you a virtual hug and I hope that you have good days as well as the tough days.

This book is dedicated to my mum and I wish she was here to read it. But the truth is, if we hadn't lost her so suddenly, I probably wouldn't have got around to writing it at all. And I don't just mean the subject matter. Grief taught me that life is short, so if I was to have any chance of fulfilling my lifelong ambition of writing a novel, I'd better just get on with it.

An early vote of confidence was being longlisted for the Bath Novel Award and if you're an aspiring writer, I'd really recommend entering this or similar competitions. Thank you, Caroline Ambrose, for running this competition, and to the mystery judge who longlisted me. Whoever you are, I definitely owe you a drink or two.

Some words on the words

The heartfelt letter from Jackie in Chapter 23 is based on one written by Caroline Griffiths, who was preparing to say her goodbyes in 2018 and asked me to look over what she was writing to her family. My sincere thanks to Tony, Phoebe and Miles for allowing me to include Caroline's moving words. She was the best, wisest friend.

Some words on facts

This is a work of fiction, so the Rosendale Centre, The Bell, The Red Lion, Masura, Sanctuary Inc. and Porthawan are all made-up places. The Cornish Night Riviera doesn't actually run on Saturdays, but it does for Henrietta. Also, I decided not to include mentions of Covid because (a) this is fiction and (b) I kind of thought Annie had enough on her plate already.

Some words on grief

To the NHS nurses and professionals who work in cancer and end-of-life care: your compassion and dedication make a huge difference to people, every single day. Thank you.

For organisations that offer support in grief and loss, there is an excellent resources section at Good Grief: goodgrieffest.com/resources-and-support

Some words on Dave the dog

The last word has to go to Lottie – my whippet-terrier-cross rescue dog and the inspiration for Dave. Sadly, train journeys are not really a cure for a nervous, reactive dog. Never mind, you're perfect just as you are, Lottie!

Your words

If you'd like to chat, you can find me on Instagram and Twitter (far more often than I should be) as @joleevers, and please do sign up for my author newsletter at joleevers.com. Thank you for taking the time to read *Tell Me How This Ends*.

ABOUT THE AUTHOR

Photo © Charlotte Gray, 2022

Jo Leevers grew up in London and has spent most of her career working on magazines, most recently writing features about homes and interiors for leading newspapers and magazines. This means she gets to visit people around the country and ask them about all the things in their homes. Some might call this a licence to be nosey . . .

Tell Me How This Ends is her debut. Whether writing fiction or interviewing people for articles, she is fascinated by the life stories that we all carry with us. She has two grown-up children and lives with her husband and their wayward dog, Lottie, in Bristol.